"You a

The Scot's eyes popped wide. "Ye daft, woman." He'd be on his way now, thank ye very much. "Besides, I have a bride." George rose shakily to his feet. Rika rose with him. Sweet Jesus, the woman was nearly as tall as he. "Arranged," he croaked, "by William the Lyon—my king."

She flinched at his words. "It matters not."

Oh, but it did. Women should be small and delicate. Submissive. Her brash demeanor repelled him...yet his body felt strangely stirred.

"Once we are divorced, you can go home and claim her. The dowry is all I want. It's mine by right, and I will have it."

What she proposed was unthinkable. Marriage was a sacrament. 'Twas not a pagan ritual to be done and undone on a whim, simply to gain the bride her coin.

"I willna do it."

"Then I hope you enjoy our island, Scotsman, for you'll be here a very long time." She turned her back on him and marched away.

Dear Reader,

Harlequin Historicals is putting on a fresh face! We hope you enjoyed our special inside front cover art from recent months. We plan to bring this "extra" to you every month! You may also have noticed our new look—a maroon stripe that runs along the right side of the front cover and an "HH" logo in the upper right corner. Hopefully, this will help you find our books more easily in the crowded marketplace. And thanks again to those of you who participated in our reader survey. Your feedback enables us to bring you more of the stories and authors that you like!

We have four incredible books for you this month. The talented Shari Anton returns with a new medieval novel. *Knave of Hearts* is a secret-child story about a knight who, in the midst of seeking the hand of a wealthy widow, is unexpectedly reunited with his first—and not forgotten—love. Cheryl St.John's new Western, *Sweet Annie,* is full of her signature-style emotion and tenderness. Here, a hardworking horseman falls in love with a crippled young woman whose family refuses to see her as the capable beauty she is.

Ice Maiden, by award-winning author Debra Lee Brown, will grab you and not let go. When a Scottish clan laird washes ashore on a remote island, the price of his passage home is temporary marriage to a Viking hellion whose icy facade belies a burning passion…. And don't miss *The Ranger's Bride,* a terrific tale by Laurie Grant. Wounded on the trail of an infamous gang, a Texas Ranger with a past seeks solace in the arms of a beautiful "widow," who has her own secrets to reveal….

Enjoy! And come back again next month for four more choices of the best in historical romance.

Sincerely,

Tracy Farrell, Senior Editor

ICE MAIDEN

DEBRA LEE BROWN

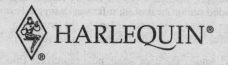

HARLEQUIN®

TORONTO • NEW YORK • LONDON
AMSTERDAM • PARIS • SYDNEY • HAMBURG
STOCKHOLM • ATHENS • TOKYO • MILAN • MADRID
PRAGUE • WARSAW • BUDAPEST • AUCKLAND

ISBN 0-373-29149-3

ICE MAIDEN

Copyright © 2001 by Debra Lee Brown

This edition published by arrangement with Harlequin Books S.A.

® and TM are trademarks of the publisher. Trademarks indicated with
® are registered in the United States Patent and Trademark Office, the
Canadian Trade Marks Office and in other countries.

Visit us at www.eHarlequin.com

Printed in U.S.A.

Available from Harlequin Historicals and
DEBRA LEE BROWN

The Virgin Spring #506
Ice Maiden #549

For James with love

Chapter One

The Shetland Islands, 1206

He was dreaming.

Aye, that explained everything.

Grit and salt stung his eyes. Icy water rushed over his body in a bone-chilling wave. He couldn't feel his legs anymore. If only he could move or cry out.

"He is perfect," a feminine voice whispered close to his ear. A soft fingertip grazed his jawline.

"Perfectly dead, I'll wager." The rough voice was a man's, the accent fair strange.

He cracked an eye to the flat, white light of dawn and tried to focus.

"You wager poorly, Lawmaker. Look, he wakes."

Nay, he wasn't dreaming at all.

He was dead.

The vision floating above him was enough to convince him. He'd heard of them, of course, in legends told around campfires late at night by seafaring Danes and Norwegians come to trade in Inverness. But he was a Christian and believed not in such tales.

Yet there she was, looming over him, waiting.

"Valkyrie," he breathed.

The vision frowned, narrowing ice-blue eyes at him.

"You're right," the male voice said somewhere at the edge of his consciousness. "He's not dead, just daft."

Oh, he was dead, all right. How else could he explain such a creature?

Two thick, flaxen braids secured with rings of hammered bronze grazed his bare chest as she studied him. She wore a helm, as might a warrior, embossed with strange runes—the kind he'd seen on ancient standing stones near the Bay of Firth—and a light hauberk of finely crafted mail.

But she was a woman, of that there was no doubt. The blush of her cheek, the ripeness of her lips, belied her garments and her hard, calculating expression.

His gaze drifted lazily along the curve of her neck and the narrow set of her shoulders. Her arms were bare and sun bronzed, adorned with more of the same hammered metal. With each measured breath, her breasts strained ever so slightly against her hauberk.

"Am I—" he rasped. "Is this—" He coughed up another lungfull of seawater, then met the Valkyrie's penetrating gaze. "Valhalla?"

Men's laughter shattered the eerie harmony of cawing terns and cormorants.

"Likely the farthest place from it," the Valkyrie said. "This is *Frideray*. Fair Isle."

His head spun and a wave of nausea gripped him. "But then…" He tried to sit up. She pushed him firmly back down onto the sand. Another icy surge washed over his numb legs and he started to shiver. "Wh-who are ye?"

"I am Ulrika, daughter of Fritha."

"Rika," he breathed, fighting to stay conscious.

At her command, a half-dozen hands clutched him and hefted him from the beach. Pain shot through his limbs, and he bit back a groan.

"Thor's blood, he's heavy," the man she'd called Lawmaker said. "We need another man."

Instantly another set of hands supported his limp, sea-battered body. Her hands. They were small, softer than the others. His head lolled to the side and found her crystal gaze.

"My ship," he mouthed, unable to make the sounds.

"Lost," she said, "and every man with it."

A searing pain twisted his gut, and he squeezed his eyes shut. "Nay, it canna be. My...my brother?"

"All."

The backs of his eyelids blazed with horrific visions of the shipwreck. The storm had come upon them in the night without warning. Biting sleet and lightning, gale-force winds the like of which he'd ne'er known in the Highlands. The howling haunted him still—a high-pitched railing, the shriek of the devil himself. The hull of their ship had shattered like a child's toy against rocks that had no reason to be there. At least not from the charts they'd carried.

His brother. His men.

All dead.

"May God have mercy on their souls," he whispered.

The woman snorted and tightened her grip on him. His eyes fixed on the hard set of her jaw as they bore him up a steep hill. She neither faltered nor slowed her pace, ignoring the labored grunts and winded breaths of her male companions.

He was vaguely aware of the landscape around him. Rocky and barren, with a chill deadness about it that was reflected in the woman's eyes. She didn't look at him, not once, until the thatched roofline of a long, low house came into view.

They stopped outside the stone structure. He sucked in a breath as his bearers dropped him unceremoniously onto a bench in the courtyard.

"You're a Scot," the woman said, and eyed him speculatively.

He nodded, trying to focus on her face. "Grant. George…Grant." His head throbbed as the white winter sky spun above him like a dervish.

"Grant," she said. "An odd name."

"I…I am…*The* Grant."

"A chieftain?" Lawmaker said. "Well, then, Ulrika, he is a good choice after all."

The woman slid a wicked-looking dagger from the scabbard at her waist. He tensed as she cut away his sopping plaid. God knows what had happened to his weapons. Likely lost at the bottom of the sea.

He was too weak to struggle, or even protest. In a matter of seconds he lay naked before her, shivering uncontrollably. Her gaze roved over him coldly, eyeing a sheep for the slaughter. Aye, well, if he wasn't already dead, he would be shortly. He mouthed a silent prayer.

"He'll do," Rika said, and sheathed her weapon. To his astonishment she covered him with a thick woolen blanket.

"Do for what?" A vision of pagan sacrifice flashed in his mind's eye.

Lawmaker stood over him and arched a peppered brow. "For her husband."

"H-husband?" His stomach did a slow roll, his head throbbed in time to the dull aching in his bones.

"Sleep now, and regain your strength," Rika said. "We've much to prepare before the wedding."

He watched her as she turned and walked away, the short hauberk clinking with the gentle sway of her hips.

Her companions lifted him from the bench.

"Wh-what's happening?" he breathed, and met Lawmaker's stoic gaze.

"Something I never thought to see." The older man smiled cryptically, then followed the woman warrior, Ulrika, daughter of Fritha, into the haze of the long-house.

"Vikings," he mouthed.

A band of bloody Vikings.

Rika sucked down the draught of mead and cast her drinking horn aside. "So, old friend, what think you of my plan?"

Lawmaker toyed with the end of his beard and looked at her for what seemed an eternity before answering. "You're sure you wish to do this?"

"It's the only way. You know that as well as I. The dowry my marriage brings with it will buy Gunnar's release."

"So it would. But we know not where your brother is held."

"Dunnet Head," Rika said. "On the mainland. I heard Brodir's men speak of it."

"You are certain?"

"Ja."

Lawmaker nodded. "Brodir will not be pleased. He expects to come home to a bride—and a dowry that will buy him fine goods and timber for ships."

Rika looked away and swallowed hard. She did not wish to think of Brodir. Not now, not ever. True, they were betrothed in the Christian way—her father had arranged it when she was a child—but Brodir had gone a-Viking months ago, and she prayed each day that some evil would befall him and he'd not return. Absently she twisted the bronze bracelets circling her wrists, and mustered her resolve.

"Brodir will return to a penniless divorcée who will no longer be of interest to him." So she hoped.

"And her brother restored to his rightful place as jarl," Lawmaker said, finishing the thought for her.

"Exactly. It will work. It must." Her brother, Gunnar, meant the world to her. He was the only family she had left. Her estranged father didn't count, of course. All she wanted from him was the dowry.

She'd do anything to free Gunnar. Anything.

Lawmaker eyed her again, silently, while she fidgeted on the bench, impatient. She must have the elder's blessing and his help. The henchmen Brodir had left behind to watch her were dangerous men. Without Lawmaker's consent, her plan was doomed.

Finally he said, "It will be dangerous—and complicated."

Rika flew off the bench in elation, ignoring the warning in Lawmaker's implied consent. "I'm prepared for danger. As for complications, I leave those to you."

"Ja, well…" Lawmaker's gaze drifted to the bed box at the end of the longhouse where the Scot had thrashed all day in a fitful sleep. "He might have something to say about it."

Rika smirked, triumphant. The Scot had little choice but to comply. "He'll do as I bid him."

"He is a chieftain, a laird. Think you he'll agree to wed you just like that?"

"Chieftain, indeed." She made a derisory sound. "He's a weakling. Look at him." Her gaze washed over George Grant's unremarkable features. "Why, he doesn't even have a beard."

Lawmaker cast her one of his ever-patient smiles—the kind he reserved for children, and for her. "Don't underestimate the man. A beard is not the quintessential mark of virility among all peoples, Rika—only ours. You've much to learn about the mainland and its folk, should you think to venture there."

"Perhaps," she said absently, and continued to study the Scot. He was more formidable than she'd first thought. Broad of shoulder and well muscled, though she hadn't seen him on his feet yet, so it was hard to judge his height. Surely he wasn't taller than she. Few men were.

Her gaze fixed on his long, tousled hair. Rich and tawny, it spilled across the pillow like a river of honeyed mead. Thin braids, like a woman's, graced each temple. Never had she seen a man plait his hair so.

She smiled inwardly. Ja, this *chieftain* would be easy to control.

George woke with a start, fumbling for weapons that weren't there. "What the devil—?" All at once he remembered—the voyage, the shipwreck, the Viking woman.

He blinked the sleep from his eyes as a barrage of peculiar sounds and smells assailed his senses. He lay in a strange sort of bed at one end of the longhouse. 'Twas more of a box, really, elevated off the hardened dirt floor.

In the center of the room a fire blazed, curls of smoke drifting lazily upward and out a hole in the roof. Strangely clad folk—men and women and children—gathered around a long table for what looked to be the evening meal.

His gut tightened as he recalled the last meal he'd eaten. A bit of bread and cheese shared with Sommerled, his younger brother.

Dead.

All of them dead.

Grief gnawed a hollow inside him. He pushed through it and, moving carefully, swiveled naked from the bed box, pulling the soft blanket with him. The sea had had her way with him. Every muscle cried out, and he grimaced against the pain.

Before his feet touched the ground, she was there. Rika, daughter of Fritha.

He stared at her, tongue-tied. She looked different without her warrior's garb. Her hair shone white-gold in the firelight, falling loose about her shoulders. She was dressed simply in a gown of pale wool, girded with the same finely tooled belt she'd worn that morning. Her hand twitched on the hilt of her sheathed dagger.

"You must eat," she said. "I'll have something brought to you."

"Nay, I willna lay here like a—" He grunted as he tried to rise. She instantly placed a hand on his shoulder to stop him. 'Twas warm, surprisingly so, given the coldness of her eyes.

"Lay back," she ordered, and pushed him down onto the soft pillows. "You're hurt and must rest."

She spoke matter-of-factly, with not a hint of compassion. Could he not see with his own eyes that she was a woman, he would not have believed it, so cool and authoritative was her demeanor.

He obeyed, and slid back into the bed box.

She called for a woman to bring food, then settled next to him on a bench, her back arrow-straight, her expression unreadable.

"You are Grant," she said.

He nodded. "Aye, George of Clan Grant—of Scotland."

"George?" She wrinkled her nose. "Not a manly name at all."

Her impertinence stunned him. "'Tis a proper Christian name. But I expect ye wouldna know of such—"

"I shall call you Grant." She turned to accept a trencher of food from a woman who bore a babe straddled across her hip.

'Twas then he noticed the scar. An angry, razor-sharp line running from her left ear under her chin. He'd not noticed it that morning on the beach. Someone had cut her throat—or had tried.

The tiny bairn squealed, his hands flailing madly. Rika reached out—on impulse, it seemed—and captured the infant's chubby fist in her hand.

A warm, bittersweet smile blossomed against her cool features. The contrast startled him. 'Twas as if she were a different person altogether.

The moment was short-lived.

Rika caught him staring at her, and the smile vanished from her lips. She scowled at the babe and waved the woman off. "Take it away."

Hmph. As he'd suspected, she had not a compassionate bone in her body. And yet…

"Here, eat." Rika thrust the trencher toward him.

The woman shot him a cautionary glance, then hur-

ried back to table. No one else seemed to pay them any
mind—save Lawmaker, who watched his every move,
and a sandy-haired youth whose twisted scowl and dark
eyes were reserved entirely for George.

Nodding at them, George grasped the trencher and
accidentally brushed her fingers. A shiver shot through
him. She, too, felt something. He watched her eyes
widen as she snatched her hand away.

He had no appetite, but forced himself to eat some
of the food. 'Twas fish mostly, both salted and pickled,
and a gruel of what smelled suspiciously like turnips.
He picked at the meal while she studied him.

As his head cleared and his strength returned, he took
stock of his situation. 'Twas not the best of circumstances he found himself in. Shipwrecked and alone,
without a weapon to his name.

His hosts, if one could call them that, were folk the
likes of which he'd ne'er seen. They spoke his tongue,
but mixed it with strange words. Norse words. Though
they were not like any Norsemen he knew. They were
grittier, more primitive—as if time had passed them by.

He counted at least a dozen men in the smoky room,
and half again that many women. Somehow, he knew
this wasn't all of them. This was but one house, and
he seemed to recall others when they carried him up
from the beach.

Fair Isle.

George knew not where it was. Only that he'd been
bound for Wick from Inverness, and a winter gale had
blown them off course, far to the north. Past the Orkneys, if he had to venture a guess. How would he ever
get back?

"You wish to go home," Rika said, reading his
mind.

He dropped the bit of fish back into his trencher and met her gaze. "That I do."

"You shall, as soon as you're fit."

"Ye have a ship then! Thank Christ." His spirits soared. They would leave immediately, of course. "Who shall take me? Whoever it is shall be well paid for his trouble."

"I shall take you, as soon as our business together is finished."

"What business?" His brows collided in a frown. Something in her voice, and the way she seemed to look right through him, caused gooseflesh to rise on his skin.

"Simply this," she said. "You wish to return home, and I can arrange that. But first, there is something you must do for me."

George set the trencher aside and sat up in the bed. "What, pray tell?" He wasn't used to dealing with women, and this one had rubbed him the wrong way from the start.

For a long moment she didn't answer, just sat there staring at him. He could almost see her mind working. Once, she opened her mouth to speak, then thought better of it.

His gaze lingered on her lips. They were lush, ripe, as they'd been on the beach that morning when she hovered over him, her breath hot on his face. He felt an unwelcome tightening in his loins and grasped the edges of the wool blanket that covered him.

Finally she spoke. "You and I shall marry."

"What?" His eyes popped wide. He thought he'd dreamed that bit of conversation she and Lawmaker had had on the beach. God's truth, it had seemed more nightmare than dream. "Say again?"

"You heard me. We shall marry." Her eyes were inscrutable, yet her lower lip trembled, belying her confidence. "I need a husband to claim my dowry. Once I have it, you may go home."

"Ye're daft, woman." He'd be on his way now, thank you very much. He glanced around the bed box for his plaid, but saw neither it, nor any kind of garment. Wrapping the blanket around his waist, he again tried to rise. This time, when Rika tried to stop him, he slapped her hand away.

"I have a bride," he said, and rose shakily to his feet. "'Tis all a—" Rika rose with him. Sweet Jesus, the woman was nearly as tall as he. "Arranged," he croaked. "By William the Lion, my king."

Her eyes widened as she stared up at him, as if he'd said or done something unexpected. She eyed him up and down, then frowned. "You're tall, Scotsman."

"As are ye." He raked his eyes over her body with a lack of tact that matched her own audacity. "Not like a woman at all."

She flinched at his words. "It matters not."

Oh, but it did. Women should be small and delicate. Submissive. A proper Christian woman wouldn't dream of talking to a strange man. Her brash demeanor repelled him, yet his body felt strangely stirred.

"About your bride, I mean. Once we are divorced you may go home and claim her. The dowry is all I want. It's mine by right, by law, and I will have it."

He shook his head, not understanding her at all. What kind of scheme was this? "There can be no divorce. Ye are mistaken. A man weds for life." He tried to move past her, but she stepped into his path.

The sandy-haired youth at table shot to his feet, eyes blazing. George had guessed the lad would be trouble.

No matter. George was about to snatch the dirk from Rika's belt when Lawmaker reached up and yanked the youth back down to the bench.

"Not always for life," Rika said, ignoring the lad's move. "Ask Lawmaker. He'll tell you. Divorce is not common, but does occur among my people and suits my purpose well."

The woman was clearly touched. "And what purpose is that?"

"I told you. I want my dowry—nothing more. Once we are wed, you shall acquire it for me from my father. When the silver is in my hands we'll declare our divorce before the elders." She shrugged. "After that, I care not what you do. Our ship will take you anywhere you wish."

George opened and closed his mouth. Twice. He shook his head again, as if he didn't understand her, but every word was clear despite her strange accent.

"Just like that," he said.

"Ja, just like that."

What she proposed was unthinkable. Outrageous. 'Twas a blasphemy against God. Did she think to use him to gain her fortune, let her think again.

Marriage was a sacrament and, at its best, an arrangement designed to secure an alliance between clans. 'Twas not a pagan ritual to be done and undone on a whim, simply to gain the bride her coin.

"I willna do it," he said.

"Fine." She stretched her lips into a thin, tight line. "I hope you enjoy our island, Scotsman, for you'll be here a very long time." She turned her back on him and marched toward the table, where all eyes were now trained on him.

"A lifetime, perhaps," she called over her shoulder, and didn't miss a step.

Chapter Two

The Scot was stubborn beyond belief.

For days Rika and her people watched, amused, as Grant worked in vain to build a seaworthy raft of driftwood and pitch and bits of rotten rope.

She stood on the cliff overlooking the beach, her cloak pulled tight about her, and observed him. The wind whipped at his hair and the loose-fitting tunic one of the men had given him to wear. His legs were bare though booted, and she knew not how he could stand for so long in the icy water, his gaze fixed on the southern horizon.

Winter was at its height. A thin crust of snow clung to the rocky outcrops and grass-covered moors of the island. Daylight was short, and no sooner did the sun rise each day then the wind waxed with a vengeance. She turned her face skyward and breathed of the salt and dampness.

All she knew was the sea, what it gave up and what it kept. As she fixed her eyes on Grant she found herself wondering what Scotland was like in the spring.

"He's given up."

Rika turned at the sound of Lawmaker's voice. "Not

yet, old man. Still he believes there must be a way. I see it in the set of his shoulders and in the way he clenches his fists at his sides.''

Lawmaker smiled and spared a backward glance to the sheep he tended on the moor.

Rika slipped her arm through his, as she often did, and huddled close. "You might have been right. This *chieftain* may not agree after all.''

"He'll agree,'' Lawmaker said, as they watched Grant in the surf. "In his own time.''

"Hmph.'' They had precious little of that. Her patience wore thin. "He's done naught but rage and pace the beach all this morn.''

"With you stood here openly watching?''

She nodded.

"Ha!'' Lawmaker shook his head. "No wonder the man's enraged.''

"What do you mean? I don't understand his anger. The solution is a simple one. He has only to agree and we can move ahead with our plan.''

"You make it sound so simple.''

"It is.'' It wasn't, but she could see no other way.

"Have you thought what you will do after?''

She hadn't, in fact. "I'll do what I always have done—take care of you and Gunnar. Until my brother takes a wife, of course.''

Lawmaker flicked her a sideways glance. "And what of you, Rika. Have you not thought about a husband for yourself?''

She frowned at him. "You know well I have not. How can you suggest it knowing how my father treated my mother? And how Brodir—'' she turned away and bit down hard on her lip "—what he did to me.'' Her arm slid from his.

"Had I known of Brodir's misuse of you—"

She raised a hand to silence him. "It's of no import now. All is behind me. Gunnar's freedom is what matters."

"Not all men are like Brodir, you know. Or your father."

That she could not believe. She sought Lawmaker's eyes, prepared to make some retort, but caught him studying Grant. The Scotsman moved with purpose up the beach toward them, eyes fixed on her, his face a grim fusion of unconcealed hate and barely controlled rage.

"*He* is," she said. "Just like them. I see it in the way he looks at me."

Lawmaker shrugged. "The man's out of his element, here in this place. Fair Isle is a world apart from his, and you a woman unlike any he has known, I'll wager."

"Ha! So he's made it plain each time I've spoken with him. This wager I shan't take."

"Have you never thought to marry for love?" Lawmaker asked.

Thor's blood, would the old man not let the subject go? "Love." She snorted. "An emotion for the weak of spirit. Men use it to bend women to their will. Some, to crush them. And I won't be crushed like an insect under a man's boot."

Lawmaker sighed.

He'd heard it all before, but she cared not, and continued. "You speak to me of love, and conveniently forget that you yourself never wed. You and I are alike, old man. We need not such weaknesses."

"Ah, but there you are wrong. I have loved, more deeply and fiercely than you can know." He looked into her eyes and smiled bitterly. "One day I shall tell you the story."

She had never seen him like this, so direct and forthcoming with his feelings. "Tell me now."

"Nay, for you are not ready to hear it. Besides, look—" He nodded toward the beach. "Your bridegroom comes."

He did come, and at a pace that caused her to take two steps back. She met Grant's gaze and saw his rage had subsided. She hardened her heart against what remained.

Hate. Disgust. For her.

She felt it as keenly as she'd felt Brodir's fist on numerous occasions. Rika knew she was not like other women, and she certainly didn't look like them. Nay, she was far from the ideal. Perhaps that was another reason she'd evaded marriage.

Who would have her?

Who, besides Brodir, who favored the arrangement only for the coin, and for the humiliation he could wreak on her?

Nay, wifery was not for her, and as Grant scaled the craggy hill before her, she took comfort in the fact that her marriage to the Scot would be mercifully short.

"Woman!" Grant called.

She did not answer.

Out of nowhere, Ottar appeared on the hill behind him, and moved with a speed Rika had not known the sandy-haired youth possessed.

"Ottar, no!" she cried.

Too late.

Grant turned on him, and Rika froze. "I must help him," she said, and started forward.

"Nay. Be still." Lawmaker grabbed her arm.

"But—"

"Quiet. I'm trying to hear what they say." Lawmaker jerked her back, and she watched, her heart in her throat, as Ottar confronted Grant. The howling wind made it impossible to hear their conversation.

"He's only ten and six," she said. "Grant will kill him."

Lawmaker shook his head. "I think not. For all his rage, methinks George Grant is not a man who'd harm a reckless youth."

"How can you be certain?"

Ottar went for Grant, and Rika shot forward, prepared to intervene.

Lawmaker yanked her back. "I'm a good judge of character."

One hand on Ottar's shoulder, Grant held the youth at bay. Rika held her breath, her arm burning from Lawmaker's steely grip, and watched as the two exchanged some unintelligible dialogue. Finally Grant released him, and Ottar scaled the cliff. Rika breathed.

"See?" Lawmaker said. "I thought as much."

Ottar shot her a dark look as he brushed past her.

"The boy's jealous," Lawmaker said.

"Jealous? Of whom?"

"The Scot. I told Ottar about the marriage."

"That's preposterous," Rika said. "Why would Ottar be jealous? He's just a boy. Besides—"

"He's smitten with you. Has been e'er since he was old enough to walk and you to lead him by the hand."

"Nonsense. We're friends."

"He's nearly a man. Take care to remember that, Rika."

She had no time to reflect on Ottar's peculiar behavior or Lawmaker's explanation of it, because Grant had scaled the cliff and now stood before her.

Rika drew herself up, ignoring her fluttering pulse, and looked the Scot in the eye. "You will agree to my plan?" She pursed her lips and waited.

"I will not," Grant said between clenched teeth.

She had expected him to yield. Could he not see that he'd lost? That she would prevail?

"In that case," she said, "there's more driftwood on the opposite side of the island. I'm certain some of the children would be pleased to help you gather it."

The fire in his eyes—slate eyes, she noticed for the first time—nearly singed her, so close did he stand. She was uncomfortably aware of his size, his maleness, and let her gaze slide to the stubble of tawny beard on his chin and the pulse point throbbing in his corded neck. Perhaps she'd been wrong to so quickly dismiss his masculinity.

Yet there was something different about him. He was not like the men she knew. She had not the feeling of foreboding she did as when Brodir loomed over her in anger. After a long moment, she realized why.

Grant dared not lay a finger on her.

Likely because he knew Lawmaker would kill him if he did. Or mayhap, as Lawmaker had said, Grant wasn't the kind of man who… Nay. They were all that kind. Besides, it didn't matter the reason. The knowledge of his reserve gave her power, and power was something she'd had little of in Brodir's world.

"How far is it?" Grant snapped, holding her gaze. "To the mainland."

"Three days' sail—by ship." Lawmaker glanced pointedly at the makeshift raft on the beach. "In fair weather."

Grant's eyes never left hers. "Three days. No so far." He brushed past her, deliberately, and stalked off onto the moor. Bleating sheep scattered before him.

Her skin prickled.

"You've not much time left," Lawmaker said to her as they watched him go.

She knew well what the elder meant. Brodir was long past due and could return any day. When he did, Rika's one chance to save Gunnar would be lost forever.

"This is one of the *complications* you mentioned," she said as she watched Grant charge a ram in his path.

"Precisely."

"Well, then, old man, I leave it to you to sort it out."

George settled on a bench in a corner of the village brew house and wondered how the devil to go about getting a draught of ale to slake his thirst.

He'd been given free range of the island, much to his surprise, and since he'd been strong enough to walk he'd covered every desolate, wind-whipped inch of it. Save sprouting wings and flying off, for the life of him he couldn't fathom any way of escape.

Damn the bloody woman and her clan.

All had been instructed—by her, no doubt, though she seemed to hold no great position in the eyes of her own folk—to speak nary a word to him save what was necessary to feed and shelter him.

What little he'd been able to learn about the place and its people, he did so from his own observation and from snatches of overheard conversations.

The village was small, housing less than a hundred folk, and sat atop a cliff on the south side of the island. Below it lay a thin strip of rocky beach, boasting a tiny inlet at one end that harbored the single craft Rika had called a ship.

'Twas not much of one in George's estimation. There was no natural timber on the island. Clearly the *byrthing,* as the locals called it, was built of scrap wood gleaned from shipwrecks. The low-drafting vessel looked barely seaworthy, but was heavily guarded all the same—likely due to his presence. Right off he saw 'twas too large for one man to sail alone.

Though sleet and the occasional snow flurry pummeled the surrounding moors, George was comfortable enough in the furs and woolen garments the islanders had loaned him, and with the food and shelter he'd been offered. He was neither prisoner nor guest, and felt a precariousness about his situation that was intensified by the fact that he had no weapons.

'Twas not the first time he'd been forced to use his wits in place of his sword to get what he wanted, though he'd feel a damn sight better about his chances with a length of Spanish steel in his hand.

He supposed he could just wait it out. If it were spring, he'd do exactly that. But few ships dared negotiate even coastal waters in the dead of winter, let alone chanced an open sea voyage. It could be weeks, months even, before another craft lit in Fair Isle's tiny harbor.

The memory of the shipwreck burned fresh in his mind, though no trace of it, save scattered bits of wood, was left along the rocky shore of the island. He'd hired the vessel and its crew out of Inverness, and had taken a dozen of his own men as escort, including his brother.

Oh, Sommerled.

He raked a hand through his hair and blinked away the sting of tears pooling unbidden in his eyes. What had he been thinking to let the youth talk him into such a daft scheme? They should have traveled up the coast by steed, as was expected.

Expected.

Sweet Jesus, the Sinclairs!

Even now, they must wonder what had become of him and his party. His wedding to Anne Sinclair, youngest daughter of their chieftain, was to take place—he mentally counted off the days—two days hence!

He'd never get back by then. He cursed, and a dozen sets of eyes turned in his direction. Not at this rate, he wouldn't.

The door to the brew house banged opened, wrenching him from his thoughts. Needles of sleet blew across the threshold instantly chilling the room. On its heels drifted another frosty presence.

Rika.

She did not see him, half-hidden as he was in the shadowed corner, as she made her way to an empty table well within his own view. The youth, Ottar, who'd made it clear to George the previous day he styled himself Rika's protector, settled beside her on a bench.

The woman needed no protector. She was half man herself. Just as he decided she was, indeed, some freak of nature, Rika threw off her heavy cloak and absently brushed the snow from her hair.

'Twas a decidedly feminine gesture, and George found himself fascinated by the dichotomy. In fact, he could not take his eyes from her. 'Twas his first opportunity to observe her undetected, and there was something about it he enjoyed.

She called for horns of mead and, once delivered,

she chatted easily with the youth. Ottar looked on her with a kind of boyish awe. God knows why. The youth had actually warned him off her. What nonsense. He had no intention of touching her, though he didn't like anyone—man or boy—telling him what he could or could not do.

No matter. The youth was harmless enough. Yesterday on the cliff, George could have snapped his neck with one hand, if he'd had a mind to. At the time, he'd been more concerned with throttling the woman. Even now, as he looked at her, he could feel his hands close over her throat. The scar she bore told him he was not the only man who would see her dead.

The brew house door swung wide again, and Lawmaker came in from the cold. He spied George immediately and nodded. Rika followed the elder's gaze and, when her eyes found George's, her fair brows knit in displeasure.

He read something else behind that perpetual mask of irritation she reserved for him, but what it was, he could not say—only that he felt strangely warmed by her cold scrutiny.

Lawmaker settled beside her. He was an unusual man—patient and clever, with an air of intellect about him that was refreshing in what was otherwise a barbaric wasteland of humanity.

Rika pulled her gaze from his and cocked her head to better hear Lawmaker's conversation. She looked up to him, relied on him. George could see it in the way she seemed to consider the old man's words before replying—as a daughter would reflect on a father's advice.

Lawmaker was clearly not her father, though he figured all important in her scheme. The elder was, in fact, the man in charge at the moment. Their laird, or jarl, was away. Gone a-Viking, the children had told him.

What surprised George most was that Lawmaker apparently condoned this marriage scheme. Mayhap the man had not the sense he'd charged him with.

Regardless, 'twas time George learned more of this plan, exactly what would be expected of him. At the moment, he had no other option for quitting this godforsaken place. He rose and moved slowly toward their table.

Rika froze in midsentence, then drew herself up to acknowledge him. Christ, the woman was irritating. "Have you something you wish to discuss?"

"Aye," he said.

She nodded for him to sit. Why he waited for her consent in the first place, he knew not. He took a place on the empty bench opposite her.

"I have questions about this proposed…marriage," he said.

Her face brightened. 'Twas the first spark of cheer he'd seen from her, and it made him feel all the more strange.

Ottar snorted, and drained the cup before him. "I've work to do," he said, and pushed himself to his feet, his eyes on George. "I'll see you later, at table?" The question was for Rika.

"Of course," she said.

Ottar quit the brew house like a young bull elk gone to sharpen his sheds against the nearest tree. The lad itched for battle, and George had the distinct impression *he* was the enemy.

"Now," Rika said. "What would you know?"

"This…marriage," he began.

She raised a hand to silence him. "'Twill be a marriage in name only, of course. And short-lived at that. You do take my meaning, Grant.''

'Twas not a question but an order, and George took orders from no one, least of all heathen women. Her confidence irked him. Yet a hint of color tinged her cheeks, and he could swear she was unnerved by the topic.

"I understand ye well." Good luck to the poor sod who dared breach that icy exterior. George was happy to have none of it.

"In name only," she repeated, louder this time.

"Name only?" A silver-haired man at the next table rose abruptly at Rika's words. "Name only?" To George's astonishment—and Rika's, too, from the look on her face—in a voice both commanding and strangely melodic, the elder recited a snippet of verse:

> "'When a man is wed
> Ere the moon is high
> He shall bed his bride
> Heed Frigga's cry'"

Hmm. What the devil did that mea—?

"He shall not!" Rika slammed her fist on the table, and her drinking horn clattered to the floor.

Now here was something unexpected. George's interest in the matter grew tenfold with her response. He watched as the silver-haired man exchanged a pregnant look with Lawmaker.

"Who is Frigga?" George asked, intrigued.

The silver-haired man smiled. "Goddess of love— and matrimony."

Rika swore under her breath.

"And who are ye, if I may ask?" George said.

"Hannes," the man said. "The skald."

"Skald?" George frowned, trying to recall where he'd heard the word before.

"He's a poet," Lawmaker said.

Rika shot Hannes a nasty look. "Not much of one, in my opinion. There shall be no—" she crossed her arms in front of her, and George saw the heat rise in her face "—bedding." She spat the word.

"Oh, but there must be," Hannes said. "It's the law." He arched a snowy brow at Lawmaker, who sat, seemingly unmoved by both the skald's declaration and Rika's outrage.

"Hannes is right," Lawmaker said finally. "It is the law. Without consummation, there is no marriage—and no dowry."

Rika shot to her feet. "You said naught of this to me before."

Lawmaker shrugged and affected an expression innocent as a babe's. "I thought you knew."

Until this moment, George had not seen her truly angry, and it fair amused him. The self-possessed vixen had finally lost control. Her cheeks blazed with color, setting off the cool blue of her eyes. Those lips he favored twisted into a scowl.

Somehow he must use this opportunity.

"If the coin is all ye want," he said to her, even as the idea formed in his mind, "ye need not a marriage to get it."

Her scowl deepened. "Explain."

"I told ye," George said. "I shall pay ye well for my transport home."

"How much?" Her eyes narrowed.

He hesitated, wondering how little he could get away with offering. His clan was comfortable, but not wealthy by any stretch of the imagination. He had his own bride-price to pay for Anne Sinclair's hand. That silver had gone down with their ship and would have to be raised anew.

Lawmaker cleared his throat. "It makes no difference, Rika, what the Scot offers. If your dowry remains intact, with your father..."

George watched as her mind worked.

"Ah, you're right, of course," she said. "It solves not my other problem."

George had no idea of what they spoke, yet the matter intrigued him more than it should.

"So marriage it is," Lawmaker said.

Hannes made for the bar. "And consummation," he called back over his shoulder.

"I refuse to submit to such a thing! He'll not touch me." Rika fisted her hands at her sides and seized George's gaze. He was certain, if she held it long enough, those crystalline eyes would burn holes right through him.

Her breathing grew labored, and George was all too aware of her breasts straining at her gown. 'Twas cold in the room, and before his very eyes her nipples hardened against the thick fabric. All at once, he felt something that startled and disturbed him.

Arousal.

He shifted on the bench and adjusted his tunic. The thought of bedding such an offensive woman—and one so tall at that—was repugnant. She was everything an alluring maiden should not be: domineering, opinionated, and with a roughness about her that was appalling in one of her sex.

Aye, should they do the deed, the hellion would likely wish to mount *him*.

His mouth went dry at the thought, and for the barest instant he recalled how her braids had grazed his chest the first moment he laid eyes on her.

Rika stiffened, as if she read his thoughts. Unconsciously she bit her lip, and George's eyes were drawn to her mouth yet again.

An unsettling thought possessed him.

Mayhap *heeding Frigga's cry* would be not so disagreeable after all.

Chapter Three

The woman disgusted him.

And intrigued him.

'Twas late and the fire in the longhouse waned, smoldering embers casting a reddish glow about the smoky room. George sat on the bench near his bed box and watched discreetly as Rika bested Ottar at some kind of board game.

She shot him an occasional glance, her eyes frosting as they met his, then warming again in the firelight as she laughed at one of Ottar's jokes.

Lawmaker sat with Hannes in whispered conversation, seemingly oblivious to everything around them. But George knew better. The old man didn't miss a trick.

Rika had avoided all of them, save Ottar, since the incident in the brew house the afternoon before. At table she'd been silent, and when George caught her staring at him, he'd read something new in her eyes.

Apprehension.

It should have pleased him. After all, decent women should fear him. Respect him. But all he felt was surprise, and a mild disappointment he was at a loss to explain.

'Twas the talk of consummation that had changed her. Of that George was certain. Her entire demeanor seemed altered since the skald's matter-of-fact proclamation.

George ran a hand through his hair and shook his head. It wasn't his idea, this bloody marriage. 'Twas hers. He wanted no part of it. He was daft to even consider such a proposal. Nay, he wouldn't do it. There must be another way.

He scanned the faces of the men still at table, and those seated around the fire on crudely hewn benches. Blowing snow whistled across the moors outside and flapped at the sealskin coverings draping the windows.

A young woman rose from the central table and caught his eye. She was small and blond, exuding a delicate beauty and an air of sensuality that George found rather appealing.

She held his gaze while she poured a draught of mead into a horn, then moved toward him with a feline grace. "Are you thirsty?" she asked, and offered him the drink.

"Aye," he said, and took it. Were he on his own shores, he'd consider flirting with this one. "My thanks." He drained the horn and grimaced at the sweetness of the libation.

"You don't like it?" The woman pouted prettily.

"I prefer a stout ale."

"My name is Lina," she said. "Perhaps I can find you some."

His gaze slid unchecked over her body, and she giggled. A chill snaked its way up his spine.

Rika.

George glanced toward the gaming table and, sure enough, found Rika's icy stare. Her hand closed over one of the carved stone pieces and squeezed. The message was not lost on Lina, who slipped quietly back to her place at table. Rika released the game piece.

George marveled at the subtlety of this power play. Aye, all had been told not to speak with him, but the islanders had grown lax on that account these past two days, and Rika had seemed not to care. Until now.

The uneasiness he'd read in her eyes just moments before had vanished. The old Rika was back. Frigid. Authoritative. Mercenary.

All a man could want in a bride.

George snorted and looked away. What in God's name had he gotten himself into? He had to find a way off the island. Lina had been friendly enough. Mayhap there were others who would help him.

He studied the small groups of men and women lounging by the fire and settled on the benches hugging the walls of the longhouse. Some smiled at him cautiously. Others scowled. He was an oddity to them. 'Twas clear the folk of Fair Isle didn't get much company.

George had lived among them nearly a sennight now, and one fact rang clear from the snippets of conversation he'd been privy to. Some sort of dissention was at work. Not all of the islanders spoke highly of their absent jarl.

Brodir was his name.

Even now, in the dim firelight, George saw two camps taking shape—those who were loyal to Brodir, and those who were not. Two of the loyalists sat watching him from their bench by the fire.

The rougher of the two, Ingolf they called him,

honed his knife on a whetstone, turning the blade slowly so that it caught the reddish light.

The other man smiled wide, revealing a nearly toothless mouth, though by the look of him he could not have been much older than George. Thirty at most. Nay, not even.

"Whatcha lookin' at, Scotsman?" the toothless one said.

George shrugged.

Ingolf continued to eye him silently, then rose and moved toward him, pocketing the stone but not the knife. The toothless one dogged his steps.

"Methinks we should join him," Ingolf said to his friend. "What say you, Scotsman? Might Rasmus and I have a few words?" They did not wait for his reply, and sat one on each side of him on the bench.

Rasmus, the toothless one, stank of seal oil and mead. George could see immediately that he was Ingolf's puppet, and would do whatever the man bid him.

Ingolf wiped his knife on his leather tunic, then held it up to the light. "Think you to wed the tall one?" he said, examining the blade.

The question caught George off guard. No one had yet spoken to him of this ill-conceived match between Rika and him, but they all knew. 'Twas the talk of the island.

Mayhap these two, unsavory though they seemed, might help him find an alternative to this sham of a wedding. George searched for the right words.

"Well?" Rasmus said, sliding closer. "Think you to wed her?"

Under any other circumstance, George would have wasted no time in teaching these two heathens a few Scottish manners. He could disarm them both in an instant and have them whimpering for mercy at his feet—and he would have done so had he not been out-numbered nearly twenty to one by their kinsmen.

"Mayhap," he said, controlling his instincts. "What of it?"

Ingolf eyed him, and his half smile turned to something more dangerous. "I wouldn't even dream it, Scotsman, were I in your shoes."

Rasmus fidgeted beside him, and let out a depraved little chuckle.

"But ye're no in my shoes, now are ye?" George said, and straightened his spine.

"We ain't," Rasmus said. "'Cause if we was, we'd be dead men, just like you."

George studied his fingernails for a moment, then shot them each a steely glance. "Are ye threatening me, lads?"

Neither replied.

The room felt suddenly over warm, the air close and rank with the stink of them. George was aware of other eyes on him.

Lawmaker's.

Was this another test then? Like that morning on the beach with young Ottar? The old man watched George closely, as he had that day, waiting to see what he would do.

Lawmaker's was not the only gaze trained to him. Two others—young men he'd overheard speaking ill of their jarl—watched him, as well.

Hang the lot of them. No one threatened him.

No one.

"The tall one belongs to Brodir," Ingolf said finally.

George narrowed his eyes at the man. "What d'ye mean?" He couldn't fathom Rika *belonging* to anyone.

"If you touch her…" Ingolf slid a dirty finger along the blade of his knife, leaving a crimson smear of blood on the hammered metal. "Be warned," he said, and stood.

Rasmus grinned over his shoulder as the two of them snaked their way to the door of the longhouse and disappeared into the night.

Lawmaker resumed his conversation with Hannes. The two young dissidents returned their attention to their mead horns, and the mood lightened.

George glanced at Rika and saw that her game with Ottar was finished. She sat rigid, her expression cool, her eyes unreadable.

What in bloody hell was going on here?

Rika poured a thin stream of seal oil onto a rag and worked it into the chain mail of her brother's hauberk. The armory had been quiet since Brodir went a-Viking last summer. Rika enjoyed the solitude, the smells of leather and burnt metal, the icy kiss of the mail where it rested against her knee.

Ottar worked beside her, carving an ancient design into a shield he had fashioned from a timber hatch that had washed ashore after a shipwreck last year.

The day was clear and cold, and Ottar had built a small fire in the smith's brazier in the corner of the small hut. Rika set the hauberk aside and warmed her hands.

"Why do you marry the Scot?" Ottar said abruptly.

She turned to him, prepared with an answer, knowing he'd ask her sooner or later. "There are things I must—"

"If you've need of a husband, why not me?" He

paused and met her eyes, which widened before she could disguise her shock.

"Ottar, you don't understand."

"I do. You need protection—from Brodir." He gouged a knot in the wood, abandoning the delicate skill required for such art. "I will safeguard you. You think of me as a child, I know. But I'm not."

Rika smiled and placed a hand over his to quell his attack on the ruined shield. "Nay. I have eyes, and I see you are a man."

He smiled, and in that moment she thought he looked more boyish than ever. One day the dark down on his chin would sprout into a man's beard, but not this year.

"Then marry me, instead," Ottar said, and set the shield and the awl aside. "We're well suited to each other. You cannot argue that."

Nay, she could not, for they spent a good part of every day together and had been naught but the best of friends for as long as she could remember.

"It's what Gunnar would have wanted were he here."

Rika arched a brow at him. Gunnar would not have wanted it, nor would he have condoned the scheme she was about to launch in order to buy his freedom.

No one knew of her plan, save Lawmaker and two of Gunnar's closest friends. All thought she was merely after her dowry as a way to thwart Brodir. She'd been careful never to speak of her plans for the silver in front of Ottar and the others. Regardless of his loyalty to her brother, Ottar's tongue was far too loose. She'd tell him when the time was right.

Ottar had worshiped Gunnar until the day her brother was taken from them—carried off in the night and sold into slavery on a ship bound for the mainland. Few believed Brodir was to blame, but Rika knew the truth each time the huge warrior looked into her eyes and grinned. The memory of him evoked a shudder.

Ottar continued to look at her, waiting for her answer. She must think of a way to crush this foolish idea without harming the youth's feelings. Lawmaker had been right, after all.

"I'm not a suitable bride for you," she said finally. "I'm not—" How could she tell him? "Brodir has already—" She fisted her hands in her lap and searched for the right words.

"I know what he's done, and had I known sooner I'd have killed him." Ottar knelt before her. "I would…marry you anyway."

A bittersweet chord tugged at her heart. "I know you would, and I'm grateful to you for the offer." But were Ottar her only choice, she would never allow such a thing. It was unthinkable. Brodir would kill him, as he would any man of her clan who dared such a bold move in his absence.

As for the Scot, who cared what happened to him? Besides, if they moved quickly, both she and Grant would be long gone by the time Brodir returned.

"Come," she said, and rose from her stool. "We've worked long enough this day. Let us take our evening meal with the others." Ottar opened his mouth to speak, and she put a finger to his lips to quiet him. "We will speak no more of this," she said, and stepped outside into what promised to be a brilliant sunset.

Ottar followed, dragging his feet in the crusty snow. Rika smiled inwardly. Honor and chivalry were rare among her folk. One day, Ottar would make a woman a happy wife. But not this year, and not this woman.

"Ho!" a voice boomed behind them.

Rika turned to see Lawmaker jogging toward them from the bathhouse, his breath frosting his peppered beard.

"I'll see you inside," Ottar said to her, and continued toward the longhouse.

She nodded, then smiled at Lawmaker.

Strange that the old man would bathe midweek. She glanced at the small hut on the opposite side of the courtyard and saw that, indeed, a whisper of steam puffed from the hole in its roof.

"It is but Thursday," she said as he approached her.

Lawmaker took her arm and led her toward the cliff overlooking the water. The sun was nearly spent. "Ja," he said, "but my old bones cannot seem to get warm. I thought a good long soak would do me good."

Rika shivered and pulled her cloak more tightly around her. "And me."

"I shall leave the fire lit when I'm finished, if you like."

She nodded, and stepped closer to him. The wind whipped at her unbound hair and chilled her to the bone, but she would not miss a winter sunset on so clear a day.

They often stood like this together, she and Lawmaker, watching as Odin's fiery orb kissed the sea. Someone else watched, as well, below them on the beach.

Grant.

He sat alone with his back to them, unaware of their presence. Rika felt a sudden stab of pity for the lone Scotsman, but quickly pushed the unbidden emotion away. Compassion, like love, was for the weak.

"Once you start down this path," Lawmaker said,

his eyes trained on the Scot, "there can be no turning back."

Rika had no intention of turning back. Gunnar must be freed. She would free him, and this was the only way she could conceive of to do it.

"You think it will not change you, this marriage." Lawmaker looked at her, and in his eyes she saw the experience of a thousand lifetimes. "But it shall."

A shiver coursed through her. "Nay, it shan't." The subject unnerved her, and she grasped at the first unrelated thought that crossed her mind. "Ingolf warned him off, you know. Last night, in the longhouse."

"Ja, but the Scot was not afraid. Far from it. Did you not see the fire in his eyes? I swear his hand itched to rip the blade from Ingolf's grip and slit both their throats. A lesser man would have tried."

Rika had seen, and was impressed by Grant's judgment and control. "Perhaps you should speak with him," she said as she watched Grant rise from the rocks and walk along the surf line.

"Tonight," Lawmaker said. "He's had time enough to think on it."

George pushed back from the supper table, sated, and made for the door. The two young dissidents who'd watched him all week offered him a horn of mead and a seat by the fire. He declined, wanting some air and a bit of solitude before bed.

The time had come to make a decision.

Today was his wedding day.

In Wick, Anne Sinclair and her family waited for a bridegroom who would not come. George closed the longhouse door behind him and sucked in a draught of wintry air.

The king and the Sinclairs would have his head. There was no way to send word to them or to his own clan about what had befallen him and his men. Mayhap they'd think him dead. Nay, no one knew they'd gone by ship. It had been a last-minute decision, made on the docks at Inverness.

He remembered the look of wonder on young Sommerled's face when his brother had first spied the bonny ship in the harbor. Stupid, stupid decision. George would never forgive himself.

All lost.

Rika's dispassionate words echoed in his mind. What kind of woman could be so callous? A woman who dressed like a warrior, who drank and gamed with men, and showed not a whit of the softness and grace expected of her sex.

He'd never agree to her plan. Never. Not if he lived a hundred years on this godless island.

"You've made up your mind," a voice called out in the dark.

George whirled toward the sound, his hand moving instinctively to the place at his waist where a dirk should rest. Damn! This lack of weaponry grew tiresome.

"Who's there?" he called back, ready for a fight, and walked toward the dark shape lurking in the shadow of the longhouse eaves.

"Lawmaker."

He relaxed. In the past week he'd formed a cautious association with the old man. He reminded George a bit of his dead uncle, a man who had shaped his thinking as a youth.

"It's a fair night," Lawmaker said. "Come and sit."

He gestured to the bench hugging the wall, and George obeyed.

There was no moon, and the stars hammered a brilliant path of light across the midnight sky. The wind had died, as was its wont after dark, and the sound of the sea filled his ears.

Lawmaker sat silent beside him, and he knew the old man waited for him to speak first. George had a dozen questions, and began with one that had been on his mind from the start. "What is your true name?"

The old man chuckled. "Now there's a question I've not been asked in years. You likely couldn't pronounce it."

"Why, then, are ye called Lawmaker?"

"It's an ancient custom we still abide. There must always be one who speaks the law, one who remembers."

"And ye are that one," he said.

"I am. Since I was a very young man."

George could well believe it. The elder had a patience and temperament well suited to such a position. 'Twas not unlike the role of the elders of his own clan.

"And Rika," he said. "In her father's absence ye are her guardian?"

"I suppose I am, as much as any man could be, given her nature."

George laughed. "She is unlike any woman I have known."

"That is not surprising."

He recalled the first moment he saw her, there on the beach looming over him. "Explain to me why a woman would don a helm and a suit of mail—here of all places, on an island where there is little threat of danger."

Lawmaker sighed. "There is more danger than you

know—for Rika, in particular. Her life has not been easy. She's fought her own battles and bears the scars of such experience.''

He remembered one such scar, and imagined tracing it along the curve of her neck.

''And we did not know, when first we saw you lying still on the beach, were you friend or foe, if you lived or nay. Rika is hotheaded, reckless even—save where men are concerned. There she tends to be overcautious.''

He looked at the old man's face in the dark.

''And with good reason,'' Lawmaker said.

George would know that reason, and that unsettled him. Why should he care?

''It's her brother's battle gear, not hers.''

''Brother?'' No one had said anything about a brother. ''Where is he? Why have I no met him?''

Lawmaker didn't respond.

''Will he no have something to say about—''

''He is gone,'' Lawmaker snapped. ''No one knows where.''

The old man was irritated, but why? There was more to all of this than he let on. An estranged father. A lost brother. An absent jarl. Whisperings among the women, and tension among the men.

There was a mystery here, and Lawmaker held the answers. George knew the elder would not reveal all to him in this night. Still he pressed for more.

''This Brodir, your jarl,'' he began. ''Rika is...'' How had Ingolf put it? ''She belongs to him?''

''Who told you that?''

George shrugged. Lawmaker knew exactly who had told him.

"Rika belongs to no man. Not yet," the old man added, and shot him a wry look.

He took Lawmaker's meaning, and the presumption annoyed him. "Why me? There are plenty of men here. If all she wants is her coin, why no wed one of her own? Someone who's willing?"

"Nay, that would be too…complicated. You are the perfect choice. You have no interest in the dowry or her. Am I right?"

He snorted. "Too right."

"Well then. What say you?"

George rose from the bench and kicked at the thin veil of snow under his boots. What choice did he have? He shook his head, unwilling to give in. There must be another way.

"Do not answer yet," Lawmaker said, and stood. "You're tense, and still angered over your situation. Angry men make poor choices."

The old man had a point.

"Go," Lawmaker said. "Have a soak in the bath-house." He pushed George toward the small hut at the end of the courtyard. A fire was lit within, and a warm glow spilled from under the closed door.

Aye, mayhap a hot soak would do him some good. At least 'twould warm his icy flesh. "Ye shall have my answer later," he called back over his shoulder, and tripped the bathhouse door latch.

'Twas hot and close inside. Steam curled from under the inner door leading to what the islanders called a sauna. George had never seen such a thing before. He noticed that the bathing tubs in the outer chamber were empty. Strange. Lawmaker had said a soak would be good for him.

No matter. He would try this sauna. George peeled

off his garments and laid them on a bench next to a coarsely woven cloak. Someone else was within. One of the other men, by the look of the garment. He sought solitude, but there was damned little of it to be had anywhere in the village.

To hell with it. The heat felt good. Already he could feel the tension drain from his body. He pulled open the inner door, stepped into the cloud of steam, and drew a cleansing breath of moist air tinged with herbs.

Ah, heavenly.

There would be a bench somewhere. A place to rest. Cautiously he took a step. Another. The heat grew intense, and a healthy sweat broke across his skin. Christ, he couldn't see a thing. Where was the bench? It should be right—

A vision materialized in the vapor. A woman. She sat with her back to him, long damp hair clinging to her nude body.

George swallowed hard. How long since he'd had a woman? Too long. In one languid motion, the vision drew a ladle of water from a bucket at her feet and poured it over her head.

She turned, and the rise of one perfect breast came into view. Water sluiced over her skin. One shimmering droplet clung like honey to the pebbled tip of her breast.

He wet his lips.

As the vapor cleared, their eyes met.

"Rika."

She gasped, but did not cover herself, nor did she look away.

He was aware of his heart dancing in his chest, of the heat, and the closeness of her. He fisted his hands at his sides because he didn't know what else to do.

Her eyes roved over him in an entirely different manner than they had that first day when she'd stripped him naked like a beast in the courtyard. Finally she turned away.

He breathed at last.

Seconds later he was dressed and stumbling out the door into the courtyard. The cold air hit him like a hundredweight stone. He felt drugged, hungover. Not himself at all.

A shape stepped out of the shadows and Lawmaker's peppered beard glistened in the starlight. "What say you, Scotsman? Will you wed her?"

Time stood still for a moment, a day, a lifetime, as the sound of the sea filled his ears.

"Aye," he heard himself say. "I will."

A sliver of moon rose over the water, and in the pearly light Lawmaker smiled.

Chapter Four

She didn't feel like a bride.

Rika stood naked before Sitryg, the woman who had been her mother's closest friend, and frowned.

"Come now." Sitryg slipped a light woolen shift over Rika's head. "Is this not what you yourself wished? To wed the Scot?"

"Ja," she said, but would not meet the older woman's eyes.

"I will say this much for him," Sitryg said, then pushed Rika down onto a stool and began to work a tortoiseshell comb through her hair. "He's fair handsome, and canny as any man I've known."

"Hmph. That's not saying much. Who have you known?"

Sitryg clicked her tongue. "Enough, girl. In a few hours he shall take you to his bed. If you're half as smart as I think you are, you'll change your mood before then."

"Why should I?" The comb pulled harder. "Ow!"

"Because it will go easier for you if you do. A man expects a compliant bedmate, not a sharp-tongued serpent in women's clothes."

At least she'd agreed to wear women's clothes. She would have preferred Gunnar's hauberk and helm. It seemed, somehow, more fitting to the occasion.

Rika crossed her arms over her chest and ground her teeth. Ja, compliant she'd be for as long as it took. And if her experience with Brodir was any indication, it wouldn't take long.

She'd do it for Gunnar. Nothing else mattered. After all, how much worse could it be than what she'd already experienced in Brodir's bed? Rika toyed with the wide hammered bracelets circling her wrists.

"I suggest you remove those," Sitryg said. "They don't belong with your gown."

Rika ignored her. She never removed the bracelets. Not ever, except in the bathhouse, and only when she was alone. A shiver ran up her spine as she recalled Grant's eyes on her in the sauna last eve.

He could have taken her then, in the heat, on the birch-strewn floor. Brodir would have. But Grant hadn't, and she knew why. She repulsed him. Disgusted him. Her size and plain features, her scars—Thor's blood, had he seen her with her bracelets off?

He'd stood not an arm's length from her and had said not a word save her name—yet she'd felt his contempt. Oh, she knew well that sensation. Her father had taught her young that she was less than nothing. She and her brother—their mother, too.

Why Fritha had stayed married to him all those years, Rika could not understand. When her mother died, it seemed almost a blessing. So peaceful did she rest on her funeral pyre, Rika longed to go with her to the next world.

Then there had been Brodir's lessons.

Rika closed her eyes and swallowed against the taste

souring her mouth. By rights, she should have told
someone and Brodir would have been punished. But
she had not. The humiliation had been too great. Too,
she feared he would exact some worse revenge. Instead,
she'd borne his abuse in silence.

And she could bear it once more at the hands of a
stranger. She must.

"Leave me now," she said, and rose from the stool.

Her pale woolen gown lay strewn across a bench in
the small cottage where she and Grant would pass their
wedding night. Most of the islanders slept in the four
longhouses that ringed the central courtyard, though
some couples built cottages of their own after they wed,
in the style of the mainlanders—and the Scots, she supposed.

"Let me help you finish dressing." Sitryg reached
for the gown.

"Nay, I can manage on my own."

"But—"

"Sitryg, please." Rika put a hand on the woman's
shoulder. Only then did she realize she was trembling.
This was ridiculous. She must compose herself. "Leave
me now. I shall see you at the ceremony."

"As you wish." The old woman covered Rika's
hand with her own. "Your mother meant the world to
me, you know. I would help her daughter in any small
way I could."

She smiled, remembering how close the two of them
had been. "I know that, and I thank you."

Sitryg squeezed her hand, then left.

Rika collapsed on the freshly made bed and whispered "I must be strong" for the hundredth time that
day. As strong as her mother had been. As strong as

Gunnar would have to be to stay alive until she could reach him.

This wedding was only the first of the trials she must endure. Her father's wrath would come later and, after she returned, she'd have Brodir to face.

The fire in the room did little to warm her. Rika rose and snatched the gown, pulled it on and smoothed it over her shift. Perhaps she wouldn't return to Fair Isle at all after Gunnar was freed. She could stay on the mainland and make a new life. Now there was a thought.

She donned her sealskin boots and secured her hair with a *kransen,* a plain bronze circlet that rested lightly on her forehead. It would have to do. She was no beauty, and it made no sense to fuss over her appearance.

Besides, what did she care how she looked? It wasn't a real marriage, after all. Following the celebration, Grant would do the deed—damn Hannes to hell—and she'd never have to suffer it again.

An image of the Scot looming over her naked in the sauna shot through her mind like a lightning bolt. It was not the first time that day she'd thought of him so. Last night in the heat and close air Rika had felt something so overpowering, so foreign, it frightened her.

Desire.

"It's time," a voice called from the other side of the door. "Your bridegroom waits."

George paced the dirt floor of Lawmaker's cottage and shook his head. "She must be mad if she thinks I'll recite such pagan words."

Lawmaker arched a brow in what George knew was exasperation. They'd been over the details of the ceremony a dozen times that day. "It's not up to her. It's the law. You have your rituals, and we have ours."

"But it's…heathen." He didn't want to offend the old man, but there it was.

"It's a Christian ceremony for the most part."

"Oh, aye? Well where's the priest then?"

Lawmaker shrugged. "The only one we had died years ago. Besides, the people like the old ways. There is little left to remind us of our ancestry. The wedding rites are something we all enjoy."

"Hmm." Well he wasn't enjoying it one bit. He supposed he should be relieved there was no priest. 'Twas not a proper Christian wedding and, therefore, 'twould not be recognized by God or king. That was some consolation. No one would have to know about it once he was home.

Home.

Again, he thought of Sommerled.

"Take this," Lawmaker said. To George's astonishment, the old man offered him the hilt of a sword.

His fingers closed instinctively over the finely crafted weapon. The weight of it felt good in his hand.

Lawmaker grinned. "It suits you."

"Why now? And why a weapon so fair?" He ran his hand along the rune-covered blade.

"Oh, it's not for you to keep. The ceremony requires that you bestow on your bride your family's sword— as a vow of protection."

George frowned.

"You have no family here, so I offer you my weapon." Lawmaker looked at him, waiting for his acceptance, and George knew from the elder's expression that the gesture was no small honor.

He was moved by the man's trust in him. "Thank ye," he said.

"Rika, in turn, will offer you her family's sword. Her brother's."

"As a sign of…?"

"Obedience."

"Ha!"

"And loyalty," Lawmaker said. "Do not scoff. I told Rika this, and I shall tell you—" Lawmaker snatched the sword from him and sheathed it. "This marriage will change you both—for the better, methinks."

He snorted. "The only thing 'twill change is my location. For if I do this thing, I expect to see the bonny shores of Scotland posthaste."

"Hmm, Latin. You are as I thought—an educated man. It will be a fine match."

"Stop saying that." The old man annoyed him to no end. He'd sent George into that sauna deliberately, knowing Rika was there. George knew it, and Lawmaker knew he knew it. Damn him.

He'd not been in his right mind when he agreed to the wedding, but by the time he'd come to his senses, the news was all over the village. He'd given his word, and he was not a man to go back on it. Lawmaker knew that, the canny sod.

"Take this, as well."

"Huh?" He hadn't been listening.

Lawmaker handed him a small, devilishly heavy tool—a hammer.

"What's this for?"

"Put it in your belt. It's a symbol of Thor's hammer. For the ritual."

He looked at it skeptically before tucking it under his belt. "What does it signify?"

Lawmaker smiled. "Your mastery in the union. And a fruitful marriage, if you take my meaning."

"Oh, aye." George shot him a nasty look, and the old man laughed. What fruit 'twould bear would be bitter at best.

"Bear with me, son. We are nearly ready."

'Twas a good thing, too. He didn't know how much more of this pagan nonsense he could stand.

"Now, about the bride-price. I expect—"

"Bride-price? Surely ye dinna expect me to *pay* for her? And with what, pray tell?" This was too much.

"Calm down." Lawmaker placed a steadying hand on his shoulder. "I was about to say, we'll cross that bridge when we come to it. When you meet Rika's father."

"Fine."

"For now, all that's needed is for you to present her with a *morgen gifu*—a morning gift, after the, uh... consummation."

George felt his eyes widen of their own accord.

"Well, on the morrow sometime." Lawmaker fished something out of a chest behind him. "Here, give her this," he said, and dropped it into his hand.

"What is it?" He examined the delicately crafted silver brooch and marveled at the workmanship. For all their roughness, these islanders were excellent craftsmen.

"Something I've had for years. It was Rika's mother's, in fact. It's time she had it."

George slipped the brooch into the small pouch at his waist and nodded.

"Well, are you ready?"

"As ready as any man who faces the hangman's noose."

Lawmaker smiled like a cat who'd cornered a tasty field mouse. "Come, your bride awaits you."

Rika turned into the courtyard and was not prepared for what she saw there.

The whole of the village was assembled and fell silent when she appeared. Hushed whispers and children's laughter rose around her, threatening to swallow her up as she walked slowly along the path that opened before her. A sullen Ottar followed in her wake, bearing her brother's sword.

She was not used to such attention, and her kinsmen's stares unnerved her. Lawmaker stood with Grant by the well at the courtyard's center. Mustering her resolve, she fixed her gaze on the old man's calming features, and moved one foot ahead of the other until she was there.

For a long moment, no one spoke. The weather was blustery, the sky white, and her thin woolen gown afforded her little protection from the chill air.

Sitryg stepped forward, and Rika stooped so the small woman could remove the bronze *kransen* from her head. It was a symbol of virginity, and after today Rika would wear it no more. Few knew why she'd ceased to do so months ago. Most of the islanders thought her strange anyway and paid her actions no mind.

Lina held the bridal crown. Fashioned from straw and last year's wheat, it was garlanded with dried flowers, and set with a few precious pieces of rock-crystal gathered from the beach.

Sitryg seated the crown, and Rika stood tall, turning her gaze for the first time on her husband.

Grant's expression was stone, his eyes cool steel. Attired in rare leather and borrowed fur, he looked every bit a Viking bridegroom. To her surprise, he wore Lawmaker's broadsword. She glanced quickly at the old man and caught him smiling.

Lawmaker cleared his throat, then nodded at the Scot. Grant stepped forward, and she fought the ridiculous urge to step back. He looked pointedly at her as he unsheathed the sword. His eyes were so cold, for a moment she thought he might use the weapon to slay her.

What did she expect?

This wedding was forced on him. The Scot hated her, and she knew he'd use that hate tonight in their bridal bed, much as Brodir had on many occasions. So be it. She was prepared. Rika swallowed hard and forced herself to hold his gaze.

Grant presented her with the weapon's hilt and she took it from his hand. Hers was shaking. She motioned for Ottar, but he did not step forward. When Rika turned to prompt him, she saw that his dark eyes were fixed on Grant and that his face twitched with what she knew was pent-up rage.

"Ottar," she whispered. "The sword."

The youth thrust it toward her. She nearly dropped it when he let it go and stormed off into the surrounding crowd. Later she would find him and again try to make him understand.

Lawmaker nodded at her to proceed.

She studied Gunnar's sword. Though it had been their father's, she had always thought of it as Gunnar's, and was now loath to part with it. She had little left of her brother, and the weapon had been one of his most treasured things.

"Rika," Lawmaker said.

She met Grant's eyes, and read something new in them. Amusement? Ja, the corner of his mouth turned up ever so slightly. Lawmaker must have explained the significance of the ritual. Her hackles rose.

She gritted her teeth behind tightly sealed lips and thrust the sword toward him. Grant's hand closed over it, and for a moment she hesitated. He jerked the weapon from her hand and smiled.

Thor's blood, she hated him. That hate fed her resolve, and her confidence. She knew men, and the Scot was no different. They fed on power and domination. Tonight's victory would be his, but she would win the war.

Lawmaker fished something out of the pouch at his waist, and Rika's eyes widened as she recognized what he held.

Wedding rings.

No one had said anything about rings.

She narrowed her eyes at him, and he merely shrugged. Hannes stood behind him, grinning.

Grant had obviously been well instructed, for he proffered the hilt of her family's sword while Lawmaker set the smaller ring upon it. She pursed her lips, and did the same with the weapon Grant had given her.

They exchanged the rings, each on the hilt of their newly accepted swords. Without flourish Rika jammed the silver circle on her finger. Grant followed suit.

There. It was done.

Save for the speaking of vows—a Christian custom Rika never much cared for. Grant raced through the lines he'd been taught, and Rika mumbled her response.

A shout went up in the crowd, and others echoed it. Lawmaker grunted, satisfied, and Rika supposed she should be happy, as well. It was, after all, what she'd wanted—the first step in her carefully crafted plan.

She turned to the crowd of onlookers and searched for the two faces she knew would be there. Erik and Leif. Her brother's closest friends. They nodded soberly when she met their eyes. The two young men shared her secret, and their stalwart faces buoyed her confidence.

"Wife," Grant's voice boomed behind her.

Her head snapped around.

The Scot had the nerve to offer her his arm. "Come, there is a celebration, is there no?"

She scowled. "I don't wish to celebrate."

"Ja, she does," Lawmaker said, and pushed her toward the path opening before them.

Her temper flared. She shot both of them murderous glances, then stormed toward the longhouse.

"Wait!" Lawmaker called after her.

She looked back, but kept walking.

"Rika, watch—"

"Unh!" She tripped over the threshold and hit the packed dirt floor with a thud. Thor's blood!

A collective gasp escaped the mouths of the onlookers.

Grant was there in an instant, looming over her but offering no help. Lawmaker pushed him aside and pulled Rika to her feet.

"What's wrong?" Grant said, obviously bewildered by the shocked expressions all around him.

"You should have been here waiting, as I instructed you," Lawmaker scolded.

"Aye, but she beat me to it. So what?" Grant shrugged.

"It's an ill omen, you fool." Lawmaker shook his head at Grant. "You were to carry her across, remember?"

Grant snorted. "She's so big, I wasna certain I could manage it."

Of all the—

Her kinsmen roared, and Rika felt the heat rise in her face. She tested the weight of the sword Grant had given her, and was sorely tempted to unman him on the spot.

Instead, she glared at him until the smile slid from his face, then she blew across the threshold into the midst of the celebration.

George followed her into the longhouse, which was already packed with people. Tables were jammed into every available space, and laden with fare—roasted mutton, bread, and a half-dozen kinds of cheese. Flagons of honeyed mead were placed within easy reach of every diner.

The air, as always, was thick and smoky. The central fire blazed. George welcomed the heat, for the weather had turned. By nightfall snow was expected and, from what the elders predicted, in no small measure.

"Ho, Scotsman!" A burly islander slapped George on the back. "Have a go at this rooftree, man, so we can see of what you're made." The man pointed at one of the thick timber pillars supporting the low longhouse roof.

George had no idea what the man wanted him to do. Rika beckoned him to the high-placed table where she sat with Lawmaker. "Nay, you need not partake of such foolishness."

"Come on, man," the islander said. "Draw that fine sword she's given you and see how far you can sink it into the wood."

George followed the man's gaze to the timber pillar, which he now noticed was riddled with scars. Still he did not understand. Men crowded around him, spurring him on.

"'Twill predict the luck of the marriage," one of them said.

"Oh, I see." George nodded his head, but he didn't see at all.

"It's a test of virility, of manhood." The burly islander slapped his back again. "The deeper you sink your weapon..." He cast a lusty smile toward Rika, who blushed crimson with rage. "Well, you... understand, do you not?"

George understood, all right. "Why not?" he said, enjoying Rika's discomfort. He drew the sword and raised it double-fisted over his head as instructed by the men. The room went deadly quiet.

Rika glared at him, her eyes twin daggers. He grinned at her, drew a breath and, with all his might, plunged the sword into the wood.

"Hurrah!" The shout went up as a dozen beefy hands slapped him on the back, a few reaching up to rumple his hair. 'Twas all fair amusing.

The burly islander grunted as he pulled the sword from the timber, carefully measuring off the length that had been embedded. Apparently, George had done quite a good job of it, for the men howled as the burly one held the weapon aloft for all to see. After George had been congratulated a dozen times over, the crowd pushed him toward the table where his *bride* waited, her face the color of ripe cherries.

"You did not have to do that," she seethed.

"I know, but I enjoyed it." He smiled again, just to taunt her. He had enjoyed it, but reminded himself that his brother was dead, and that he was far from home.

Too far. 'Twas easy to forget amidst such revelry who he was and why he participated in such pagan rites.

He scanned the faces in the room, and nodded at those he recognized. Most of the men seemed to accept him, which he thought odd. Others—Ingolf, in particular—spared him naught but menacing glances.

"Here," Rika said, and pushed a strange-looking vessel toward him. "The bridal cup. You must drink from it, and I will do the same."

The handles were carved into the likeness of a fantastical sea creature. Never had he seen such a thing. George grasped the handles, brought the cup to his lips, and drank. What else? Honeyed mead. Another cheer went up. He screwed his face up as the sweet liquor hit his senses. Nay, there was no hope of a decent ale for fifty leagues.

Three days' sail.

He passed the cup to Rika and she drained it.

"There," she said to Lawmaker. "It's done. All rituals complete."

"All but one," Hannes said, and rose from his seat on the opposite side of the table. "Grant," he said, "your hammer."

"Nay." Rika visibly stiffened beside him. "I won't have it."

"It's custom," Hannes said, and the crowd cheered him on.

George wondered what, exactly, this custom signified, to cause her such distress. He rose at their beckoning, slipped the hammer from his belt and handed it to the skald.

"It's ridiculous," Rika hissed, and turned to Lawmaker as if he would put a stop to Hannes's antics.

George had no idea what was about to happen, but 'twas clear Lawmaker had no intention of stopping it.

Hannes moved behind Rika, whose fists were balled on the table. So profound was her anger, it radiated from her like an icy heat.

"Get it over with, poet," she said to the skald.

Hannes placed the hammer in her lap, and every man, woman and child in the tightly packed room let out a howl.

Lawmaker smiled.

"What does it mean?" George leaned behind the fuming Rika to ask him.

"Hannes invokes Frigga, who is also the goddess of childbearing."

George could not stop his eyes from widening.

"The gesture is meant to bless the bride's…er, womb." Lawmaker arched a brow at him.

"I see," George said, and decided he'd best have another cup of that insufferable mead, after all.

Hours of feasting and drinking ensued, during which Hannes recited a host of verses—many of them love poems, to Rika's enormous displeasure.

George relaxed for the first time since he'd arrived on Fair Isle, and decided, after all, that this marriage was no great burden. 'Twas harmless, really. A pagan rite, nothing more. Had he agreed to it immediately, he might have been home by now.

His obligations to king and clan, and to the families

of his men who'd perished at sea, weighed heavy on his mind. Surely they'd sail on the morrow. His bride was as anxious to secure her dowry as he was to return home.

As for tonight…he'd make the best of it.

Rika sat not inches from him, but had barely glanced in his direction all evening. He leaned over and whispered in her ear, "This was no my idea, ye know."

His closeness startled her, and she drew back. "I know. It will all be over soon." Her expression was cool, but her eyes were troubled.

"No soon enough," he said, and wondered why this much celebrating was really necessary.

She whispered something in Lawmaker's ear, and the elder rose. "It's time!" he shouted over the din. "The night is on us."

"Time for what?" George asked to no one in particular.

Rika's grim, pale expression gave him his answer. "Oh, the—"

"Ja," Rika said, cutting him off. "We will retire now to our…" She drew a breath, and if George didn't know her for the icy thing she was, he'd think it was for courage. "To the cottage," she finished weakly.

Without preamble, he and Rika were whisked from the bench and carried outside on the shoulders of a small throng of drunken islanders.

'Twas snowing. Billowy white flakes blustered down on him, clinging to his hair and garments. He sucked in a breath and realized, too late, that he'd had far too much mead. His head began to spin.

Moments later, the door to a small cottage at the other end of the courtyard was kicked open, and Rika was dropped unceremoniously onto the bed within. George was set on his feet in front of her.

Before he knew what was happening, three men relieved him of his weapons, his boots, and his tunic, leaving him next to naked in naught but his leggings. He snatched a fur from the bed and held it in front of him. He wasn't usually this modest, but the strangeness of the situation unnerved him.

Two women hovered over Rika, and when they drew back he saw that she, too, had been stripped of her outer garments. Her undershift was thin, nearly transparent. In his mind's eye he saw her as she'd been in the sauna last eve—her skin pearled with sweat, her hair damp and clinging to the curves of her body.

He drew a sobering breath.

One of the women, an elder, said, "Remember what I told you, girl."

Rika did not respond, nor did she move a muscle. Hannes and Lawmaker and the few others packed into the tiny cottage fell silent. Finally she tipped her chin at George and said, "Do it then. Get it over with."

He looked at her, uncertain of her meaning.

She set her jaw and eased back onto the bed. "I'm ready, Scotsman. Finish it."

"What?" he croaked. Truth dawned, and his mouth gaped. "Ye mean…" He glanced at the others in the room, and shook his head. "She canna mean what I think she means?"

"Ah, what's that?" Lawmaker said, his face as innocent as a babe's.

Oh, nay. Surely they didn't expect…

"It must be witnessed," Hannes said. "It's the law."

George stood speechless, clutching the fur.

"Go on then," the burly islander said, and slapped

him on the back for what had to be the hundredth time that night.

"With all of ye here? Ye're daft." In truth, since the third or fourth flagon of mead he'd been thinking he wouldn't mind it so very much. And why not? Any port in a storm, so the Inverness sailors were fond of saying.

But this, this was unthinkable.

Rika sat up in the bed. "You must, or it won't be legal. Am I right?" She looked to Lawmaker for confirmation. "Unless of course, we don't have to do it at all?" Her face lit with hope.

"We've been all through this," Hannes said. "Have we not?"

"Ja, we have," Lawmaker said. "But it need not be witnessed. That's an ancient custom we rarely practice. I, myself, shall attest to the legality of the marriage when the time comes. Now, let us away."

"But—" Rika flew from the bed as Lawmaker herded the onlookers from the room. "Nay, you must stay!" Her eyes widened in what George could swear was fear. "Sitryg, Lawmaker, do not leave me here alone with him."

Lawmaker paused in the doorway and cast her a hard look. "He's your husband now. You must trust him, as he has trusted you in agreeing to this bargain."

She started toward the door, and on impulse George reached out and grabbed her braceleted wrist. Her whole body went rigid at his touch.

"Remember, too, what I have told you," Lawmaker said to her. "Not all men are the same."

George looked into the blanched face of his bride and, as Lawmaker closed the door on them, wondered what the devil the old man meant.

Chapter Five

All men *were* the same.

Rika backed onto the bed in the cottage, drawing her legs up under her, and waited. And waited.

Grant stood for what seemed a lifetime with his back to her, the fur wrapped around his waist, warming himself by the small peat fire blazing in the hearth.

The moment she had been dreading had come at last, and now that it was here she was anxious to have done with it.

"What are you doing?" she asked lamely, not knowing what else to say.

"Trying to clear my head."

This surprised her. Brodir had never been concerned with such matters. In fact, he'd been deep in his cups most every time he'd taken her.

"Perhaps this would go…better for you, were it not entirely clear."

He turned to look at her, and she could tell from his expression he thought it a strange thing for her to say. Their eyes locked, and he let the fur slip from his waist.

Thor's blood!

Grant was nothing like Brodir.

Heat suffused her face as the Scot dispensed with his leggings and cast them aside. His eyes raked her up and down, and she braced herself for what would come next.

He moved toward her in the firelight, and for the second time in as many days she was acutely aware of his size and strength. He exuded a feral maleness that startled her.

Lawmaker was right. She had underestimated the Scot.

Rika drew herself up to meet him, fisting her hands at her sides. Fear was not an option. She would never give him that satisfaction. Never. Let him take her and be done with it.

Her pulse raced as he eased himself onto the bed beside her. "Do it," she demanded. "Do it now."

He cocked his head, studying her face. Why did he hesitate? Thor's blood, just do it!

All at once his expression softened. "Never in my life have I taken a woman against her will, and I'm no about to do so now."

Her heart stopped. Of all the words he might speak, those were the last she expected to hear. "But…you must."

"Nay, lass." He shook his head. "Ye dinna want me, and…well…" He shrugged.

The truth of it stung more than any blow Brodir had e'er dealt her. Grant didn't want her. Her belly tightened. She knew all along he didn't, so why did it hurt? She should be relieved, elated, even, but she wasn't.

Something else occurred to her. "It doesn't matter what you or I want. It's the law. You heard the elders— without consummation the marriage is not legal and I cannot claim my dowry."

He shook his head. "This coin is of great import to ye—to willingly give up your virginity to a man ye canna stand, and one you'll ne'er see again."

She closed her eyes against the rage of memories blasting across her consciousness. There was no reason to keep the truth from him, for he was about to learn it for himself. "I am no maid, and therefore give up nothing."

The silence that followed was unbearable. She felt her cheeks blaze hot. Finally he said, "We can say that we did it, and no one will be the wiser."

Rika opened her eyes.

He really didn't want her.

She almost laughed. That would never have stopped Brodir. His hate stoked his lust, and he wreaked it on her not as a lover, but an enemy.

Nay, she did not understand the Scot at all.

"Lawmaker sees all," she said. "The old man will know we lie."

Grant laughed, and warmth flooded his eyes. "Aye, methinks naught gets past him."

Rika smiled, unable to help herself, and worked to instill a measure of gentleness in her words. Everything depended on the Scot's cooperation. "Will you do it, then, as agreed?"

"Aye," he said, and slid his hand across the furs to cover hers. "I will."

The warmth of his touch startled her. She drew her hand away and, gathering her courage, stripped her shift off over her head.

Grant sucked in a breath.

"I will not struggle," she said, and eased back onto the pillows. "Do as you will."

For a long time he did nothing—he simply sat there

looking at her body in the softness of the fire's glow. She feared to look at him, but curiosity overcame her apprehension and she stole a glance.

His face was shadowed in the firelight, his hair awash in gold. Her gaze drifted lower, across the muscled expanse of his chest, which rose and fell with each measured breath he drew. His body was hard and lightly furred, all burnished gold as if the sun had kissed him.

Her own breathing grew quick and shallow under his scrutiny. And when their eyes finally met, what she read in his stirred her blood.

Desire.

Nay, it could not be.

Yet even as she formed the thought, his hands trailed lightly over her thighs. She gasped at his touch.

"I willna hurt you," he breathed, and slid closer on the bed.

How could she believe that? She tensed as he leaned over her, and when she looked into his eyes she knew she'd believe anything he told her.

"Wha-what are you doing?"

"Just this," he said, and his mouth covered hers in the gentlest of kisses.

The world slipped out beneath her, and she floated weightless in the tender wash of the kiss, his breath hot and sweet, his tongue smooth as glass as she opened to him.

What was happening?

"Rika," he breathed against her mouth. "Put your arms around me."

She obeyed without thinking, and he deepened the kiss. His body settled atop hers, the weight of him solid, comforting, nothing like Brodir's oppressive bulk.

His mouth moved over her skin like a firebrand, and she gasped with a spiraling sensation she could not comprehend.

"Touch me," he whispered in her ear. It was not a command, but a plea, invoked with such sweetness she could do naught but respond.

Her hands roved his back and buttocks with a will of their own. He moaned in pleasure, and his surprising response spurred her on. She kissed him with a ferocity that shocked her, clawed at his back as he thrust against her.

"Grant," she breathed, lifting her hips to meet his.

"Will ye no call me George?"

Her eyes flew open.

Thor's blood, what was she doing?

Her body stiffened beneath him. Ja, she would submit, but never would she succumb. Oh, she'd heard about men like this, though she'd not believed it. They wielded pretty words and tenderness like a double-headed ax. Their weapons were tenfold more deadly than the brutal domination at the core of Brodir's armory.

She tried to push him off her, but when his mouth slipped to her breast and he began to suckle, all thoughts of stopping him vanished.

"George," she breathed involuntarily, and fisted handfuls of his hair. Heat spread from her center like molten steel.

His thighs parted hers in one swift motion, and she knew the inevitable had come at last. He was ready, and so was she, yet it was not the velvety tip of his manhood that brushed against her—it was his hand, his fingers playing her like some rare instrument.

"Don't." She struggled against him.

"Aye," he breathed against her lips before his tongue continued its silken exploration of her mouth.

Nothing in her experience with Brodir prepared her for Grant—for the unbearable urgency mounting within her, centered at the place where his fingers worked their magic.

Her heart thrummed in her chest, her limbs writhed beneath him, and when she felt certain she might die from the pleasure he wrought from her, he spread her thighs wide with his own and drove himself inside her.

She drew breath with the shock of it, and knew naught but him—his scent, his power, the slick heat of his skin as she bit into his shoulder. He cried out and thrust again.

A bright-edged wave of something that was, until this moment, unfathomable gripped her, jolting her near senseless. Somewhere at the edge of consciousness she felt not submission, but a visceral power that surged beyond all sensation as Grant found his own pleasure.

In her.

George pulled a fur over the sleeping woman beside him, and wondered what the hell had come over him. The hearth fire burned low, and in its waning light he looked at Rika, daughter of Fritha, with new understanding.

Her naiveté had stunned him, for true to her word, she was no maid. Her kisses were artless, her response to his own surprising passion uncontrived.

She was, in her lovemaking, as open and straightforward as she was in her other dealings with him. Nothing like the women he knew at home.

He shouldn't want her, but he did.

Even now, his desire for her surged anew. This could

not be. 'Twas the drink. That was it. What other reason could there be for this irrational hunger? He'd bedded dozens of women, but never had he felt the ache of wanting that consumed him now.

He knew if he touched her, chanced the simplest caress, she'd wake and look at him in wonder, as she had when first he'd touched her, as if he'd done something remarkable.

As if she'd never before been made love to.

The tall one belongs to Brodir.

He understood now what that meant. The jarl was her lover. What kind of a man was he to have never shown her pleasure? For clearly this had been her first experience of such things.

His gaze drifted to the scar on her throat, and he recalled the panic in her eyes when first he kissed her. What had this Brodir done to evoke such fear in a woman who styled herself fearless?

The bracelets.

He'd tried to remove them before she drifted off to sleep, but she'd grown panicky again and had refused. He hadn't pressed the issue.

Now, one slender, bronzed arm splayed across the pillow over her head. He leaned over her and slowly, carefully, tripped the latch on the bracelet.

She sighed dreamily. He froze. The bracelet fell away onto the pillow when she turned and reached for him in her sleep.

"Sweet Jesus," he breathed, catching her wrist in his hand.

She was horribly scarred. Aye, she'd been bound, and on more than one occasion. What kind of a monster could do such a thing?

Absently he drew her wrist to his lips and planted a

gentle kiss on the purplish scar, then laid the bracelet to rest on the chest flanking the bed.

His anger surged.

Christian or pagan, a man who abused a woman so deserved a slow and painful death. George wished the whoreson were here now, so he could teach him a lesson in—

What the devil was wrong with him?

What did he care what went on between these heathen people? 'Twas none of his affair. He had his own bride waiting, in Scotland, and she, unlike Rika, was everything a woman should be—so the king had promised.

George shook off the momentary stupor. He must forget this Viking woman. What had happened between them tonight was brought on by drink—nothing more. He hadn't even wanted her, not at first. She'd insisted. What could he do? He was a man, after all, not a monk.

He edged away from her and squinted in the near dark, looking for his clothes. Ah, the bastards had taken them. Fine. He'd pass the night here, but would freeze to death before he touched her again.

A shiver shot up his spine. With the fire gone out, 'twas cold as a tomb in the cottage. He burrowed under the furs and turned his back on her, edging as far from her as he might without falling off the bed. Tomorrow they'd sail for her father's island, and in no time he'd be home.

After a while he drifted into an uneasy sleep, and dreamed of serpents bathing in a bridal cup of mead.

Rika dressed at dawn in the everyday garments she'd stashed under the bed the afternoon before. Grant was gone, but his scent lingered on her skin.

She'd bathe quickly before breaking her fast. It was Saturday, and the bathhouse fire would be lit, the tubs filled with heated water, the moist air of the sauna redolent with herbs.

The sealskin drape on the window flapped in the rising wind. She drew it aside and was blasted with sleet. A shiver raced up her spine. Donning her cloak and boots, she took one long look around the room. The rumpled bed stared back at her accusingly.

"You enjoyed it," she whispered to herself. Nay, she hadn't. She couldn't. It was horrible. It was...

Wonderful.

She'd wanted him, and he her.

Rika shook her head fervently and pulled her cloak tight about her. It would never happen again. Never. She tripped the door latch and walked into a blizzard.

Thor's blood, where had the weather come from?

They couldn't sail in this. The courtyard was deserted; everyone must be inside. Her bath would have to wait. Rika jogged to the main longhouse where she took her meals and burst inside.

"There you are."

In the entry she stamped the snow from her boots, and turned toward Lawmaker's familiar voice.

"Come and break your fast. Your husband waits."

Husband.

She bristled at the old man's words, but knew there was no escaping it. Grant sat beside him on the bench, and from the look of their full trencher, it appeared neither had yet eaten.

Grant didn't spare her a glance as she crossed the room and seated herself facing him. Fine. She had naught to say to him, either, and was glad for his disinterest.

What they'd shared last night—what he'd done to her, rather—meant nothing. Not to her certainly. Nor to him, from the cool expression he bore.

It was over now, and time to move ahead with her plan.

Sitryg brought a flagon of mead to the table along with two drinking horns.

"Nay," Grant said, and waved her off. "None for me."

"But you must," Sitryg said. "A bride and groom partake of honeyed mead—together—until the moon is new again."

Grant scowled at the old woman, and for the first time Rika shared his sentiment.

"It's your honeymoon," Sitryg said.

Rika shot her a dark look and pushed the flagon away. "Go, and take this back to the brew house."

Sitryg flashed a loaded look at Lawmaker, and left without a word.

"The blizzard," Rika said, changing the subject. "Can we sail?"

Lawmaker shook his head. "You know as well as I we cannot."

"Why the devil not?" Grant said. His expression twisted into a mask of disbelief.

"What, are you so eager to repeat your last experience at sea?" Lawmaker arched a brow at him. "Was losing a brother not enough for you?"

Grant ground his teeth, and behind his stoic expression she read his pain. Compassion was not an emotion she fostered. It led to weakness, especially where men were concerned. Still, a curious wave of empathy breached her well-schooled heart.

She pushed the emotion away, and focused instead

on the weather. She wanted nothing more than to quit this place. Every day they waited was another day of bondage for her brother—and another day closer to Brodir's return.

"It's not the snow, but the wind that is the danger," Lawmaker said, and Rika knew he was right. It would blow the *byrthing* to bits before they lost sight of the island.

Grant rubbed the tawny stubble of beard on his chin. Rika recalled the feel of it on her skin and shivered.

"How long must we wait?" he said.

Lawmaker shrugged. "Who can say?"

Grant swore under his breath, some Christian curse she'd never heard. It sounded wicked, whatever it meant. She must remember to ask him about it, although now was clearly not the time.

She watched him as he stared at nothing in particular, then wet her lips absently, remembering their coupling.

He'd wanted her.

Perhaps not at first, nor afterward. Certainly not now. But last eve, for one fleeting breath of eternity, the ardor of his kisses, the passion in his eyes, had been for her.

Grant caught her watching him and, for an uncomfortable moment, she held his gaze. What did she expect to see in those steely eyes? Love?

What nonsense.

Men didn't love, they controlled. Oppressed. She was smart enough to know that, and knew—too well, perhaps—how to beat them at that game.

She broke his stare and began to pick at some of the food on the trencher. "What now, old man?"

"Ah, well." Lawmaker cleared his throat authoritatively. "Methinks your hu—"

She shot him a look icier than the blizzard without.

"Uh, Grant, I mean—" Lawmaker paused and nodded to him "—has something for you."

Rika frowned at them both. "What?"

Grant looked equally befuddled, then his face lit up. "Oh, right." He drew something from the pouch at his waist and slapped it on the table before her.

"What's this?"

"'Tis your…" Grant looked to Lawmaker, apparently for help. "*Morgen gifu?* Aye, right. Your morning gift."

How dare he? Her eyes widened, and she felt suddenly over warm. "I…I don't want it."

"Suit yourself." Grant slid the trinket toward Lawmaker. "I was just doing as instructed."

"Take it," Lawmaker said, and pushed it toward her. "At the least, have a look at it."

She arched a brow at him in annoyance, then glanced at the gift. It was a piece of jewelry—a silver brooch. Something about it seemed familiar to her. She picked it up and turned it over in her hand.

"What's wrong?" Grant said, reading her suspicion.

She shook her head. "Nothing. It's just…" Where had she seen this before? She narrowed her eyes at Lawmaker, and he cast her one of those all-innocent looks she loathed. "Nothing," she repeated, and set the brooch on the table. "I won't accept it, is all."

"Fine," Grant said. "It doesna matter a whit to me."

She could murder the old man. Had she known he was going to meddle like this… "Tell him, old man. Tell my *husband* why I can't accept such a gift. He doesn't know, does he?"

Lawmaker shrugged. "The morning gift compensates the bride for her…availability to her husband."

Grant's eyes widened. "Ye mean..."

"Exactly." And she had no intention of ever allowing him into her bed again. "So you see why I won't accept it."

"Aye, fine." The Scot put up his hands in a gesture of compliance. "I could no agree more."

Her blood began to heat, and she knew if they continued the conversation it would reach dangerous temperatures. She rose to take her leave, feeling the need for that bath more than ever.

"What I said last night, about trust," Lawmaker said quickly.

"What about it?" She was not in the mood for more of the old man's preaching, nor was Grant from the sour look on his face.

"It seems you have taken my advice."

She frowned. "What do you mean?" Save Ottar and her brother, she trusted no man, especially the Scot. Lawmaker, himself, was fast losing her good opinion.

She turned to leave, and Lawmaker caught her wrist.

Her wrist.

Thor's blood, her bracelet!

She wrested herself from Lawmaker's grip and protectively covered her bare wrist with her hand. Where was her bracelet? Her eyes flew to Grant's.

He looked at her expressionless, his eyes unchanged. Cool slate, like the sea on a winter's day. "I...it fell off. In the bed," he added. "I set it on the chest."

He lied.

Her cheeks grew hot, serving only to fuel her anger.

"I've work to do," she said flatly, then threw her cloak around her shoulders and made for the door.

"We can use the time," Lawmaker called after her.

She turned in the open doorway, sleet blowing past her into the room. "What time? For what?"

"Until the weather clears and we can sail," the old man said. He turned to Grant. "The Scot has much to learn if he would woo your father into giving up your coin."

She hadn't thought of that. Lawmaker was right: Grant knew nothing of their culture. The unclaimed brooch sitting on the table was evidence enough.

"You must indoctrinate him," Lawmaker said.

"Indoctrinate?" Grant scowled, and shifted restlessly on the bench. "I dinna wish to be indoctrinated."

Rika drew herself up, taking strength from his displeasure and from the biting sleet whipping at her garments. Oh, how she loved the winter. Whatever had she been thinking to wonder about Scotland in the spring?

"Your wishes do not concern me," she said. "Your training begins today."

Chapter Six

He simply wouldn't do it.

"Why should I?" George let the question hang there, and ignored the two young warriors who'd spent the better part of an hour trying to convince him to comply.

The dark one, Leif, said, "If you master our ways, 'twill ensure a fruitful meeting with Rollo."

Rollo. Rika's father. George doubted the man could be more difficult to deal with than his sharp-tongued spawn of a daughter.

The air in the brew house was hot and close. Packed with men, the small building reeked of wet wool, sweat and the cloying odor of mead.

Erik, the fair one, called for another flagon of the stuff, and George screwed up his face.

"You wish to go home, do you not?" Erik said.

George thought the question so absurd, he didn't bother to answer.

Leif whispered something to Erik, and Erik said, "Methinks Rollo's dwelling is not so far from your own."

"What?"

"A few days' ride," Leif said. "A sennight at most."

"Ride?" How could that be? George had assumed Rika's father lived on some other island—in the Shetlands or Orkneys. It hadn't occurred to him that they'd be sailing straightaway to— "Her father lives in Scotland?"

Both men nodded.

"On the mainland, at any rate," Erik said. "Whether it's held by Scots or Norse, one never knows from one day to the next. Rollo's wife is a Scot, and his loyalties lie with those from whom he can best profit at any given moment."

This was news, indeed. George might be out of this mess sooner than he'd thought. Once they landed on the coast, what was to stop him from hanging this dowry nonsense and going his own way?

He'd been bound for Wick, which was off the northernmost tip of the mainland. Mayhap they'd sail right into the town's harbor. Ha! The thought brightened his spirits.

"So," Erik said. "You'll allow us to teach you some of the things you'll need to know?"

George was barely listening. He was thinking of August Sinclair, and Anne, his bride-to-be.

"We'll start with some simple games," Leif said.

"What?" What the devil were they going on about? George turned his attention back to the two young men. "I told ye both. I need not learn your ways."

A loud belch cut the air behind him. "He's too stupid, if you ask me."

George turned slowly, bristling at the familiar voice. Ingolf sat at the table behind him with the doltish

Rasmus and a half-dozen other men. Brodir's men, so George had come to learn.

"No one asked you," Erik said. "Ignore him, Grant."

George was unaccustomed to ignoring insults, especially those delivered by ill-mannered heathens. He sized Ingolf up, and wished he still had Rika's brother's sword or that handy hammer tucked into his belt. The weapons had been stripped from him after the celebration.

"Scots are not built for it." Ingolf drained the drinking horn in his hand. Mead ran in rivulets down his heavily bearded chin. "The Viking way, our skills, cannot be learned. One is either born to it, or one is not."

Bollocks. He had a mind to teach this unschooled heathen exactly what the Scots were built for. "What kind of skills," George said, and looked to Erik and Leif for an answer.

Leif shrugged. "Tests of wit and strategy."

"Bah. Tests of manhood." Ingolf scowled.

"Those, too," Leif said.

George turned his back to them.

"I told you," Ingolf's voice carried over the din in the room. "He's not man enough."

Brodir's men laughed behind him, and George's blood boiled. 'Twas time he imparted some lessons of his own. "When do we begin?"

Leif and Erik smiled. "Straight away," they said in unison.

"Besides," Erik said. "What else is there to do in weather so foul?"

The youth had a point, George thought. He must do

something beyond sitting on his arse all day, or he'd go mad.

The door to the brew house banged open, and Rika blew in with the wind. Ottar pulled the door shut behind them, and the two settled on a bench across from George. Rika spared him not a glance—not that he expected her to.

'Twas the first he'd seen of Ottar since the wedding. The angry youth had avoided the bridal feast. No small wonder. George had stepped into a role Ottar fancied himself filling. Or so it seemed, by the fierce protectiveness he displayed toward Rika. The youth glared at him.

Rika was strangely quiet. He hadn't seen her since they'd broken their fast that morning. The incident over the bracelet had enraged her. He saw that she'd recovered it from the cottage. Both hammered bronze bands were strapped snugly in place over her wrists.

At first he'd thought Brodir made her wear them, then he realized the truth. She wore them because she was ashamed for anyone to see what that animal had done to her. He'd read the humiliation in her eyes, and sheer will alone had prevented him from offering a word or a look of comfort.

Looking at her now, he marveled at her stoic behavior. 'Twas as if last night and this morning had been like any other for her. That Valkyrie's shell of hers was tough as burnished leather, but he knew what lay beneath it. He knew her warmth, her passion, the feel of her yielding beneath him.

George, she'd called him—just the once—in the heat of their lovemaking. His Christian name had never sounded so exotic as it had when breathed from her lips.

As of the dawn, he was merely Grant. She hissed the word as if it were some blasphemy.

Now that he knew her better, he realized she had to work at maintaining her indifference. She was not so comfortable in her icy skin as she would have the world believe. There was a natural femininity about her that one could see if one looked.

And he was looking.

Nonetheless, she took pleasure in crushing to dust any attributes exemplifying her sex. Compassion, tenderness, generosity. Oh, she'd been generous with him between the furs last night.

God's truth, he couldn't stop thinking about her. He needed a diversion. Something to keep his mind occupied while they waited for the weather to clear. Mayhap these tests of strategy would provide some amusement.

"Your drink," a feminine voice said.

Lina.

She was all the diversion a man could want.

George looked up into the girl's doelike eyes. She set the flagon of mead on the table and batted her lashes prettily at him.

"Our thanks," Leif said, and winked at her.

Lina was a woman a man could truly appreciate. And one he had no problem understanding.

"I have found a keg of ale." Lina smiled demurely at him. "In the storage shed. 'Tis a bit young, but methinks you would prefer it." She leaned closer so that her breasts were level with his eyes. "Would you not?"

Oh, he understood her perfectly.

"Only, I cannot lift it." She batted her lashes again. "It's far too heavy for my delicate frame."

George grinned. He was familiar with a woman's

wiles. They connived, manipulated, never came right out and told you what they wanted.

"But not for mine," an icy voice said. Rika appeared out of nowhere and towered over Lina's small form. "Go on—" she pushed the girl toward the door "—and I'll be along directly to help you."

George opened his mouth to speak, but she cut him off.

"As for you, Grant, meet me in the courtyard. There are things I would show you before we sail."

She turned her back on him, snatched her cloak from the bench, and quit the room with the same blast of chill air she'd come in on.

"Our work together can wait," Leif said to him. Erik merely smiled.

George filled his drinking horn with mead. As the honeyed liquor burst upon his tongue he decided that some women had wiles, and others simply did not.

Rika waited for him near the stable, under the cover of an open shed. Her favorite pony nickered softly in the straw beside her and nudged her hand for the treat he knew she had brought. She opened her palm and the pony made short work of the small turnip. She smiled and scratched his head.

"It wouldna hurt to do more of that, ye know." His voice startled her. Grant stood in the snow outside the shed watching her.

"Do what?" she snapped, annoyed that she'd not heard him approach.

"Smile. No matter. 'Tis just...ye look more..."

She tensed, waiting for him to finish the thought.

"Christ, forget that I said it." He moved under the overhang and studied the pony with more than mild interest. "What in God's name is it? 'Tis no like any colt I've e'er seen."

"It's not a colt, it's a horse full grown."

"Go on. It canna be."

"Ja, of course he is." She frowned. The Scot had much more to learn than she could ever teach him if he didn't even know a colt from a horse.

"He's too small to be full grown."

She clucked her tongue. "He's the biggest and sturdiest on the island."

"Ha!"

"Lawmaker imports them from the Shetlands. Shetland ponies we call them."

Grant reached out and stroked the pony's neck. "Fair Isle, where the women are big and the horses small."

Rika bristled and bit back the curse she was tempted to let fly. The unschooled idiot wouldn't have understood it anyway, she surmised.

"Follow me," she said curtly, and stalked off toward the moors, heedless of the wind and sleet.

It was the first time she'd been alone with Grant since last night. Now she wondered at the wisdom of it. Being with him unsettled her, made her feel... strange. Not like herself at all.

After a short, steep hike to a ridge top, she stopped and turned, prepared to wait until Grant caught her up. He nearly plowed her over.

"Thor's blood!"

"Whoa, sorry," he said, displaying not a hint of breathlessness.

He was fit, she'd give him that. More so than most of her kinsmen, who whiled away the winter months indoors, growing soft and flabby.

Grant had not an inch of spare flesh on him. He was

pure muscle. A dizzying image of him naked and powerful, spreading her thighs wide with his own, caused her to suck in a breath.

He could have forced her last night, but he had not. He'd wooed her with gentle kisses and caresses so soft his fingers might have been dove's wings.

Oh, she must stop these thoughts!

They rushed over her unbidden and unwelcome, at the slightest provocation. She must get hold of herself, and quickly. Difficult days lay ahead, and she would not allow one night with a stranger to befuddle her thinking.

Or alter her convictions.

Men used women for their own purpose, and this man was no exception. A home and a bride awaited him in Scotland, and she must remember that the things he did here and now he did solely to speed his return to them.

"What is that place?" Grant said, snapping her out of her thoughts. "Down there." He pointed at the graveyard on the moor below them.

"Some of my ancestors rest there. Come, there are things you might learn." She started down the other side of the ridge toward the graveyard, and Grant bounded along beside her, the wind whipping at his hair and clothes.

He seemed not to mind the weather, and that struck her as odd. She envisioned Scotland as a lush, green place, sheltered from ravaging winds and the sea's fickle temper.

Sleet bit at her face, and she pulled the collar of her cloak higher to protect herself from its icy blades.

"Here, take mine," Grant said. "It has a bigger hood." Before she could protest, he whipped off his cloak, wrapped it snugly about her and pulled the hood low over her face. ''There.''

Their eyes met, and his flashed a hint of the warmth they'd held last night. For the barest moment it seemed they were truly husband and wife. She looked away, and the spell was broken.

''Thank you,'' she said awkwardly, and continued down the slope.

A few minutes later they stood amidst the graves, a sea of ships bound for other worlds. Each mound was ringed with stones set in the shape of a Viking long ship.

Grant marveled at their construction. Apparently Scots did not practice this custom. ''Some have the cross,'' he said, rather amazed, nodding toward a grave that bore the Christian symbol.

''Ja, we are not as godless as you imagine. True, we practice the old ways, but most of us are Christian.''

''So Lawmaker has said.'' He ran his hand over the rough stone of the ancient cross. ''And ye? Are ye a Christian?''

The question took her by surprise, and she found herself hesitating. Why? Did she care what he thought? Did she wish her answer to please him?

''I was,'' she said, dismissing her concerns. ''Until my mother died and my father left. After that—'' she shrugged ''—I cared not for any god.''

''When was that?''

She turned away and stared out to sea. ''Long years ago. I was still a child.''

''And Lawmaker watched over ye e'er since?''

''Lawmaker—and Gunnar, though he is the younger of the two of us.''

''Where is your brother, Rika?'' He moved closer

and pulled her hood aside so he could see her face. "Why did he leave ye alone?"

A flood of memories washed over her. God, how she missed him. "He was... Brodir's men came and—" She caught herself before spilling the truth. What was she thinking?

Rika snatched the hood and pulled it over her face, then made for the circle of standing stones near the beach. Grant jogged after her. As she reached the outer circle, he grabbed her arm.

"Let go of me." She shot him a warning with her eyes.

"Tell me about Brodir."

Her heart leaped to her throat. His grip on her tightened. "What are you talking about? Let me go."

"Nay. What is he to ye besides your jarl?"

"He is nothing." She wrenched herself free and realized she was trembling. "Less than nothing. Don't speak his name again."

"Why not? What did he do to ye?" Grant edged closer and she backed into one of the towering stones.

"Move away," she said, and tipped her chin at him.

"I'm no inclined to." He placed his hands on the stone, hemming her in. "Those marks on your wrists. He did that to ye, didn't he?"

Whoreson. He *had* lied. He'd slipped the bracelet from her wrist while she slept. "He did nothing. Now move away." She pushed against his chest, but he was as immovable as the stone cutting into her back.

"He's no your lover, then, as Ingolf said."

"Ingolf? What lies has he been spreading?" She pushed at him again, but it was useless.

"He said ye belonged to Brodir. That if I touched ye—"

"Stop it!" She tried to sidestep him, but he gripped her shoulders like a vise. "I belong to no one! No one, do you hear?" Her breath came in ragged gasps. She fought to control the anger boiling within her.

He caught her chin and wrenched it high so she'd have to look at him. "He forced ye, didn't he?"

Oh, God. "Stop it!"

"Didn't he? Say it."

"Nay!" A sting of tears glassed her eyes. She'd be damned if she would cry.

"The marks on your wrists, the scar on your neck— 'twas his doing."

She shook her head vehemently as Grant's fingers traced the path along her neck Brodir's knife had journeyed the night before he'd left for the mainland. Sleet turned to rain, pummeling her face and washing away the tears she could not stop.

"Don't," she breathed, reading the intent in his slate eyes.

Too late.

His mouth covered hers in a kiss that was neither tender nor controlled, and that screamed with a frantic possessiveness that shocked her nearly off her feet.

Her instinct to fight him crumbled instantly under the weight of some deep longing that she did not understand. A need for him that was more than physical. A yearning for closeness, for—

She broke free of him and ran.

Lightning flashed overhead, and a crackling thunder split the air. She threw off his cloak, and hers, and scrambled up the ridge, the wind lashing at her hair, icy sheets of rain battering her on.

By the time she made the village, she was soaked to the skin. Ottar stood in the closed doorway of the longhouse, waiting for her, as she knew he would be. She slowed to a walk in the courtyard and tried to catch her breath, rein in her wild emotions.

"Rika, what's happened?" Ottar cast aside the bit of bread he'd been eating and rushed to her.

"Nothing, I'm fine." She pushed past him.

"Where's your cloak?"

"Nowhere. It's…" They reached the cover of the eaves, and she collapsed against the whitewashed stones of the longhouse. "I lost it."

"But—"

Grant rounded the corner, clutching her sopping cloak, and stopped short when he saw the youth.

Ottar whipped a blade from his belt. "Blackguard! Did he hurt you?"

"Nay. Ottar—" She grabbed his arm. "He's done nothing. Sheathe your weapon."

Grant approached them. "Your cloak…*wife*."

The muscles in Ottar's forearm tensed at Grant's words. "Go inside now," she said, and pushed the youth toward the door. "I would speak to my—to Grant, alone."

After Ottar had gone, she realized she had nothing to say to the Scot. His kiss had stunned her, but it was her reaction to it that made her afraid.

They stood there, silent, in the rain until the light went out of his eyes and the warmth of her indifference returned, buoying her strength.

All was right again.

He held the door for her, and she went inside to join the others.

"You're not concentrating," Lawmaker said. He snatched the carved game piece from the board and placed it back where it had been before George had moved it. "Try again, and this time think what you mean to accomplish."

"Aye, I know, I know." George ran a hand through his hair in exasperation. "I must capture your king before he escapes to the edge of the board."

"Exactly," Lawmaker said. "And you have twice as many attackers as I do defenders. So, get on with it."

"It's no like any chess I've e'er played." And he'd played plenty, against some of the finest minds in the Highlands.

"I told you, it's not chess. The game is *tafl.*"

George made a derisory sound in the back of his throat. "Well, whatever the devil it is, I canna concentrate with *her* lurking over me and grunting every time I make a move." He glanced over his shoulder at Rika, who eyed the board with an arched brow. "See what I mean?"

Lawmaker shrugged. "She's your wife. She's entitled to lurk."

He swore under his breath and moved the carved game piece for the third time.

"Good." Lawmaker nodded, satisfied at last.

Rika snorted.

"Och, what now?" George had had enough of her arrogance. She'd been in a foul mood since their walk that afternoon. And while what had happened between them had been his fault, he grew tired of her unrelenting punishment. At supper, she'd snapped at him over the slightest infraction against their customs.

Customs he was beginning to hate.

Leif and Erik had spent the whole meal lecturing him in Norse history—tales of bloody battles, for the most part. The two young men sat watching him now, and he wondered—not for the first time—what stake they had in this dowry business. 'Twas not for nothing they offered their friendship.

The two of them, along with Rika and Lawmaker, were thick as thieves. Meanwhile, Ingolf slouched in the corner with his rat-pack, watching Rika's every move.

George mouthed a silent prayer for clear weather. The sooner they sailed the better. For him and for Rika, too, he suspected.

"It's your move, Grant." Rika poked him in the back.

"D'ye think ye can do better?" He shot her a nasty glance. "Here, take my place and show me how 'tis done."

George started to rise, but she pushed him firmly back down on the bench. "Nay, you must learn to master this game if you're to win my father's favor."

So he'd heard a dozen times that night.

"Perhaps you should play against him, Rika." Lawmaker rose and offered her his seat. "It would be an excellent test of his concentration." George could swear the old man suppressed a smile.

"Pff! Nay, I will not play him."

George had sought all afternoon for a way to soften the tension between them, for it served no purpose and only made for misery in the close quarters mandated by the weather. Perhaps this *tafl* was a way to ease her out of her mood.

Lawmaker asked her again, and George recognized his opportunity. "Dinna force her," he said. "After all, women have no the wit for games of strategy. 'Twould only embarrass her."

He hoped she wasn't armed. Looming there behind

him, 'twould be easy enough for her to slit his throat. He resisted the urge to turn around, but did not have long to wait for her reaction.

"Out of the way, old man," she said, and plucked the elder from his seat.

"As you wish." Lawmaker put his hands up in defense and sidestepped out of her way. He smiled discreetly at George, then moved to the hearth where Leif and Erik sat grinning in amusement.

Fine. He'd play her if that's what everyone wished.

"It's your move," Rika said, and propped her elbows on the table.

This was going to be fun.

George was good at games, particularly those that required forward thinking. Lawmaker had taught him all the moves and basic strategies, and George was certain he could beat her without much trouble—should he wish to.

He did not.

'Twould be better to let her win. It might brighten her mood. Besides, women truly did not have a mind for such things. Oh, he'd seen her best Ottar, but the youth was smitten with her, and for certain let her prevail so he might win her favor.

George moved one of his pieces and stole a glance at her while she studied the board.

He felt a strange remorse for his actions that afternoon. He should never have mentioned Brodir—and should have known she would deny the jarl's mistreatment of her.

George didn't know what had possessed him. He'd felt suddenly angered by the whole affair, and couldn't stop himself. What had he expected? That she would collapse in his arms and beg him to protect her from the brute?

Any ordinary woman would have.

Rika, daughter of Fritha, was no ordinary woman.

She moved her king with confidence and raised a brow at him.

"Who taught ye to play?" George moved one of his men in turn.

"Lawmaker, after my father abandoned us."

"Why did he go, your father?"

Her expression darkened, as it did each time Rollo was mentioned. "He remarried when my mother died."

"Ah, right. A Scot."

"Who told you that?"

"Erik. Or Leif." He shrugged. "I canna remember which."

"I allow them to school you, but do not bother them with unnecessary questions."

"I'll ask what I—"

"*I* shall tell you the things you need to know."

Haughty bitch. Perhaps he'd not let her win, after all. He had a mind to beat her soundly, in fact, and studied the board while she made her next move.

She called for more mead, and the old woman Sitryg brought another flagon to their table. George hadn't seen Lina since that morn. It amused him that Rika found the girl threatening. He had no real interest in the lass. She was entertaining only in that she provided such a marked contrast to Rika.

He lifted a game piece from the board.

"I wouldn't make that move," she said.

"Why not?" The woman was increasingly irritating. The move would put him in a position to win, and she knew that. The scheming little vixen. Mayhap she was not so unlike Lina, after all. "My move stands," he said, more determined than ever to best her.

"Suit yourself." She dropped one of her pieces onto a square that did absolutely nothing to protect her king. She had lost the game already but did not see it.

George grinned at her, and slid one of his attacking pieces toward her king.

Rika arched a brow. "Careful."

He laughed, savoring his triumph over her, but three moves later the smile slid from his face.

"Raichi!" she cried, and stood. "You've lost, Scotsman."

"But—" George stared at the board, incredulous. How the devil had she done it? A few of the men who watched them laughed.

"Perhaps you should go back to playing chess." She sauntered around the table, dragging her finger across the edge of the board. "What was it you said earlier?"

He ignored her, shaking his head, going over the moves in his mind again.

Lawmaker's steady hand lit on his shoulder. "He said that women had not the wit for games of strategy."

Damn her! George rubbed a hand over his stubbly beard. Finally he relented and looked her in the eye.

Rika stood tall, smiling down at him—nay, gloating. His blood boiled.

"One must conclude," she said, "that until now the only women he's known were witless, indeed."

George swore under his breath, as she turned her back on him and took a seat by the fire between Erik and Leif.

"I told you she was an unusual woman." Lawmaker settled onto the seat she'd vacated. "Come," he said, and moved the game pieces back into place. "Let us start again."

Chapter Seven

The weather worsened.

Rika feared they would never sail. She stood at the window in the small cottage where she and Grant had spent their wedding night, and stared out to sea.

Gunnar went missing nearly a year ago, and it was months before she'd pieced together the evidence of foul play and Brodir's involvement. By then, Brodir had installed himself as jarl, and few would listen to her accusations.

She was alone in this. She and Lawmaker, and the few young warriors who remained loyal to Gunnar. Where was he now? she wondered. In some work camp at Dunnet Head, cold and starving—or dead, mayhap?

Nay, she refused to believe that. Gunnar was alive. He was young and strong, and nearly as willful as she. Ja, he was alive, and Rika would find him and bring him home.

She drew a cleansing breath of sea air, and let the sealskin cover fall back into place over the window. Her bed lay untouched from the previous night. She'd had trouble sleeping ever since she and Grant had...

Oh, that was days ago now. Why couldn't she stop

thinking of it? At her request, Grant slept in his usual place in the longhouse. She could not bear to be near him at night, and so she slept in the cottage alone, with the door barred—just in case.

Not that she expected company from Grant. She'd made it clear to him she wanted no dealings with him save what was necessary for his instruction. He'd complied with her wishes all too readily. That was something, at least, they agreed on.

Her kinsmen seemed to think naught of this arrangement. They'd always thought her unusual, and she'd done little to convince them otherwise. Most accepted Grant readily and didn't question her motives for wedding him.

On Fair Isle a woman with no family was free to choose her own mate if the one chosen for her had been gone as long as Brodir had. More often than not, men who went a-Viking never returned.

All save those in on her plan had no idea Grant would be leaving—and she with him. The truth would come out the day she and Gunnar returned to Fair Isle. Until then, it was her secret, to be shared only with Lawmaker and those loyal to her brother.

A knock sounded at the door.

Rika drew back the bolt and opened the door cautiously. Ingolf and his men had it out for her, and she'd been careful since the wedding not to be caught alone with him and his cronies.

Lawmaker's bright eyes peered at her through the cracked door. "Come," he said. "There is something afoot I think you'll wish to see."

She didn't wait for an explanation, just grabbed her cloak, threw it around her shoulders, and followed him into the courtyard.

"The Scot does battle this morn with all comers."

"What?" She grabbed his arm. "Where? With whom?" Thor's blood, what if he were killed?

Lawmaker smiled. "Not to worry. Mock battle. Leif and Erik have been instructing him in the use of some of our weapons."

"Ah." Her pulse slowed. That was a spectacle she did, indeed, wish to see. She took Lawmaker's proffered arm and he led her to the longhouse flanking the stable, the one used for odd work and weapons practice in winter when the weather was bad.

The house had been cleared of the few bits of furniture it normally housed. Only the central fire remained, to both warm the room and serve as an interesting obstacle to be negotiated during battle practice.

Her kinsmen packed the benches on each wall and stood three deep in the doorway. The Scot's indoctrination to their ways provided the folk of Fair Isle endless entertainment. In fact, they'd followed Grant's progress with a relish she'd not seen since the quarterly games Gunnar used to hold when he was jarl, to encourage fitness and sportsmanship.

Wagering was at a peak. Her kinsmen bet on everything from Grant's skill—or lack thereof—at the *tafl* table, to his memory for verse, which was a pastime much revered in her culture.

Rika pushed her way through the crowd and squeezed onto a bench next to Lawmaker. "What's happening?" she said, and tried to make sense of the knot of men hovering around Grant at one end of the longhouse and around Ottar at the other.

"They are nearly ready." Lawmaker nudged her. "Look, he makes a splendid Norseman, do you not agree?"

Rika's eyes widened as Grant stepped forward.

She did agree.

He was clad only in breeks and boots, his chest bare, his long tawny hair loose about his shoulders. He bore a *halberd,* a spear whose linden-wood pole was as long as most men were tall. Grant was far taller than most men, and the weapon seemed dwarfed in his grip.

Ottar was similarly garbed and armed, but appeared a gangly youth next to the Scot.

Rika was annoyed at this matching of boy against man. "Ottar has no chance against the Scot. Grant has two stone on him at least."

Lawmaker seemed unperturbed. "Ottar has more at stake. It is a good match, and one that is long overdue."

Rika watched as the two opponents circled each other. "You speak in riddles, old man. What has he at stake? I don't understand."

"Nay, you wouldn't. You're a woman."

Rika snorted.

"Ottar hovers on the brink," Lawmaker said. "He has the body of a man—well, nearly so—coupled with the hotheaded emotions of youth. A dangerous combination. His pride is easily wounded."

"Hmm, methinks you are right."

"Of course I'm right."

She smirked at the old man and turned her attention back to the match.

Ottar was as tense as she'd e'er seen him, circling Grant as a predator would its prey, jaw set, eyes afire. Grant, conversely, appeared relaxed, loose, and lighter on his feet than she would have expected for a man of his size.

The two of them parried awhile, jabbing and ducking, taking care to avoid the central fire. Matches usually lasted until the first serious blood was drawn. However, the definition of what was serious and what was not was left up to the audience. Glancing around the room, Rika spied more than a few who she knew thirsted for serious blood sport.

Ingolf among them.

And she suspected he cared not which of the two combatants did the bleeding.

Ottar grew impatient with Grant's lack of offense, and moved in to strike. Rika gasped as the youth's blade grazed the Scot's chest.

The crowd let out a collective roar.

She breathed again when she realized it was just a scratch. A thin red line materialized 'neath his curling chest hair. To her amazement, Grant nodded at Ottar and smiled. Was he not angry?

Brodir would have been furious had a youth of Ottar's inexperience drawn first blood. Brodir might have killed him over the insult. Not in public, mind you. He'd find some private place for his revenge.

Rika shivered, remembering the times she had crossed him.

Ottar's confidence exuded from every pore. He grew bold and reckless, and more than once nearly backed into the fire pit. Grant worked him around the room, allowing the youth an occasional harmless strike.

Again Lawmaker was right.

To Grant this was merely an afternoon's amusement—a chance to hone his skills with a foreign weapon. But to Ottar, it was serious business. He was hell-bent on besting the Scot. She could read it in his eyes, in the fierceness of his expression.

Grant read it, too, and she wondered how the Scot would deal with him. She knew what Brodir would do, or any man of her clan. He'd crush the youth at the first opportunity.

Dominate. Destroy.

That was the way of things on Fair Isle. The Scot, she surmised, was not much different in his thinking. All men were the same.

Or so she'd thought.

Grant backed Ottar toward the fire. She held her breath when the youth nearly slipped. He used the butt of his spear to brace himself from falling, leaving his right side unprotected. Grant had his chance. And did not take it.

Rika was astonished.

An instant later, Ottar regained his balance and delivered an unexpected jab to Grant's torso. Unexpected to all, save Grant. He saw it coming in time to thwart it. She read the hesitation in his eyes.

Then something extraordinary happened. Grant froze, his decision made, and Ottar's blade licked him cleanly across the chest. Blood seeped from the wound, and a shout went up amongst the men.

Rika was on her feet, choking back a cry, and would have rushed to aid the Scot had Lawmaker not grabbed the skirt of her gown. "This is men's business," he said. "Do not interfere."

Interfere? Grant was hurt. She must go to him and—

Rika stopped dead. Thor's blood, what had she thought to do?

Grant looked at her, breathless, sweat beading on his brow. After a long moment that made her insides tingle, he smiled. A smile she would remember.

In the ensuing uproar, Ottar was lifted off his feet by a throng of men and carried on their shoulders as befit a victor. The jubilation on his young face made her heart swell with new-found admiration.

Not for Ottar, but for Grant.

"You are a fortunate woman, Ulrika," Lawmaker said. "Only you do not know it yet."

Night fell and the wind died. The rain had stopped hours ago, and Rika prayed the weather would hold. She took one last glance at the clearing sky before stepping into the warmth of the longhouse.

Spirits were high and the honeyed mead flowed. Ottar sat by the fire, at his feet a knot of younger boys who bid him tell them one more time how he bested the Scot that afternoon. Likely, the tale would be told a dozen times more before the night was over.

Lina brought him a plate of sweet cakes. Her eyes washed over him with predatory intent. Ottar smiled wide. The vixen was far more dangerous to the youth than was Grant, though Ottar was too stupid to see it.

"Come hither, girl!"

Rika turned toward Hannes's voice and was surprised to see Grant sitting with him at a gaming table in the corner.

"So, you have not yet tired of the *tafl* board?" She felt good tonight, better than she had in a long time, and spared the Scot a rare smile. His behavior at the mock battle that afternoon had won him her respect, and that was something she bestowed not lightly.

"I'd be willing to give it another go," Grant said, "but beware, Lawmaker has schooled me in some of the finer points of the game." His eyes flashed mirth, and his cheeks were tinged with a ruddy glow. She'd ne'er seen him so...relaxed.

If she didn't know better—how he loathed their hon-

eyed drink—she would swear he was in his cups.
Hmm. Mayhap that silly chit Lina had discovered a keg
of ale, after all. Of course there had been no barrel that
day Rika accompanied her to the storehouse. It was
deceitful ploys like that which caused men to think
women underhanded.

"Nay, there will be no gaming tonight for you,"
Hannes said to Grant. "You have yet to master the task
I set for you days ago."

"Which is?" Rika nudged the skald aside so she
might share his bench.

"Och, I told ye I canna do it." Grant refilled his
drinking horn. "The words mean naught to me, and are
too bloody hard to pronounce."

What on earth was he talking about?

"I taught him some verse to recite for your father,"
Hannes said.

"Really?" Now this impressed her. Few of her own
kinsmen took the time to learn such things.

"And a poem," Hannes added.

"Aye, let me see if I can remember it." Grant
drained his drinking horn and rose from his seat. No
one paid him any mind, and Rika was grateful. She did
not wish to see him make a fool of himself in front of
the others. He cleared his throat ceremoniously and began.

His accent was terrible, and though he butchered the
words he did not falter. He was confident, and her father liked confidence. She was beginning to think Grant
would win Rollo's favor after all.

Then, on the third stanza, she recognized the poem.

Her teeth clenched instinctively behind thinned lips.
The Scot rambled on, and with each new stanza her
temperature rose. Her reaction was not lost on Hannes.

Finally Grant collapsed onto the bench and grinned. "I'll be damned if I know what it means, but I did a fair job of it this time, did I no?"

Rika's face flushed hot.

"What's the matter?" Grant frowned at her reaction, and looked to Hannes for some explanation. "Did I say it wrong?"

"Nay, 'twas dead-on, was it not, Rika?" The skald's face was a mask of pure innocence. He no doubt learned that little trick from Lawmaker.

"You're skating on thin ice, old man." She shot him a deadly look.

"I got the words right," Grant said, and looked at her with what she believed was honest bewilderment. "Hannes said ye would like the poem. That I should recite it to ye at the first opportunity."

"Oh, did he?"

Hannes sputtered beside her. "I didn't exactly say that—"

"Did he tell you what it meant?" she snapped, and eyed Grant for the slightest sign of duplicity.

"He did."

"I ne'er actually said that—"

"Quiet, old man." If Hannes so much as opened his yaw again he'd be eating her fist.

"He called it a *drottkvoett*—a warrior's meter. 'Tis a poem paying tribute to some great victory. Am I right?"

The blood in her veins hardened to stone. "A great victory for the warrior in question, ja."

"Well then—"

"Won not on the battlefield, but in the bridal bed."

Grant's face reddened. "Oh. I hadna thought of

that.'' He reached for the flagon, but Rika snatched it from the table.

''Methinks you've had enough. As for you, poet—'' she cast Hannes an icy look ''—school's over.''

Both of them sat there like idiots. Grant was clearly drunk. Thor's blood, that's all she needed—a husband who couldn't hold his liquor. Her father would laugh him right out of his house.

Rika moved to an open bench as far from the Scot as she could get. On the way, she sniffed at the flagon. Hmm, 'twas mead after all. She handed it off to the nearest man, and he hiccuped in response.

She mouthed a silent curse.

Tomorrow they would sail, clear weather or not. She was sick of this waiting. And the longer they delayed, the greater the chance of others discovering their plan.

Grant had promised not to speak of their bargain, and so far he'd kept his word. But honeyed mead had a way of loosening a man's tongue, and secrets were never long kept on Fair Isle, given the close quarters in which she and her kinsmen lived.

Ingolf dogged her every step. Even now, he sat in a corner watching her, honing his knife as he had that first night when Grant had come to them. How much, if anything, did he know? And what did he plan?

Had there been a way to send word to Brodir, Ingolf would have done it in a heartbeat when her plan to wed the Scot became known. But no one knew Brodir's whereabouts, not even the trusted few he left behind to keep a watchful eye on things in his absence.

Besides, no one sailed in winter save to avert some pending disaster, and her marriage to the Scot hardly qualified as that. Lawmaker and the other elders would have had to agree to any such voyage, and Ingolf knew enough not to dare ask.

Lawmaker had set guards to watch the *byrthing*. She cast Grant a sideways glance and saw that his head was lolled back against the wall, his eyes barely open. The Scot, no doubt, thought the guards were there for his benefit. Ha! As if he could sail such a vessel on his own.

She met Ingolf's gaze head-on.

The guards were for him and his cronies, should they think to commandeer the ship and sail in search of their jarl. Rika smiled at him, and the blade of his knife stilled on the whetstone.

She was exhausted, and longed for sleep. Perhaps she'd stay in the longhouse tonight with the others. The cottage sat off the far end of the courtyard, isolated from the other houses.

Ingolf moved the blade over the stone again in a slow circular motion, his eyes riveted to hers. If some evil should befall her out there in the night, no one would hear her cries for help.

Rika closed her eyes and drew a deep, calming breath. *Get hold of yourself, Ulrika. This nightmare will be over soon.*

George watched the two of them through slitted eyes. Rika looked drained, as if she hadn't slept in days. Ingolf's gaze burned into her with a malevolence that kept George perpetually on his guard.

'Twas long past the hour at which Rika normally retired to the cottage. Mayhap tonight she wouldn't go. George prayed she would not.

No one else seemed aware of Ingolf's malice toward her. Not even the youth Ottar, who was always the first to rush to her defense when danger reared its head. The boy was a good ally for Rika to have, but he was just that—a boy—and had not the experience to deal with vermin like Ingolf and his henchmen.

Besides, the youth had other dangers to thwart this night. Lina sat on Ottar's lap and tittered prettily at every word he spoke. George suppressed a smile. A boy had to grow up sometime, he guessed. Ottar would grow fast in that one's clutches.

A bittersweet chord tugged at his heart. He was reminded of another youth. His brother, Sommerled. Oh, how he missed him. A wave of raw emotion gripped him, and he gritted his teeth against the agony it wrought.

He must get home.

That's what mattered. He'd been on Fair Isle nearly a fortnight. By now his clan would have sent riders to look for him and for Sommerled. Mayhap they'd stumble on the news of their taking to ship from Inverness. News of the wreck.

Mayhap they thought him dead.

He ought to be dead.

It wouldn't bring his brother back, but 'twould be just payment for his own negligence. He breathed a silent curse and vowed to rid his mind of this misery. There were other matters to deal with now. Once he was safe in Scotland and had made good on his contract with August Sinclair, he could grieve without distraction. But for now—

Rika shot to her feet, and George's mind snapped to attention. He let his head loll sideways against the wall, feigning drunkenness, and peered through a fringe of lashes at Ingolf and his pack. The henchman was on his feet, his dagger in hand.

George's own hand closed surreptitiously over the hilt of the dirk he'd been allowed to carry since that afternoon at the match. He would have preferred a broadsword, but the dirk would do. Not that he couldn't dispatch a man like Ingolf with his bare hands. But given the heathen's half-dozen friends eager for a piece of him, the weapon was an added comfort.

Rika spared George's seemingly lifeless form not a glance as she snaked her way through the tables toward the door. On the way, she slipped a short ax from the belt of a passed-out kinsman and shot Ingolf a backward glance.

A warning.

As soon as she was out the door, Ingolf and his pack followed in her wake. George watched them until they quit the room, then bolted to his feet.

"Ho!" Hannes started beside him. The skald had been dozing. "Where are you off to, lad, with so grim a look on your face?"

"Nowhere. Go back to sleep."

He suspected that Rika would rather have cut off an arm than beg protection from any man, but he didn't intend to offer her a choice in the matter.

No one else questioned him as he moved swiftly to the door and stepped into the night, the dirk itching in his hand. He squinted in the dark. Aye, 'twas as he'd feared.

Rika stood backed against the well in the middle of the courtyard, brandishing the short ax, Ingolf and his men spread out in a half circle around her.

In five strides George was there.

Ingolf whirled on him.

"Dinna even think it," George said, and had the

point of his dirk against the henchman's throat before Ingolf could even blink.

The others drew their weapons, and George tensed, prepared to take them all.

"Not so fast," a voice called from behind him.

Erik.

George pushed Ingolf away.

"What have we here?" The Norseman flanked George. Leif and a half-dozen others whom George did not know fanned into a line behind them.

For a moment no one said a word.

"We were just having some sport is all." Ingolf nodded casually at Rika, then sheathed his weapon. "With the new bride."

"Ja, well, we'll reserve that for her husband, eh?" Erik said, and beckoned Ingolf toward him. "Come, let us share a flagon and leave the newlyweds to their pleasure on this fine, clear night."

The weather *had* cleared, George realized. He glanced up and marveled at the spray of stars peppering the sky.

A moment later, he and Rika were alone. She cast the ax into the dirt and turned away from him, bracing herself against the wide lip of the well.

"Ye may have need of this later," George said as he retrieved the ax from the dirt and offered it to her. "I would feel more assured of your safety if ye kept it."

"What concern of yours is my safety?"

He moved up behind her and sensed her anger—nay, not anger. Fear. She was trembling. George leaned the ax against the well and gripped her shoulders.

She tensed under his touch. "What do you want?"

"Nothing. Just to make certain ye're all right."

She shrugged out of his grasp. "Why do you care?"

"Because—"

Why did he care?

Merely because she was a woman, and in no small danger from Ingolf and his men? Or because she was his wife? As ludicrous as it seemed, he had to admit there was some truth to this last explanation.

"Promise me ye'll take Ottar with ye should ye venture away from the village."

She turned and frowned at him. The moon was not yet risen, and her eyes reflected the pale light of the stars. "I would thank you for what you did for him today."

"For Ottar? I did naught. The lad bested me fair and square." He patted his chest gingerly. "Aye, and it still stings."

"No Norseman would have done such a thing."

He looked into the silver depths of her eyes and read something new there. "I am no Norseman."

All at once he was aware of the blood heating in his veins, of his heart beating strong in his chest. His mouth went dry, and he longed to quench his thirst.

"Nay," she breathed. "You are not."

He dipped his head to kiss her.

"Look!" Rika sidestepped him and pointed to the northern sky. 'Twas as if someone had dumped a bucket of icy water over his head.

George followed her gaze. "Sweet Jesus, what's that?" A tingle of horrific fascination snaked its way along his spine as he fixed his eyes on a living veil of red and green shimmering against the midnight sky.

"The northern lights," she said. "Aurora borealis. I, too, know some Latin."

He stared rapt at the eerie display. "I have heard of this, but never in my life had thought to see it."

"It comes only in the winter months, when the sky is clear and the weather cold." She shivered, and he instinctively stepped closer.

"Is it always this brilliant?" He watched as the veil of color waxed and waned, washing across the sky in a seductive dance of light.

"Nay, it is not. In truth, the red is strangely rare. Only once have I seen it before. The night my brother was—" She hesitated. "The night he left."

A film of tears glassed her eyes, and for some unfathomable reason, it pained him to see her so distraught. No sooner did his arm slip around her shoulder than she turned into him, clutching his waist and burying her face in the hollow of his neck.

He kissed her tears away and, before he could stop himself, his lips found hers.

Chapter Eight

It was the drink in him, but she didn't care.

Rika's lips parted to the gentle prodding of Grant's tongue, and she lost herself in his honeyed kiss.

"You're drunk." She made a show of trying to push him away.

He knew she didn't mean it.

"I'm not." Grant pulled her tight against him and kissed her again.

This time she kissed back.

His hands roved her body and began to work the magic that no man, save him, had worked on her before.

Why did she allow it?

When he rolled his hips against hers she felt his hardness and his heat. It was by sheer will alone she mustered the strength to break the kiss.

"You were right," she breathed against his lips.

"About what?" He kissed her again, more passionately this time, and she knew if she did not stop him now she'd succumb to his lovemaking all over again.

Rika felt blindly behind her for the ax resting against

the well, and drew the weapon slowly upward between their bodies. "This."

Grant jumped back. "Christ, woman, what are ye about?"

The hint of fear tinging his voice brought a smile to her lips. "It seems I might have need of it after all, to—what were your words? Ensure my safety."

He ran a hand through his tousled hair and looked again to the northern sky. But the lights had gone out, and with them the passion in his eyes.

She'd been right to stop him.

"I...I'm sorry," he said.

"No matter." She hefted the ax over her shoulder and turned toward the cottage.

"About the poem, I mean."

She glanced back at him, and knew from his sober expression he was not toying with her.

"I didna know what it meant."

"I'm certain you did not."

The moon rose over the sea and caught him in its light. For the barest moment she thought him the most beautiful man she'd e'er seen.

She had decided not to tell him but suddenly changed her mind. "The poem speaks of a warrior's strength and a valor born of love for his new wife."

He said nothing to that, but as Rika made her way to the cottage and locked herself inside, she felt his eyes on her, and knew that, once again, Lawmaker had been right.

This marriage would change them.

Had changed them already.

It was up to her to ensure it did not change them overmuch.

* * *

Dawn came, and with it an incredible calm.

The sea spread out in all directions, a silvered mirror reflecting the sun's white light. George stood on the cliff overlooking the beach and counted the hours until they would sail.

He'd hardly slept last night, and wasn't certain which had been more responsible for keeping him awake—Ingolf's threats or Rika's kisses. He told himself it didn't matter. They'd sail on the night tide and in three days' time Fair Isle would be but a memory.

As agreed, he hadn't spoken of their planned departure to anyone. The two young dissidents, Leif and Erik, seemed to know all about it, though. More, even, than George knew himself.

The other islanders naturally assumed that he, as Rika's husband, would claim her dowry at some point. They had no idea how soon that day would come—or, rather, that it would never come. Once their ship reached the mainland, he would be a free man.

"You are thinking of your homeland."

He whirled, startled, and met Lawmaker's gaze. "D'ye always sneak up on a man like that?" 'Twas damn unsettling.

Lawmaker smiled. "What is it that you most miss?"

Together they turned toward the sea and stared out across the water toward Scotland.

"It doesna matter what I do or do not miss. I am a laird, and have many obligations—to clan and king, and to the father of the woman to whom I am betrothed."

"Ah. You are a man who takes his duty seriously."

"Most seriously."

Lawmaker nodded. "I would not have expected less.

Tell me about this bride, this woman who waits for you.''

"Anne Sinclair?" He shrugged. "I know her not."

"And yet you are intent on taking her to wife?"

"Of course I am. I must. 'Tis all agreed.'' How could the elder think he'd do otherwise?

A pelican drafted low along the surf line and dove with graceful precision upon its breakfast, an unwitting school of perch.

"Is she remarkable, this Anne Sinclair?" Lawmaker said.

George thought it an odd question. "So my king tells me. But of what consequence is her remarkability? As long as she is obedient and fair of face, she will suit me well."

"Will she?"

He frowned at the old man. "Why would she not? What more could a man ask in a wife?"

"There is much."

"Oh? Such as…"

Lawmaker raised a peppered brow at him. "A sharp mind, for instance. Courage. Strength of character."

George laughed, and together they turned onto the rocky path leading back to the village. "Those things a proper wife dinna make. I would have a woman obey me, unconditionally. Fear me a little, if that served to fortify her obedience."

"I see. You would not have your wife challenge your thinking in any way?"

"Ye mean like *she* does?" He nodded at the row of longhouses in the distance. Rika stood, fists on hips, barking orders to Leif and Erik. "Nay, I would not. 'Tis no a woman's place to question a man's decisions."

Out of the corner of his eye, he saw the edges of Lawmaker's mouth curl into a smile. "Ofttimes a woman's questions can lead a man to better answers."

The old man was daft. George knew what he wanted in a wife—exactly the opposite of what Lawmaker suggested. His gaze raked over Rika as they approached.

Exactly the opposite of her.

And yet…

He watched as she hefted the end of a chest Erik was dragging and helped him to set it on a bench. Last night in the courtyard she'd faced Ingolf and his men with valor, not fear. Her courage had fortified his own.

Och, he was as daft as the old man.

The woman meant nothing to him. Aside from his occasional physical response to her, which was not something a man could always control, he was entirely certain he loathed her.

She glanced up at him suddenly, and smiled.

Didn't he?

"Come," Lawmaker said. "Let us take to my cottage and break our fast together. I expect the others have already eaten."

George shook off the unsettling feelings eating away at his convictions, and followed Lawmaker past the central courtyard and into his tiny abode.

The air was damp and musty. Bread and cheese sat on a trencher on the table. His stomach growled.

"Sit, eat." Lawmaker threw off his cloak and gestured to the bench.

George obeyed. The remnants of a peat fire smoked in the brazier behind him, giving off just enough heat to warm the cottage. He hadn't donned a cloak that morning, and didn't realize how cold he was until he sat down.

"I have something for you," Lawmaker said.

"Aye?" He devoured a hunk of cheese. "What?"

"This." To George's astonishment, the old man handed him his weapon—the strangely runed broadsword he'd loaned George for the wedding.

"I dinna understand. 'Tis your weapon, is it no?"

Lawmaker set the sheathed sword on the table before him. "It's yours now. Methinks you will have need of it before our voyage is over. Or even begun."

He remembered well the malice smoldering in Ingolf's eyes last eve. "There are some who would stop us from sailing. Is that what ye mean?"

"They would if they could, but they'd dare not try. They are small in number and should we wish to, we could call a score of kinsmen to our aid—though I'd prefer not to risk such bloodshed. Besides, as long as your tongue's not wagged, no one knows we sail." Lawmaker looked at him hard. "And once we've made the mainland, there will be other dangers. But you know that."

The elder's penetrating gaze unnerved him. 'Twas almost as if the old man read his mind about abandoning them once on Scottish soil.

"Take it." Lawmaker pushed the weapon toward him.

His hand closed over the finely crafted hilt, and a stab of guilt twisted his gut. "What about ye?"

"Oh, I have other swords. Besides, my fighting skills are not what they were. I've no need of so fine a weapon."

'Twas an honor George couldn't refuse. He met the old man's eyes and nodded. "All right, then. Thank ye."

"We set sail as soon as the night is full on us."

"Does it have a name?" George unsheathed the sword and held it aloft, marveling at the workmanship. "I've heard that Norsemen name their weapons."

Lawmaker pointed to a runic inscription on the weapon's hilt. "She is called *Gunnlogi*—Flame of Battle."

"Battle Flame," George repeated. "I like it." He ran a hand over the runes peppering the blade. "And this? What does this say?"

"It's a series of spells—for luck."

He eyed the spidery engraving and frowned.

Lawmaker laughed. "Don't worry. No longer do we invoke such magic."

"That's comforting. I think." He sheathed the sword and returned his attention to breakfast.

"This may be the last opportunity for us to speak alone before we sail." Lawmaker settled on the bench beside him. "There are things I would have you know."

"What things?" He cast the bread he'd been eating back onto the table.

"About Rika's father."

"Ah, the infamous Rollo."

"Ja, the very same. Make no mistake, Grant, he is a shrewd man."

George snorted. "No shrewd enough to marry off his daughter before she took matters into her own hands."

"She was betrothed."

"What?" His heart skipped a beat.

"Rollo saw to it before he left Fair Isle."

"But then, why—"

"To Brodir."

George looked at him, incredulous. "When I asked ye about that before, ye said she wasna."

"Nay, I said she *belonged* to no man. There's a difference."

"No where I come from. Her father will have my head—and hers. She'll ne'er get her coin."

Not that he intended to ever meet her father. He was not hungry anymore, and pushed the trencher away.

"Relax. You shall win his respect and gain the dowry. It matters not what covenants were broken between him and Brodir."

Brodir. The heathen who raped her. Her *betrothed*.

"Rollo looks out for his own interests. An alliance with a Scottish laird is a boon too precious for him to cast aside."

George pushed back from the table, his gut roiling, sick of the whole scheme. "I will see ye at the ship."

Lawmaker nodded, and rose with him when he made to leave. "Ja, tonight, and don't forget this." Lawmaker nudged the sheathed broadsword toward him.

Bloody tricksters, the lot of them. He picked up the weapon and eased the shoulder baldric over his head. "Tonight," he said, and left the door gaping as he stormed off into the chill of the morn.

A finger of afternoon sunlight streamed through the window warming the otherwise cheerless cottage. Rika carefully arranged her brother's hauberk and helm on top of the cloak she'd spread on the bed, then reached for Gunnar's sword.

"I thought we sailed in search of a dowry, no a battle."

She whirled toward Grant's unmistakable voice. He stood in the open doorway, eyeing the possessions she'd assembled on the bed. "Thor's blood, do you never knock before entering?"

"We are marrit, are we no?" He sauntered into the room and closed the door behind him. "I didna see the need."

The forced casualness in his expression and offhand tone of his voice put her on her guard. "What do you want? I'm busy here."

"I can see that." He grazed a hand over the polished chain mail, then pushed it aside and settled onto the bed.

"Get off! Get out of here now."

He ignored her and picked up Gunnar's helm. "This might come in handy, after all."

"What do you mean? Here, give me that." She went for the helm.

"No so fast," he said, and snatched it out of her reach. "Methinks 'twill take more than board games and poetry to win your coin. I might be able to use this."

She frowned at him. "What's happened? Why do you say these things?" A chill uneasiness washed over her.

"Naught has happened. I just wish to be prepared. Your father expects another man in my place." He flashed her a cold look. "A jarl."

She clenched her teeth, prepared for another confrontation. She'd be damned if she'd allow his prodding to reduce her to tears, as it had that day on the moor.

"Your *betrothed*."

The way he said the word made her want to wretch. "Ingolf again. I told you not to listen to him."

"Nay, 'twas not Ingolf."

"Who then?"

"Your guardian—Lawmaker."

Rika cursed under her breath.

"On our wedding day, did ye conveniently forget about your obligation to this man?"

She snatched Gunnar's helm from his hand, placed it on top of the hauberk and bundled them both into the cloak. "I owe him nothing. He's lower than a dog."

Before she could move from the bed, his hand closed over her wrist, his eyes fixed on the bracelet. "On that last account, I willna argue."

"This matter is of no consequence to you." She wrested herself out of his grasp and continued to gather up the few things she'd need for the voyage.

"Methinks it is. Especially if it's no a chest of silver that awaits me, but your father's sword."

She made a derisory sound. "You don't understand our ways. If you did, this *betrothal* would not concern you."

He crossed his arms behind his head and eased back onto the pillows. "Enlighten me."

"Thor's blood, you are a nuisance." She pulled up a stool and sat down, resigned. "It's true, I was promised to him—long ago when Brodir and I were children. But you must understand, it's not a custom widely practiced among our people. Engagements are a Christian habit that suit not our style of living."

"Go on."

"If a man and a woman are to wed, they simply marry. There is no waiting once the woman's father has agreed."

"Why then—"

"When I came of age I would not have him. Besides, Brodir is gone and may never return." Oh, if she were only that lucky. "My people know that. Why do you think so few opposed our marriage?"

He frowned, and she could see his mind working. "So, with Brodir gone, ye are…fair game."

"Precisely." Although she was loath to think of herself in those terms. It was…degrading. She rose from the stool and continued with her packing. "My father will see it that way, as well." At least, she hoped he would. "You have naught to fear from him."

"I fear no man." He shot to his feet. "But neither will I be played for a fool. What else have ye no told me?"

She watched as the pulse point in his neck throbbed in time to her own escalating heartbeat. She gathered up Gunnar's things and set them by her satchel near the door. "Nothing. You know all that you need to carry out your part of our—"

He grabbed her arm, and she froze.

"Bargain?" he said. "I had better. For if ye've lied to me…"

Blood heated her face. "Then what?" She jerked out of his grasp. "What will you do?"

She tipped her chin at him and stood statue-still as he traced the line of her scar from ear to throat with his fingertip. A shiver snaked up her spine.

"Ye dinna wish to know."

Before she could come back with some smart retort, he turned and left. She slammed the door after him and slid the bolt.

Think he to threaten her? She ran her hand over the hilt of her brother's sword.

Let him think again.

Chapter Nine

Their departure was surprisingly uneventful.

George stood aft and watched until the dark shadow of Fair Isle melted into the blackness. He drew a breath and could no longer smell the sheep, the fermenting grain of the brew house, or peat fires smoldering in longhouse braziers.

All that remained was the brackish sea air, and a whiff of pickled herring wafting from the barrels stacked amidships. Their cargo was precious. Preserved fish, cheese and kegs of mead, dozens of yards of homespun cloth.

Erik and Leif had secretly stashed the goods in an unused cave along the rocky bluff, a few barrels at a time over the past week, in the wee hours before dawn when all were abed. It had been dead easy to roll them down the hard packed beach the last few yards to the ship.

Lawmaker thought to trade it all for horses once they reached the mainland. George didn't have the heart to tell him that for the lot they'd be damn lucky to get a nag or two—not enough mounts to carry them all.

He was surprised how few men it took, after all, to

sail the *byrthing*. 'Twas a small ship, meant for trading in coastal waters, and sported but a single square-rigged sail. Save for the massive keel, which extended high out of the water both fore and aft and was carved into the shape of some mythical sea creature, the vessel little resembled the Viking ships he'd seen at harbor on the mainland.

Because their cargo took up so much space, only four sets of oars were used on the *byrthing,* and only then, Erik had told him, for specialized tasks such as docking or steering the bow into the wind during a storm.

They were only six in the end. He and Rika and Lawmaker; Erik, Leif and the ever-present Ottar. George had expected more hands for such a voyage. As he gazed south at the midnight expanse of sea that lay before them, a chill washed over him. Gooseflesh rose on his skin.

He pulled his fur-lined cloak tight about him and recalled his last sea journey. It had been what…a fortnight? Three weeks since the wreck? It seemed months since that ill-fated voyage. A lifetime since he stood on the deck of the coastal frigate with Sommerled and drank of the salt air.

Once they made the mainland, if he never saw another ship again, 'twould be too soon.

Lawmaker huddled with Rika ahead of the sail. Every few moments he'd point skyward, and Rika would nod her head. Everyone knew that Norsemen were excellent navigators. George had heard tell of their strange instruments and wondered if any were useful by night. He had naught better to do. Mayhap he'd join them and learn something.

Erik, Leif and Ottar were busy trimming the sail to best catch the wind. George had already asked them once if they needed his help. Ottar had made it clear they did not. 'Twas fine with him.

He skirted the cargo and joined the navigators.

Lawmaker clapped a hand on his shoulder. ''Ah, here you are. Do you read the stars?''

''Only those spinning above his head when he's in his cups,'' Rika said.

He smirked at her in the dark. ''Verra funny.'' She'd been avoiding him since their confrontation in the cottage that afternoon. The moon was not yet risen. He could not read her expression, but felt her chill demeanor.

''Well, I shall leave you two to it,'' Lawmaker said. ''There are things I must discuss with the lads.'' He nodded behind them where the others worked, then joined them.

George stood silent for a time, gazing at the brilliant map overhead. As a boy he'd thrived on pagan legends describing the constellations, but his parents had forbid such tales as they kept a devoutly Christian household.

''So,'' Rika said abruptly. ''Do you read them?''

''What, the stars? Aye, certainly.''

''Tell me, then, what is that?'' She pointed overhead to a familiar grouping.

''Och, that's easy. 'Tis the Plough.''

''Ha! You're wrong, Scotsman. It's called Woden's Wagon.''

'''Tis not.'' He frowned at her. '''Tis the Plough.''

''And the Lady's Wagon is there—'' she pointed again ''—with Tir, the Nail, at its tip.''

''Tir?'' The woman knew nothing, just as he'd suspected. ''Nay, ye're wrong. That's the pole star.''

She clucked her tongue.

"She's right," Lawmaker called out as he coiled a length of walrus-skin rope atop a barrel behind them.

"Of course I'm right," she snapped.

"But—"

"And Grant is right, as well."

"What?" Rika turned to George, and he shot her a nasty glance he was certain she could not see in the starlight.

"You're both right," Lawmaker said. "There are as many names for the stars as there are peoples on the earth. Each race conjures its own tales of the night sky."

The old man had a point, though George had never thought of such a thing before. He'd always assumed that his view of the world was the right one. The only one. By God, it ought to be. He was a Christian, after all.

Rika stared rapt at the sky as if she waited for it to reveal something promised yet long in the coming. Aboard ship, away from the island, she seemed more of a mystery to him than before.

Never had he known a woman to take to ship—for any reason. The sea was a man's domain, fraught with adventure and unexpected peril. Ulrika, daughter of Fritha, likely did not see it that way at all.

Her strange beliefs and unconventional behavior flew in the face of the very foundation on which he was reared. His fascination with her was dangerous. She corrupted his sense of what was right and wrong, of what a woman should be.

The only woman he had ever known well was his mother. She was a quiet thing, so fragile in body and spirit that, after his father died, George had taken it upon himself to protect her from the world outside their home.

A blast of wind rushed over them, and he heard the chattering of Rika's teeth. The urge to put an arm around her and shelter her from the elements was nearly too strong to resist.

But resist it he did.

She had made it plain to him, time and again, that she sought not a man's protection. Nay, not even his kindness. Mayhap she'd ne'er known such comforts, save for the friendship bestowed on her by an old man and a boy.

He stared at her in the dark and willed her meet his gaze. After a moment he felt her eyes on him and he smiled.

What kind of a woman was she, to venture forth on such a journey? A fool's mission.

A woman of intellect, of courage.

A woman of character.

He turned away from her and shaded his eyes against the salt spray blowing over the bow. Vega rose in chilling brilliance on the southern horizon.

The shores of Scotland seemed far, indeed.

Dawn ushered in a fog so dense Rika could barely make out the water beneath their low drafting vessel. She squinted ahead into the diffuse light, pulling her cloak tight about her, and tried in vain to discern the position of the sun.

"We're lost." Grant's voice sounded behind her.

"We are *not* lost." She didn't bother turning around.

He moved up beside her, shrouded in mist, the waxing wind ruffling his damp hair. "How d'ye know? I for one canna see a bloody thing."

"I don't need to see."

"Then how d'ye know where—"

"I know." She cast him a sideways glance, dismissing his concern. The Scot knew less about sailing than even the simplest child. She supposed she should remedy that. Although why she should bother...

"Oh, all right." She drew the braided sealskin cord from around her neck and thrust it toward him. Few were allowed to handle the precious stone dangling from the cord's end, but she'd make an exception this once. "Here. This is how I know."

Grant's eyes widened as she dropped the stone into his palm. "What's this? Some heathen magic?"

She smirked at him. "It's a *sunstone*. You led me to believe you were skilled in the ways of navigation."

"Nay. I said I knew the stars."

"Ja, well, one cannot use the stars by day. Mayhap you were searching for the Plough when your ship was scuttled." As soon as the words slid from her lips she was sorry she'd said them.

His expression hardened, but in his eyes she read pain. The loss of his brother weighed heavy on his mind. As did the loss of her own. "Grant, I—"

"Show me how this works," he said abruptly, and held the sunstone aloft.

She swallowed her apology and launched into an explanation of how the crystal worked.

"Andalusite. Hmm." Grant fingered the crystal in wonder. "It catches the light then, and shows the position of the sun, even in a fog?"

"Ja, but..." Rika peered at the crystal and frowned. "It tells us little today, so dim is the light." She fished a small homespun pouch from the pocket of her cloak. "Here, we shall try the lodestone."

"Lodestone?" For lack of a better place to put it, Grant hung the crystal around his neck and opened his palm in time for her to spill the contents of the pouch into his hand.

"I will show you," she said, and knelt. A few seconds later, she'd pried the lid off a small keg of mead resting at the edge of their cargo.

"What, are ye thirsty?"

"Nay." She arched a brow at him. "Open your hand."

Grant did as she instructed, and she plucked the iron needle and the dark heavy stone from his palm. "Watch." She stroked the needle across the stone three times in the same direction. "All right, now hand me the straw."

Grant proffered the short length of straw, watching her every move with an interest that surprised her. She inserted the needle into the hollow straw and set it to float on the sloshing surface of the mead.

"There. You see?"

Grant's eyes widened as the straw aligned itself with the prow of the *byrthing*. He snatched it out of the mead, turned it around, and set it to float again. As she knew it would, the straw again aligned itself with the prow of their vessel.

"Bloody hell," he breathed.

Rika smiled. "The needle points north-south every time."

"I have heard of such a thing, but never thought to see it." He looked at her, and she was drawn in by the warmth of his eyes. "Ye were right, then. We are in no danger of losing our way."

Oh, but they were. She felt it as surely as she felt

the familiar heat spread from her center. His eyes lingered on her lips overlong, and her mouth went dry.

"What's this?" Lawmaker's voice boomed from behind them.

Rika snapped from her momentary stupor.

"Get that out of there! It will taint the cargo." Lawmaker leaned down and snatched the floating straw from the mead.

Grant pressed the lid back onto the keg, while she slipped the lodestone, the needle, and straw back into their pouch.

"Well then, is our bearing sound?" Lawmaker asked her.

"Ja, dead on south."

"Good." The old man nodded satisfaction, then clapped a hand on Grant's shoulder. "Take heed, son. There is much you might learn from Ulrika, should you wish to."

Grant flashed her a look that spoke new understanding. "Aye, it seems that there is."

She felt the warmth of his admiration, and her own heat spread, despite the chill weather.

"Come," Lawmaker said to Grant. "Ottar needs help trimming the sail—though he won't admit it."

Grant smiled at her, and she felt the edges of her own mouth turn upward. She watched as he followed the old man aft and disappeared into the fog.

Hunkering down between a couple of kegs of cargo, she pulled her cloak tight about her, eluding the frigid wind. A thunk sounded from one of the kegs. Rats? Surely not. Then again, God knows what Lawmaker had packed inside some of them.

With luck, two days hence she'd catch her first glimpse of the mainland. Rika drew a breath of salt air and held it in her lungs. She'd sailed before—lots of times, in fact—but only to the Shetlands. Never south.

South was where her father lived, and in all the years since he'd abandoned her and Gunnar, never once had she ventured in that direction. Until now.

She exhaled slowly. All had gone according to her plan. Soon, God willing, she'd be reunited with her brother. The trials yet to endure she ignored for now. It was enough to know that at the end of it, Gunnar would be freed.

Oh, how he'd chastise her and Lawmaker for daring such a scheme. Rika smiled inwardly. She suspected she'd changed much over the year, since Gunnar's abduction. Mayhap he'd see her with new eyes.

As Grant had seen her this morn.

She peered aft into the mist and could just make him out, working with Ottar to secure the vathmal sail with ropes of oiled walrus skin.

An uneasy peace had settled between them, and it pleased her, though why she could not say. She told herself it was because she needed him to gain her coin, and that all would go smoother should they strive to get along. That was true enough, but there was more to it.

She liked him.

Her admiration had grown out of a begrudging respect she was compelled to afford him. He was a good man—for a Scot. Not that she had ever known any Scots. That day at the match, Lawmaker had said she was lucky. Mayhap she was.

A blast of salt spray hit her full in the face. She scrambled to her feet, choking.

"Are ye all right?" Grant called out to her. He started toward her, but she waved him off.

Thor's blood, she must stay focused. She'd gone soft in the head since the night Grant bedded her. His noble actions of the past weeks served only to befuddle her thinking further. She must hold fast to her convictions, rid herself of the tender feelings blooming inside her. Such feelings were dangerous. They weakened a woman's resolve, left her open and vulnerable.

Ja, they were as dangerous as succumbing to Grant's feigned admiration. For that's surely what it was. Feigned. He had his own motives, she must remember. Just as she had hers. The brief moments of intimacy they'd shared meant nothing—to him or to her. Once her dowry was secured, she'd rid herself of the Scot and be glad of it.

The fog thinned, and she could see him clearly now. He worked closely with Ottar, though the youth's sour expression told her Grant's help was not appreciated.

Dark clouds massed overhead. Rika glanced skyward and a premonition of something evil snaked through her. All the light went out of the sky.

"The weather's turning," Lawmaker called to them. "We'd best secure the cargo."

Rika steadied herself on the gently pitching timbers and whispered a prayer for the weather to hold. A Christian prayer. One her father had taught her long ago.

"Look to your head, man!"

George ducked a split second before Erik dropped the sail; the vathmal sheet came crashing down. The *byrthing* pitched starboard and he lost his footing.

"Bloody—unh!" He crashed backward into a row of kegs.

"Grant!" Rika's voice barely carried over the deafening roar of the wind. "Where are you? Are you hurt?"

"Nay, I'm..." He pushed the heavy sailcloth aside and scrambled to his feet. "I'm fine."

Rika grasped the front of his soaking tunic and pulled him toward her, inspecting him for signs of injury. She looked half-drowned herself with her gown soaked through—where was her cloak?—and her sopping hair plastered to her face.

He almost laughed. "D'ye no believe me? I'm fine."

"Rika!"

She let him go and turned toward Lawmaker's voice. The old man worked to secure a couple of barrels rolling around near the front of the cargo.

George sidestepped her and rushed to help him. "Och, these are heavy. What in God's name have ye packed into them?" A blast of seawater hit him full in the face. Bloody hell! They were mad to continue in this weather. The storm had come upon them out of nowhere late that afternoon.

"There, that's it." Lawmaker fastened a length of rope around the barrels and tied them to the rest of the cargo while George held them fast.

The *byrthing* pitched again. He grabbed for something, anything, to steady himself. The wind raged like a madman, drowning out all other sound. As if she would devour him whole, the sea rose up on all sides like some living, breathing predator.

Visions of the wreck that had cast him into this hell flashed across his mind in hideous bursts of color. The screams of his men, the terror in Sommerled's young face. A thousand times over George felt his brother's hand slip from his own and watched, helpless, in his mind's eye as the sea claimed him.

"Grant!" Lawmaker waved him toward Leif and Ottar and the others who huddled around the naked mast.

He made his way toward them, stepping carefully between the barrels, hanging on to whatever he could as the *byrthing* rolled and pitched beneath his shaking legs.

Lightning flashed overhead, illuminating for a second the grim faces of his companions. Rika was not among them. He wiped the icy salt water from his face and peered, slit eyed, toward the stern. "Where is she?"

"She's there." Ottar pointed to the stacks of sopping homespun nestled between rows of kegs at the rear of the cargo.

The woman was impossible. She should be here, with them, clutching the mast, where they could protect her from the storm. "What the devil is she doing?" George shook his head, amazed at her lack of regard for her own safety.

"God knows," Lawmaker said.

Without a second thought, George started toward her.

Ottar grabbed his arm. "Nay. I'll go."

George wrenched out of the youth's grasp and pushed him back into the mast. Ottar lunged at him.

"Idiots!" Lawmaker said, brushing past them. "Both of you stay here. I'll go!"

"Fine," they said in unison. George caught Ottar's murderous glare before the two of them grabbed hold of Erik and Leif's outstretched hands.

"What now?" he cried.

Leif shook his head. "We wait it out."

"And if it doesna pass?"

The three youths exchanged sheepish glances.

He realized that none of them was an experienced seaman. What had they been thinking to chance such a voyage in the dead of winter? This dowry scheme of Rika's was insane. Och, he was as much at fault as any of them. He'd have done anything to get off that island.

George narrowed his eyes against the icy needles of rain and salt spray blowing over the side. Where was Lawmaker? "What's keeping th—"

A flash of lightning lit the sky, and the words froze in his throat.

Lawmaker stood backed against the low-timbered sides of the *byrthing,* clutching the top rail, the tip of a dagger poised at his throat.

Ingolf's dagger.

A split second later George's dirk was in his hand and he was snaking toward them through rows of barrels and stacks of homespun.

Rika lay sprawled at Ingolf's feet and, as the sky lit up again, he saw her slip her own weapon from its sheath. His gut tightened. Three more strides. Two.

"Rika, wait!" Ottar cried, and tried to push past him.

The *byrthing* pitched again, and they all tumbled to port. George was the first to his feet. One barrel lay between him and Ingolf, who had Lawmaker pinned to the side. Rika crawled toward them on hands and knees, her weapon gleaming in the sharp flashes of light.

"Stay put!" he cried, and skirted the last barrel. Its top flew off. A split second before Rasmus shot from the barrel, ax in hand, George lurched sideways.

Rika screamed.

"I'll kill him!" Ingolf cried, and thrust the dagger at Lawmaker.

"Nay!" Rika lunged at him.

George shot forward, barely aware of Rasmus thudding to the deck behind him under Ottar's weight. A second later, Erik and Leif flanked him, weapons drawn.

"Turn the ship around!" Ingolf edged his dagger higher on Lawmaker's throat. "I'll kill him, I swear!"

"Do it!" Rika cried. "Erik, turn us around." She knelt at Ingolf's feet, her own dagger poised in midair.

"Nay." Lawmaker shook his head. "Don't turn back."

One more step.

"Grant, no!" Lawmaker caught his eye, and George hesitated. "The dowry, get it for her." The elder smiled, then grabbed Ingolf by the throat.

The henchman lunged. Rika screamed as Ingolf's dagger slipped neatly between Lawmaker's ribs. A second later, to George's astonishment, Lawmaker cast himself backward into the sea, pulling Ingolf with him. Erik and Leif exploded across the deck as George lunged for Rika.

"Nay!" she screamed, and eluded his grasp. "Lawmaker!"

An enormous wave crashed over them, pummeling George backward into a roil of bodies—Rasmus, Ottar and the rest. By the time he got to his feet, she was halfway over the side.

"Rika!" He shot forward and grabbed her wrist. Too late.

She hung there, half in the water, struggling against him. "Let go of me! I must save him. Let go!" With each roll of the ship, she went under, shrieking and sputtering.

George held her fast, his heart pounding, his lungs

burning against the blasts of sea water threatening to choke him.

"Let go!"

Lightning flashed, so close the sopping hair on the back of his neck prickled. For a moment their eyes locked, but 'twas not Rika's fearless gaze he saw— 'twas Sommerled's, eyes wide and terror-glazed.

She jerked herself from his grasp, and the sea swallowed her whole.

"Rika!" Ottar pulled himself up beside George and shrieked her name over and over.

George's hand was still outstretched, as if he thought by some miracle the sea would cough her up and she'd take hold of it once more.

Another wave rolled toward the boat like a dark phantom. Rika's head broke the surface just before the water hit them. He could save her, she was that close.

Instinct drove him to reach for her. Then he froze.

What if she drowned?

He'd be free, would he not? Free of the bargain. Free of her. Free to go home—if he survived.

The icy wave crashed down on them, and through the stinging spray he saw her hand shoot from the water, reaching out to him, fingers splayed, the eerie light of the storm beaming off her braceleted wrist.

Chapter Ten

He would let her drown?

So be it.

The sea sucked her under, and this time she did not struggle. Why should she? Lawmaker was dead. Gunnar, too. She must stop fooling herself. A year in hard labor in the dank caves at Dunnet Head. She'd heard tell of the beatings, the torture. What man could survive such abuse?

Nay, they were both lost to her, and there was not another on this earth who cared whether she lived or died. The look in Grant's eyes when she slipped from his grasp, for a moment she had thought...

Nay, she'd been wrong.

Rika let her body go limp, and mustered the courage to suck the chill water into her burning lungs.

And then his hands were on her. Grant's hands. Strong and sure, circling her waist, pulling her tight against him. Together they broke the surface and her lungs exploded. Thor's blood, she could not get enough air. She fought him, choking and sputtering.

"Be still!" He pulled her under with him, and something slipped around her waist. Rope. They crashed to the surface again and she sucked in air. Grant pulled the tether tight. "Put your arms around me, woman!"

"Nay!" She beat at him with her fists. "Let me go!"

She knew he would not. Grant slipped his arms under hers and pulled them along the tether, hand over hand, toward the ship, which bobbed like a cork in the dark water.

Ottar and Leif hung over the side, their hands outstretched, reaching for her. Erik held the other end of the line to which Grant had tied her.

The wind screamed. The sea raged. Her legs were numb, her fingers ice. She was barely aware of them hauling her into the *byrthing*. The deck pitched beneath them, and she went down hard on a rolling keg of mead.

"My…head." Rika felt blindly along her damp scalp. Her eyes, glued shut, stung with salt.

"Dinna move."

Grant. The calm authority in his voice made her head stop spinning. The Scot had saved her life.

She cracked an eye and was instantly blinded by the light. "The…storm…"

"'Tis past."

Her throat burned. "How long?"

"A few hours. Ye hit your head on a barrel. 'Tis a wee bump. Ye'll be fine." She squinted up at him as he knelt before her, proffering a cup. "Here, drink this."

"What is it?"

"Water."

Her stomach lurched, and she waved him off. "I've had my fill of that."

"Try this, then." Ottar's wet boots came into her

line of sight. He squatted beside her and Grant and offered her a ladle. "It's mead."

"Ah, good." She tried to sit up, and both of them moved to help her. "I…I'm fine. Leave me be."

The two exchanged a look she could not read, and allowed her to right herself on her own. The sweet libation brought her to her senses. "Ah, that's better."

She blinked into the sun until her eyes focused. The *byrthing's* sail billowed white against the unbearable blue of the sky. Perhaps she'd dreamed the storm.

"Where's—" Lawmaker's name died on her lips. She remembered now.

"He's gone," Grant said.

"Nay." She shook her head, not wanting to believe. Ottar's filming eyes and the empty ache she felt inside told her it was true. "Nay," she breathed, and met Grant's sober gaze.

"Aye, lass, 'tis true." He pulled her to her feet and held on to her until she felt steady on the gently rolling deck.

She closed her eyes and breathed deep of the salt air. Oh, God, what would she do now?

"Grant, she should rest," Ottar said.

"Nay, I'm fine." She pushed past them both, gripped the top rail and blinked at the southern horizon. Was that land she spied? "Where are we?"

"On course, by some miracle," Ottar said. "Erik says—"

She spun toward the *byrthing's* bow. "Erik! Leif! Where are they?" The events of the previous night crashed over her. "Ingolf, Rasmus. How did they—"

Grant stepped in front of her, blocking her way. "The lads are well. Erik and Leif are sleeping—over there, on a pile of homespun."

"And—"

"Tied up." Grant nodded toward the center of the cargo, where the back of Ingolf's dark head lolled against one of the barrels.

"He lives?" Rage boiled up inside her. Grant read it in her eyes, and placed a steadying hand on her shoulder.

"But then—"

"Nay," Grant said. "I know what ye're thinking, but there was naught to be done. Lawmaker was dead before he hit the water."

A sick feeling welled inside her as she remembered the flashing lightning reflected off Ingolf's blade.

"Erik fished the murderer out," Ottar said, and cast Ingolf a deadly look. "God knows why."

Grant's gaze drifted out to sea and his expression tightened. "Because no man should let another drown."

He was remembering his brother. She recognized the anguish in his eyes and felt the staggering weight of his pain. He held himself responsible for Sommerled's death.

She, too, felt responsible—for Lawmaker's untimely demise. He had purposefully sacrificed himself for their mission. Rika closed her eyes and offered up a silent prayer for his soul.

"Rasmus is still out cold." Ottar's voice wrested her from her entreaty. He drew himself up straight and tall before her.

Rika pushed her own pain away and smiled at him. "You did well last night. Thank you."

The youth wiped a hand across his ruddy, tearstained cheek and beamed at her.

"Aye, ye did," Grant said.

The two exchanged glances, and Rika sensed a fragile sort of peace between them. It pleased her.

Ottar glared over the barrel tops at their captives. "We should have killed them both straightaway. What good are they alive? They're Brodir's men."

Grant snorted. "Aye, all the more reason to slit their bloody throats."

"Yet you yourself would not have let Ingolf drown." Rika arched a brow at him.

Grant shrugged.

The Scot's initial reaction evoked in her a strange sense of satisfaction. Still, they were not killers. Lawmaker himself would not have condoned murder. She lusted for vengeance more than any of them could know. But she would wait and let Gunnar decide a fair punishment. "Nay, we will not touch them."

"But—" Ottar silenced himself at her upraised hand.

"Make certain their binds are tight." She caught herself rubbing her own braceleted wrists. Grant looked at her with a heady measure of understanding. It unnerved her, and she turned away.

"Come," she said to Ottar. "I wish to check our bearing." The sun was enough of a gauge, and the islands to the southwest, but she needed the diversion. Her thoughts raced, and she was not yet ready to confront them.

The pouch at her waist was still damp, but intact, and she drew comfort from knowing the lodestone was safe within it. At least that was something.

She was alone in this now. True, she had Ottar and Erik and Leif—but while the youths were valiant and loyal, they had neither Lawmaker's wisdom nor his foresight.

Rika gripped the top rail and ground her teeth. *Once*

you start down this path there can be no going back.
The wind toyed with her hair. Absently she reached
back and began to braid it.

It was up to her now.

She'd see them safe—and Gunnar, too, God willing.

George stood starboard and squinted against the setting sun. The sky warmed red then cooled to violet as
the brilliant orb slid behind the dark silhouette of the
islands.

"Orkney," Ottar said.

George arched a brow at him. "How d'ye know?"

"It must be. Lawmaker said we'd pass east of the
islands near to the third day."

"So he did." George felt the old man's loss as
keenly as did the others, and that unsettled him. He
gripped *Gunnlogi*'s hilt. The sword would ne'er leave
his side again. Had he worn it from the start, Lawmaker
might still be alive.

"We're nearly there, then," Ottar said.

"Aye."

"A day at most? What think you?"

George met the youth's gaze and read something in
those dark eyes he'd not seen before. Uncertainty. The
events of last night had had a sobering effect on them
all.

'Twas the first time Ottar had asked his opinion on
any matter. The first time, in fact, the youth had shown
him any measure of civility. His hotheaded pride and
misplaced rivalry had quelled with the storm.

Erik and Leif had consulted George throughout the
day, as well. They were boys, he reminded himself, and
though he was a foreigner and traveled with them not

quite of his own free will, he was older, more experienced, and they looked to him for advice.

Ottar waited, his anxiety manifest in the twitch of his beardless cheek.

"Aye, a day," George said, and saw the tension drain from the youth's expression. In that moment, Ottar reminded him much of his brother Sommerled—the exuberance of youth all but crushed under the sobering weight of manhood.

For Sommerled, that exuberance was extinguished forever.

"Erik is preparing some food. Are you hungry?"

George wasn't, but he supposed he should eat. "I could do with a bit of something."

He turned his face into the wind and his eyes to the sea, which had gone a pearly slate under the darkening sky. The first stars blinked at him low on the horizon, their violet backdrop cooling to indigo.

"Shall I wake her?" Ottar said.

"Rika?" His gaze was drawn to her sleeping form, curled like a cat on a bale of homespun nestled amidst the kegs. "Nay, let her sleep."

Ottar smiled—George felt it more than saw it—then made his way aft to where Erik and Leif were rearranging some of the cargo. Aye, much had changed between them since he'd pulled Rika from the sea.

Why had he done it?

Looking at her now, he wondered that he had ever hesitated. In sleep she seemed small, defenseless—a woman like any other. Oh, but she was not like any other.

A gust of wind blew her cloak open and, without thinking, he knelt beside her and smoothed it back over her damp gown. She'd lost her boots in the water. Her feet were ice. Quickly he stripped off the fur wrap covering his tunic—'twas nearly dry—and wrapped it around her feet.

She stirred, a tiny sigh escaping her lips.

He had an overpowering urge to lie down beside her, cradle her in his arms, brush a kiss across her temple. But he did not. He told himself he'd have braved the chill waters to save her no matter who she was. 'Twas the Christian thing to do. He would have done it for anyone.

All at once, he recalled the shipwreck—watching in horror as Sommerled pitched over the frigate's top rail into the churning water. George had leaped after him but caught a foot in some twisted rigging hanging off the side. He'd managed to grab Sommerled's outstretched hand as the youth worked madly to keep his head above the surface, but the drowning ship lurched starboard and his brother slipped from his grasp.

"Sweet Jesus," he breathed.

"There is naught sweet about him," Rika said, startling him. She opened her eyes and fixed them on his. He could see in the waning light that she'd been crying. "He is a cruel and merciless God."

For a long time he just looked at her. "Aye, that he is."

She shivered and pulled her cloak more tightly about her. Fisting his hands at his sides, he willed himself not to help her. Then her eyes lit on the fur wrap covering her feet. Their gazes locked.

After a long moment she said, "Thank you."

He nodded, then rose, suddenly uncomfortable under her scrutiny.

"Why did you do it?"

"The fur?" He shrugged. "Och, 'twas just that your feet—"

"Nay, not that. Last night—" She sat up and looked at him with those guileless eyes. "Why did you fish me out?"

Why had he?

The answer he'd prepared for her died on his lips. He shrugged stupidly.

"Grant!" Ottar's voice carried over the rushing of sea and wind. "Come—eat with us." The youth waved him over.

He stood there a moment longer, looking at her in the last of the light, wondering what she was thinking. Then he left to join the others.

The cawing of seabirds woke her just before dawn. It was a frigid morn. Her bare feet burned with cold as she stood near the *byrthing's* prow and watched the sun rise. Shrouded in a whispery veil of mist, she saw it, and her breath caught.

Land.

"We shall finally have done with this hellish voyage," Grant said as he came up behind her.

"Ja."

"Where d'ye plan to put in?" He eyed her in a way that made her suspicious of his intent.

"Gellis Bay," she said, visualizing the crude map Lawmaker had drawn for her in the snow the afternoon before they sailed. "We seek the man MacInnes."

"A Scot. Fine. But there must be dozens of Mac-Inneses. 'Tis a fair common name in the north. If that's all ye've got to go on, then—"

"Thomas MacInnes, and he lives just above the

bay.'' Lawmaker had described the place to her many times.

"Ye're certain?''

She nodded. "Lawmaker said he would not be hard to find. His is the only family for leagues and leagues.''

"It doesna surprise me. 'Tis a godforsaken place.'' His face brightened. "Gellis Bay it is, then.''

"You know the place?''

"I know of it.''

Thank God. He was the only one of them who did. Brodir had taken all of the charts of the mainland with him when he left. She had thought to rely on Lawmaker's memory to guide them. Now she'd be forced to rely on Grant.

"It lies just there—'' he pointed to the rugged, mist-cloaked coastline "—due east of Dunnet Head.''

She bit back a squeak, and her eyes widened involuntarily.

"Ye know it? Dunnet Head?''

"Nay, I do not.'' She shook her head fervently and turned away from him. "I've never heard of it.''

"Ye could have fooled me.''

She risked a glance back at him, and caught him frowning, studying her. Not once since they'd sailed had she or Erik or Leif even mentioned Gunnar's name. She had thought to tell Ottar of their plan once they were at sea, but now that Ingolf and Rasmus were aboard she dared not breathe a word of it.

"Are ye still intent on this harebrained scheme of yours?''

"Wh…what scheme?'' For a moment she wondered if he'd read her thoughts. "Oh, collecting my dowry you mean?'' She drew herself up and faced him. "I am most certainly intent on it.''

He muttered something unintelligible under his breath.

"And you shall help me. We've come all this way, and at no small cost." Lawmaker's death lay heavy on her conscience.

"Aye, there's that. All the same, 'tis a fool's mission, and one that is not mine."

"You gave your word—husband."

Their eyes locked.

He said nothing, and she feared with Lawmaker dead the Scot would abandon their bargain. In the short time he'd lived among them, Grant had shown them all he was a man of his word. A man of honor.

But such virtues were bought and sold cheap on Fair Isle, and Rika had little experience with them since Brodir's rise to power. She had thought to rely on Lawmaker's strange bond with the Scot to ensure his compliance. But with her guardian dead, who knew what Grant intended?

She was in a precarious situation, and she knew he knew it.

"What d'ye intend for them?" Grant nodded toward their captives.

Rasmus snored loudly, whistling as he sucked breath through his near toothless mouth. Ingolf was awake, she realized, and she wondered what, if anything he'd overheard of her conversation with Grant.

"MacInnes shall keep them for us until we return from my father's house." She'd thought long and hard about what to do with them, and this seemed the only answer. She prayed Tom MacInnes was the friend Lawmaker had made him out to be.

Grant shrugged. "'Tis of no import to me what ye do with them. I was merely curious."

Ingolf twisted his head around and grinned at them. "More cowardice than curiosity if you ask me."

Rika started toward him.

Grant grabbed her arm. "Stay away from him. He's dangerous."

"Not trussed up like a goose he's not." She wrested herself free and approached Ingolf, her hand resting comfortingly on the hilt of her sheathed dagger. Just in case.

Grant followed.

"I would speak to him alone," she said, and shot one of her well-practiced jaded looks over her shoulder.

"Suit yourself." Grant pulled up a keg out of ear-shot—a dozen paces from where Ingolf and Rasmus lay bound—settled atop it, and stared across the gray water toward land.

Rika knelt before the henchman, taking care not to get too close. "As I said, you'll remain with Tom Mac-Innes until we return for you."

"Who's we? You and the Scot?" Ingolf smirked in Grant's direction. "You're a fool, woman. Surely you don't think he means to keep his word?"

Rika stopped breathing. "What do you mean?" Her hand twitched on the dagger's hilt.

"Think you I'm a dolt like this one?" Ingolf kicked at his companion's feet. Rasmus snorted a few times but did not wake. "Husband or no, the man will ne'er stay with you now that he's on his own turf."

She was tempted to slit his throat, but stilled her hand.

"If you return at all, 'twill be alone, with but your snot-nosed dogs." He meant Ottar, and Erik and Leif.

Surly whoreson. "*When* I return, it will be with—"

She bit her tongue a second before saying Gunnar's name.

"Who?" Ingolf narrowed his eyes. He might have already guessed her plans for the silver, but the questioning look on his face told her that he had not. Ingolf lunged against his bonds.

Rika fell backward as the ship lurched.

"I'll enjoy watching Brodir punish you, you bitch—after he's had a bit of sport." His eyes raked over her, and her stomach did a slow roll. "Perhaps he'd allow me a go. Why not? You're damaged goods now."

"Shut your mouth before I shut it for ye." Grant stepped over her and poised the tip of Lawmaker's sword at Ingolf's throat.

Rika scrambled to her feet, pleased by Grant's intervention.

"Ho! What's this?" Erik jogged toward them from the stern, Ottar and Leif in his wake.

"'Tis naught," Grant said, and sheathed his weapon. "This one needs a lesson in manners, is all." He cast her a stony look, then retreated to his perch on the keg.

"Look!" Ottar stopped short and pointed southwest off the starboard bow. "The mainland! There, peeking out from the mist."

They all looked. Even Ingolf twisted his head around in an attempt to see. Rika drew a sobering breath. Salt and sea and something else.

"Scotland," Grant said. "I can smell it on the wind."

Chapter Eleven

He was home.

Thank Christ.

George and the youths worked the oars while Rika stood on the prow and guided them into a tiny, sheltered bay. The fog was thick and deadly chill. He rowed faster, harder, putting his back into it, working to stave off frostbite and still his chattering teeth.

He caught a glimpse of the desolate shoreline as the mist swirled and eddied about them, thinning for the barest moment only to swallow them up again.

'Twas impossible to make out landmarks. While he'd ne'er journeyed this far north before, he was good with maps and remembered well the shape of the coastline from the charts he'd seen on the Wick-bound frigate.

George had directed them to put in as close to his recollection of where Gellis Bay lay as they could manage, given the fact that none of them could see a bloody thing.

"Hold!" Rika called from the prow. Through the mist he saw her peer ahead into the whiteness, a hand raised in caution.

The *byrthing* scraped bottom and lurched to a stop.

"Ja, this will do." She turned and bade them disembark.

Ottar was the first ashore. He kicked at the sea-tumbled rocks peppering the beach and screwed his face into a frown. "This is it?"

George vaulted over the top rail into the shallows. "Aye, lad, this is it." On shaking legs he waded ashore then dropped to his knees. He dug his hands into the sand, relishing the feel of it between his fingers.

Scotland.

Near enough, at any rate.

Who knew what king held these distant lands? They'd best be bloody well careful. The fog, mayhap, was a blessing after all.

Erik tossed him the end of a thick-braided rope. He and Ottar secured it around a jagged boulder halfway up the beach. "That should hold her," he said, and the youth nodded.

"What about them?" Leif nodded at the two bound henchmen.

George waved him ashore. "Come, we shall decide who's to stay behind and watch them. I dinna trust them on their own."

"Since when do you give the orders?" Rika's head popped up from the center of the cargo.

"Since we landed in my country—wife."

Even at twenty paces, he could see her sour expression.

He waited on the beach for her, wondering why in hell he didn't just bolt. He had Lawmaker's fine weapon, but neither mount nor coin. Soaked to the skin and bone cold, it seemed not the best of ideas at this point.

Rika appeared at the *byrthing's* prow, and George

squinted through the fog to make certain he was seeing what he thought he was seeing.

Aye, he was seeing it, all right. She had donned men's clothes—breeks, boots, and a belted tunic from which hung her brother's sheathed sword. Her hair was swept back off her face and refashioned into two severe-looking braids. But for the lack of hauberk and helm, she looked much the same as she had the day he first laid eyes on her.

He caught himself smiling, and that troubled him.

A minute later she stood beside him on the rocky beach. "What are you staring at?"

"Your…attire."

"This is a foreign place. We know not who or what we'll encounter. It seemed…prudent. Besides, it's drier than my gown."

He could not argue with her logic, but said nothing.

"What now?" Ottar said. His face was flushed ripe as cherries from the cold.

George realized that the icy temperatures would do them all in should they not find shelter, and soon. Three days in an open ship in the dead of winter—they were lucky to have made it this far. He realized they were all looking at him, Rika too, as if he knew something they did not.

George shrugged. "Why ask me? We're here on her account." He arched a brow at Rika and waited to see what she would do.

She drew herself up and fixed that annoyingly authoritative expression on her face—the one that made him want to slap her, or kiss her, he was never certain which. "We shall…" She hesitated, peering into the fog up the beach, then down. "We shall find Mac-Innes."

"Just like that," he said.

"Ja." She tipped her chin at him, but he read an uncertainty in her eyes that belied her confident exterior. Nay, 'twas more than that.

'Twas fear.

"Lead the way, then." He swept an arm inland and waited for her to take the lead.

The three youths watched, disheartened by their lack of a better plan.

George felt rather satisfied, smug even. The woman had no idea what to do. She'd not thought this far ahead. As he strode up the beach in her wake and watched her study the elusive bits of cliff and rock peeking out of the fog, he realized just how defenseless she was.

Damn her.

"All right," he snapped. She stopped and turned, arching a brow at him in question. "Stay here, the lot o' ye. I'll scale the cliff and see what's on top."

The youths muttered their agreement.

"You will not," Rika said. "Think you I'm that big a fool?"

"What, d'ye think I'd leave ye here in this—"

"In a second."

The thought had crossed his mind, in fact.

"I will go with you," she said.

"Fine." He turned to the youths. "Go back to the ship and wait for us there. Mind ye keep a watchful eye on the other two. We willna be long."

Ottar protested, but Rika waved him off.

"Come on," Leif said to him. "I'm not at ease leaving Ingolf and Rasmus so long on their own. Someone should go back."

Ottar frowned, resigned, and followed Erik and Leif back to the *byrthing*.

"Shall we?" George said, and nodded toward the cliff.

Rika strode off ahead of him.

An hour later they were still wandering on the moor above the beach, no wiser about their location than they'd been when first they landed. There was not a soul in sight—nor was there any evidence of habitation. Neither sheep, nor croft. Not so much as a wagon track or a hoofprint. The only sounds they heard were the wind and the sea, and the occasional cawing of a tern.

George noted a marked change in Rika's behavior since leaving the ship. She was wary, almost fearful, and had stuck uncharacteristically close to him on their reconnaissance, venturing no farther than a few paces from his side.

There was something about this last bit he liked.

A frigid wind gusted through them and his teeth began to chatter. His hands and feet were ice. He looked at Rika and realized she, too, was shivering. "Here," he said, and opened his cloak to her. A second later she was clinging to him.

He reminded himself that she was far out of her element here. The landscape was not so unlike Fair Isle's, but this was a foreign land, and she, a woman alone.

How could he leave her?

How could he not?

'Twas madness. He was, what, a two-day ride from Wick? Barely a sennight's walk. As he held Rika in his arms, warming in her embrace, he thought of Anne Sinclair.

His bride.

Och, what did it matter? He was already a fortnight late for the wedding. What was another sennight?

"Come on," he said, and took her hand. "Let's go back to the ship. When this damnable fog lifts, we'll find this MacInnes and go from there."

She looked up at him, her face ruddy from the icy wind, her eyes vitreous. "Truly? You will keep your word?"

He met her gaze, but didn't answer. "Come on," he said finally. "Let's go."

They could hear Erik's shouts long before they reached the cliff's edge. Tiny alarms went off in George's head.

"Something's happened!" Rika scrambled down the rocky slope and took off at a run.

George sprinted ahead, drawing his sword as he ran.

"Rika! Grant!" Leif's shrill voice carried through the mist. "Here! We're he—"

George collided with the youth and nearly lost his footing. "Bloody Hell! What—"

"Ingolf and...and Rasmus," Leif said, trying to catch his breath.

Rika skidded to a stop on the flat, slick rock beside them. "Where are they? Where?"

George spun right then left, brandishing *Gunnlogi,* peering into the whiteness.

"Gone," Leif said. "Long gone."

"Oh God, we must find them!" Rika started forward, and George grabbed her arm. "Let go of me!"

"It's m-my fault."

"Ottar!" Rika stiffened in George's grip as Ottar staggered out of the mist, grasping his bloodied thigh. Erik was right behind him. Both youths collapsed at their feet, gasping for air.

Panic shone in Rika's eyes as she took in the blood dripping from their wounds and weapons.

"It's…it's nothing," Ottar said. "A flesh wound."

"Here, let me see." Rika knelt before him. Ottar grimaced as she tore away the fabric of his breeks and inspected the wound.

Leif sheathed his weapon, and Erik followed suit.

"Are ye hurt?" George spared a quick glance at both lads. They seemed fit enough if a bit bloodied.

"Fine," Leif said. "Just scratches really."

"Me, as well." Erik scrambled to his feet.

"What happened?" George lowered his sword and watched as Rika finished bandaging Ottar's wound with a strip of cloth torn from her tunic. "Tell me."

Ottar looked up at him. "Erik and…and Leif were on the beach, scavenging a bit of driftwood for a—a fire. I—was supposed to be watching I-Ingolf, but…" The lad gritted his teeth and looked away. George recognized too well the pain of self-reproach in his eyes.

"He…drifted off," Erik said. "And…"

Ottar waved Rika away and struggled to his feet, swearing when she tried to help him.

"We were close by, thank God, when they slipped their bonds." George read fear in Leif's tight expression. "Ottar wounded Rasmus, but we couldn't overcome them, even three against two." All three youths looked away, shamed.

George's heart went out to them. Christ, they were barely men. Against seasoned killers the likes of Ingolf and Rasmus they'd stood not a chance, and were probably lucky to be alive.

'Twas his fault, not the youths'.

He cursed himself twice—once for leaving them alone, and again for not having killed Brodir's men when he'd had the chance. He clapped a firm hand on Ottar's shoulder. "It might have happened to any of us, lad. God knows we've had damned little sleep these last days."

Ottar shrugged his hand away.

"You'll be fine," Rika said. "A bit sore, perhaps. As for Ingolf and Rasmus…we must go after them, find them."

Surely she wasn't serious?

"Ja," Leif said. "They can't have gotten far."

"Hang on." George sheathed his weapon as he considered their options, and following two murderers into the mist in a strange land was not one of them. "The fog's too thick. We'll ne'er find them. Besides, 'tis of no great import now. We've other problems to deal wi—"

"You don't understand!" Rika spun toward him, her face white with alarm. Never had he seen her so distressed.

Regardless, his decision was made. "It matters not. So they're gone. No harm done. We'll get your coin, and ye shall return home."

"Nay, nay." Her eyes glassed, and she bit her lip so hard it raised a droplet of blood.

There was more here than met the eye. If anything, she should be glad to be rid of them. "What d'ye fear? Retribution?"

She strode off toward the cliff, but kept changing direction. 'Twas plain she had no idea what to do next.

George caught her up. "Dinna fash. As long as I'm with ye, I'll see ye come to no harm."

As soon as the words left his lips, he wondered why he'd said them. He was daft—gone soft in the head over this whole affair. If he were smart, he'd leave them now and get on with his life.

Rika stopped short as a spray of rocks tumbled onto the beach from the cliff just above them. George glanced up, and froze dead in his tracks.

"Thor's blood," she breathed.

A good-sized man dressed in breacon and boots and a fur-lined cloak stood on the rocky promontory above them, mist swirling around his bonneted head. A broadsword swung from his beefy hand.

George slipped *Gunnlogi* from his shoulder baldric.

"Who are ye, and from whence d'ye come?" the man called down to them.

Rika backed against George. Unconsciously, he wrapped a protective arm around her waist.

"We...we hail from Fair Isle," she called up to the man. "I am Ulrika, daughter of Fritha."

"Fritha, ye say?" The burly man squinted at her through the mist.

"Ja. And this is—"

George squeezed her, hard. "What, d'ye intend to introduce us all?" He stepped in front of her, brandishing *Gunnlogi*. "And who might ye be?" he called out to the man.

He was a Scot, surely—clothed in the fashion of a Highlander, his speech thick with a comforting brogue. And yet... George tensed as two other similarly garbed men stepped out of the mist and flanked the stranger. One whispered something in his ear.

Here it comes. Scots they may be, but these men were no friends. He cast cautionary glances to Ottar and Erik and Leif, who'd fanned out beside him and Rika. They nodded, weapons at the ready.

Rika inched forward and clumsily drew her brother's sword. Damn her! He scanned their surroundings for a suitable place to safeguard her. All hell was about to break loose. The last thing he needed was a headstrong woman on his ha—

"I am MacInnes!" the stranger called down to them.

What? George swapped wide-eyed looks with Rika.

The stranger sheathed his weapon, and his companions did the same. "Come, Ulrika, daughter of Fritha—" he beckoned her scale the cliff "—ye are welcome here."

"*You* are Thomas MacInnes?" Rika stared at the craggy faced Scot. Up close, he looked older than first she'd thought him to be.

"Aye, but most call me Tom." He nodded at Grant and the others. "We saw your ship early this morn, off St. John's point, and figured ye'd make for the bay."

"Ye sought us out then." Grant stood between her and MacInnes, eyeing the stranger and his kinsmen, his weapon still in his hand. "Why?"

MacInnes shrugged. "To find out who ye were and what ye were about. We get few visitors here. Most ships put in at Wick, or around the head to the west."

"Dunnet Head?" Rika held her breath.

"Aye. D'ye know it?"

She shook her head with far too much vigor. "Nay, I do not."

MacInnes cocked his head to see past Grant and looked her up and down. "Ye dinna look much like your dame. More like your sire, methinks."

Rika shivered, stunned—less from the cold than from MacInnes's words. "You knew them?" When first she'd called her name out, she'd read the surprise in his face. It was as if he already knew her. "But... how?"

"Och, we met years ago on Fair Isle, long before ye were born."

"You've been there?" Ottar ignored Grant's look of caution, and sheathed his sword. "To Fair Isle?"

"Aye, many times, but no since I was a young buck. There is a man there who was once like a brother to me. He was the law speaker." He eyed the weapon in Grant's hand, then arched a brow. "Lawmaker, we called him. Surely ye know him."

Rika nodded, her belly tightening. "He is my guardian."

"Aye, he spoke of ye often in the many letters I received from him over the years. How fares he?"

"He is dead," Grant said. "Lost at sea in a storm, two nights past."

Rika fought to keep her composure as the dark memory gripped her. She stepped out from behind the protection of Grant's body in time to see the two Scots lock eyes.

For a moment no one spoke. The wind rushed up and over the cliff, chilling her to the bone. She staved off a shiver. "May he go with God," MacInnes whispered.

"There were two others in our party," Grant said, ignoring the sentiment. "Have ye seen them?"

"Nay, we've not." MacInnes glanced at his kinsmen, and they shrugged. "They'd be fools to slog off in this soup—" he nodded at the mist-shrouded moors behind him "—without a local guide."

"They...escaped," Rika said, nearly biting her tongue. How much should they tell him? He was most certainly the friend of whom Lawmaker spoke. Still...

MacInnes frowned.

"One was responsible for Lawmaker's death," Grant said. At last, to her relief, he sheathed *Gunnlogi*. "They were our prisoners."

"I see." MacInnes pulled the edges of his breacon tighter about him, and shivered. "Come on, we'll catch our death out here. My house lies less than a furlong east. What say we continue our talk over a hogshead and a hot meal?" He turned and she started after him.

Grant grabbed her arm. "What about the ship?"

"We've a full load of cargo," Erik said, nodding down to the beach. "Homespun, grain, and kegs of mead."

MacInnes's brows shot up. "Mead, ye say?"

She nodded.

It was clear from Grant's expression he was not pleased with Erik revealing so much. But what did it matter now? They were only five, and this MacInnes, friend or foe, surely had enough kinsmen at home to overtake them and the ship should he wish to.

"We thought to trade the homespun and grain for horses," she said, thinking that confidence might serve them well in this situation. "And the mead."

"I've not had a decent draught o' the stuff since last I visited your fair island."

"Will you trade with us then?" Erik said. "For horses?"

MacInnes looked at her, and she held her breath. "'Tis a bold proposition, lad. D'ye ken how rare a good mount is in these parts?"

Grant had warned her of this, but she'd not listened.

"I'd first hear more about why ye've come, and about these...prisoners." MacInnes started east, and she followed, wrenching herself free from Grant.

"Mayhap we could manage an agreeable trade, though I canna say as I'd be willing to part with my bonny steeds." He shot a shrewd look back at her. "I'll send some men for the cargo."

Rika exhaled. Though it was not the promise she'd hoped for, it was a start. She jogged ahead and caught him up. "And the ship—can you mind it for us for a time?"

MacInnes's brows shot up. "Mayhap." He glanced back at Grant. "If ye tell me why ye travel with a Scot, and why he bears Lawmaker's weapon."

She tripped, stunned by MacInnes's canny recognition of *Gunnlogi*. Grant rushed up behind her and saved her from a fall. There seemed no sense in hiding the truth. MacInnes obviously knew Lawmaker well. "Grant is my…husband," she said. "Lawmaker made him a gift of the sword."

MacInnes stopped short, and eyed Grant with new appreciation. For some unfathomable reason, Rika felt her chest swell with pride. MacInnes's blue eyes flicked to the sword. "Such a gift is no made lightly," he said. "I'd know more of ye, Grant."

"Aye," Grant said, his expression stone. "And I'd know more of ye."

They trudged for nearly an hour across the wet, windswept moor, mist swirling about them. She could barely see a half-dozen paces ahead, but MacInnes seemed to know exactly where he was going.

More of his kinsmen joined them along the way. Grant had been right about that. Earlier, he'd whispered to her that it seemed damned unlikely MacInnes would approach a strange ship with but two men as escort. Nearly a score accompanied them now, along what looked to be a footpath, running up over craggy ridges then down again.

The wind burned her face and breached her garments. She wiggled her toes in Gunnar's oversized boots and realized she couldn't feel them anymore. When would they get there?

MacInnes's men looked at her strangely, whispering among themselves. A few made rude comments. Some of the words she didn't understand, but she could well imagine their meaning. Absently she traced the line of her scar from ear to throat.

"Ignore them," Grant said, watching the strangers with eagle's eyes. He'd strayed not two paces from her the whole long walk, and once rested his broad hand on the small of her back as they trudged over some uneven ground.

For years she'd relied on no man for protection. But today she found herself comforted by Grant's presence, and more than a little thrilled by his cavalier and possessive behavior.

Because MacInnes had been Lawmaker's friend, she was tempted to give him her trust. But a dozen years had passed since the two had last seen each other, and Rika knew that much could change a man's loyalties in that amount of time.

Ottar and Erik and Leif took to the burly Scot immediately. She reminded herself they were young and out of their element, and looked for any anchorage on which to ground themselves.

Grant was wary, and that wariness caused her to reserve a final judgment of the strangers.

As if he'd read her mind, Grant took her arm and said, "If he offers more than a sway-backed nag for the whole of the cargo, he's either a fool or he's what he says he is—a friend.''

''Were he truly a friend, would that surprise you?''

He shrugged. ''Stranger things have happened. But beware. Stay close by me when we reach his demesne.''

She smiled inwardly, and trudged on.

A short time later, through the thinning mist, she saw it. A great house of timber and stone surrounded by a low wall.

''My home,'' MacInnes said, looking back at her. They stopped outside the wall. ''Wait here, whilst I confer with my wife.''

Most of MacInnes's men disappeared into a low building flanking the main house. Rika guessed it was a barracks of sorts or a stable. Six stayed with them, finding seats on the low wall. Grant continued to watch them.

Moments after MacInnes entered the house, the door swung wide again and a woman, his wife, no doubt, strode into the courtyard to bid them welcome.

''My dear,'' the bright-eyed woman said, extending a long white hand to her. There was no hint of disapproval or even amusement in her expression as she surveyed Rika's bedraggled garments and weapons. ''Ye look wet to the skin. Aye, and ye're surely exhausted.''

Until this moment, Rika hadn't allowed herself to recognize the magnitude of her fatigue, but the woman's warm demeanor and sympathetic smile breached the last of her defenses. Rika took her hand. ''I am, on both counts, if truth be told.''

''Come inside, then,'' the woman said. ''A chamber is being prepared for ye and your husband.'' She flashed her eyes at Grant, and beckoned him follow.

Husband.

Rika risked a backward glance at him. Grant arched a brow at her, then followed them inside.

After an uncomfortable night sleeping on the floor of the tiny bedchamber he shared with Rika, George spent the day helping MacInnes's men relieve the *byrthing* of its cargo.

Rika seemed safe enough in the house with MacInnes's wife. The couple had no children of their own, and the mistress fawned over her as one would a daughter.

George suspected Rika was unused to such attention. He took pleasure in seeing her doted upon. 'Twas a small thing, but to Rika he knew it meant much.

Late in the day, five mounts were brought from the stable for his inspection. He could not believe MacInnes's generosity. The steeds were loaned, not given, but the gesture was still no small thing. It seemed they owed much to the Scot's friendship with Lawmaker.

George caught himself thinking of the elder more than once that day. He missed him. 'Twas as simple as that. But he knew he could not dwell on such thoughts. He had plans of his own to carry out.

Now that Rika was safe and apparently among friends, George thought for the hundredth time about leaving. After supper, when all but a few had retired, he had a look at MacInnes's charts.

Wick was no more than a day's hard ride from there—two, mayhap, given the inclement weather. 'Twould take him a minute at most to saddle a mount and be gone. 'Twas a fine, clear night. Why not?

He rose and made a show of stretching sleepily. Ottar sat by the hearth fire with two of MacInnes's men, swapping lies and fantastical tales. They paid him no mind as he slipped from the great hall into the corridor.

A handful of short tapers lit the passageway. Instead of making for the chamber he shared with Rika, he turned toward the unguarded entry of the fortified house.

"Grant." MacInnes's voice stopped him dead. He turned and saw their host leaning against a far doorway. "Come and share a pint with me. It's no often I get the chance to mingle with men from the south."

What else could he do? A few minutes later George was settled by the fire in the kitchen, a cup of mead in his hand.

"Your wife should be in bed," MacInnes said.

"What?" He shot to his feet. "Where is she?"

"Sit down, man, she's well." He nodded toward a window draped in deerskin. "She's outside is all—in my wife's garden. 'Tis bitter out, though, and I fear she'll catch her death."

He strode to the window, lifted the covering and peered into the night. Rika sat with her back to him on a crudely hewn bench amidst the frozen remains of last season's vegetables. The moon cast a pale light upon her. She seemed well enough.

George let the window cover drop and took his place by the fire. "She has a mind of her own."

MacInnes laughed. "Aye, I can see that."

George swilled his mead in silence while MacInnes openly studied him. With their host yet awake, 'twould be hours before he might make his escape. So be it. He was enjoying the warmth of the fire and the sweetness of his drink.

"Ye are a laird, so the lads tell me." MacInnes's directness did not surprise him.

"Aye."

"What takes ye so far afield? Fair Isle is a strange destination for a lone Scot."

George met the man's gaze, and wondered how much Ottar and the others had told him. MacInnes was no fool. George weighed how much of the truth he'd be obliged to impart. "I…I am newly wed."

"That much is evident."

George arched a brow at him.

"There is a sweet tension yet between ye." MacInnes nodded toward the garden where Rika sat. "And a newness that canna be hid."

The man's perception unnerved him and he knew it showed on his face.

MacInnes smiled. "Enjoy it, son." He drained his cup and set it on the raised hearth, then drew himself up, as if he were about to say something of import. "So ye go to claim her dowry."

George stiffened.

"When women get together, they talk." MacInnes shot him a wry glance.

George shrugged, trying to remain casual. "Aye, that's our plan."

"And a fine one it is. There's just one thing about it that doesna make sense." MacInnes willed George to his gaze. "Why now? In the dead o' winter? Why no wait till spring?"

He couldn't think of a good answer for MacInnes's question, so he said nothing.

"Och, no matter. 'Tis none of my concern. I was just curious, is all." MacInnes swept a flagon off the kitchen's massive wooden table and refilled George's cup. "I know him, ye know—Rika's father."

"Rollo? Aye, ye said as much yesterday."

"He's a strange one, and none too friendly."

"So I've been told."

MacInnes rubbed a hand over his short, thick whiskers. "His place is no far from here. Mey Loch—to the southwest, barely a half day's ride."

George stared into the fire, sipping his mead, trying to quell his curiosity. He could not. Finally he said, "Tell me about him. About Rollo." He looked at MacInnes. "What kind of man abandons his own children?"

MacInnes's brows shot up at George's question. "Why, a man who thinks they're no his."

George's mouth gaped. He started to speak, but MacInnes cut him off.

"Ye didna know?"

He shook his head. "I'll be damned. Ye mean to tell me Rika and her brother are..." So Lawmaker was her father, after all.

"Och, nay." MacInnes waved a hand in dismissal. "They're Rollo's spawn all right. He just would ne'er believe it."

Now George was truly confused.

"Lawmaker didna tell ye? Hmph. That's just like him. What about your bride? Did she no share the tale?"

He shook his head. "If indeed she knows of what ye speak, it seems not to sway her mind. She holds naught but contempt for her sire."

MacInnes looked at him for a long moment. Finally he said, "I know not for what reason Lawmaker would withhold the truth from her, but I will tell it to ye now for methinks ye can make use of the information in your dealings with Rollo—and with Rika."

"I would be most grateful to ye." George slid forward on his stool, elbows braced on thighs, surprised by the magnitude of his interest. He told himself 'twas just idle curiosity. For what did it matter how much he knew or did not know? After this night he'd ne'er see Rika again.

MacInnes blew his nose into a rag, and began. "Lawmaker and Fritha were in love."

MacInnes's simple declaration startled him, though when he thought about it he was not entirely surprised. "Rika's mother was Lawmaker's lover?"

"Nay, I didna say that. They were *in love,* but ne'er lovers. There's a difference."

"Oh, aye. Go on."

"Rollo knew it, but he thought that once he wed her, he could sway her affection away from Lawmaker and toward him."

George nodded, understanding. "But he could not."

"Exactly."

"So what happened?"

MacInnes shrugged. "Rollo took his vengeance the only way he could—he treated Fritha badly. And when Rika and her brother were born, he swore the bairns werena his."

"And he treated them ill as well," George said.

MacInnes nodded.

"Why did Fritha no leave him? It seems a common enough custom among their folk."

"I canna say. But after Gunnar and Rika were born, Rollo grew more violent. Lawmaker feared for their safety. He knew Fritha and the bairns would fare better were he gone. So Lawmaker came here, to Gellis Bay, to live with me and mine. When we got word that Fritha had died, Lawmaker returned to Fair Isle. By then, Rollo had gone."

"So he took them in—Rika and Gunnar."

"That he did. For love of Fritha, he raised them as if they were his own."

George slipped his hand into the pouch tied at his waist and fingered the silver brooch Lawmaker had given him for Rika's morning gift.

It's something I've had for years. It was Rika's mother's, in fact. It's time she had it.

MacInnes stretched and yawned. "'Tis a sad tale, but an enlightening one. I leave it to ye to decide whether to tell it to you wife or nay. With Lawmaker gone..." He brushed a gnarly hand across his eyes. "Och, may-hap 'tis of no import now."

George rose with him. "I thank ye. And methinks 'tis of great import." Although he knew he'd not have time to share the tale with Rika, nor did he wish to. What difference could it possibly make now?

"I leave ye to it, then," MacInnes said, and nodded toward the garden. "I'm for bed."

George thanked his host and watched as MacInnes ambled down the corridor toward the stairs leading up to his chamber.

The kitchen fire had died to embers. MacInnes's small dog lay curled on a rug by the hearth twitching, dreaming. George strained his ears, listening for sounds of men still awake in the great hall. Only snores echoed down the long corridor. All were finally abed.

All save Rika.

He paused by the draped window and willed his hand stay put by his side. What purpose was there in disturbing her now? If he were smart he'd get out straight away, under the cover of night—make Wick by the day after tomorrow.

Two days hence he could sup with his new bride. Wed and bed her and get on with his life.

His loins tightened at the prospect of such an evening, but 'twas not the promise of Anne Sinclair's delicate beauty that fired his blood. 'Twas the gritty reality of the woman sitting alone in Tom MacInnes's dead winter garden.

Of its own accord, his hand lifted the deerskin window drape. She was still there, shivering in the cold, her cloak wrapped tight about her, her head uncovered and her hair loose, a silver fall of silk in the moon's eerie light.

He moved silently to the door and tripped the latch, all the while telling himself he was the biggest of fools.

She turned and saw him. "Grant." She smiled at him as if she were surprised to see him. "I thought you to be halfway to Wick by now."

What was she, a bloody mind reader? George stepped out into the snow and shivered under her scrutiny.

"Nay," he said. "No tonight."

Chapter Twelve

She knew what he intended.

The primal look in his eyes confirmed it.

Grant closed the distance between them and pulled Rika to her feet. Had she wished to protest—and she did not—there was not the time.

He kissed her, hard. As he had that day on the moor, with a fury and a possessiveness that thrilled her. Rika more than allowed it. She wanted it. Burned for it.

She burned for him.

How could she?

Shame and desire warred in bright fusion inside her. How could she want for this manhandling? The thought sickened her, yet her body betrayed her sensibilities, and she gave herself up to his strength, his surety. Heat spread like honey from her woman's place as his hands moved over her breasts.

"Come to bed with me," he breathed against her lips.

His sweet plea and the memory of their bridal night caused gooseflesh to rise on her skin. Oh, how she wanted him. She grew bold and ran her hands down his back to his buttocks. Grant moaned dreamily in response.

"Just this once," he whispered. "One last time. Come to bed."

She stiffened in his arms.

"What's wrong?" He brushed a lock of hair from off her face and looked into her eyes. "I know ye want it as much as I."

She pushed against his chest, but he drew her even closer, if that were possible, and kissed her again despite the litany of protests dying on her lips.

One last time.

The short-lived nature of their relationship was driven home to her. Nay, one could not even call what they shared a relationship. 'Twas a bargain. Plain and simple. And made under duress—on both their parts.

He used her—as all men used women.

Merely to slake his lust.

"Stop it," she whispered halfheartedly as he moved against her, holding her fast so she'd feel the full measure of his desire.

"I will if ye truly wish it, but ye do not." He kissed her again, with more urgency, and she was swept up in the haze of her own passion.

"Grant, nay," she breathed. 'Twas madness. She must not succumb. She must stay focused.

"Tell me ye want me," he groaned, his hands moving lower.

"Nay, nay." She broke the kiss and shook her head. Oh God, why wouldn't he stop? They stood in the snow on a dead chill night, yet all she felt was his heat—and her own.

She was dangerously close to giving in.

Mayhap she should?

Her submission to his animal lusts might serve to hold him to their bargain—might keep him with her long enough for her to claim her dowry.

She kissed him back, and let her arms slip around his neck.

"Aye, that's it." He backed her toward the open kitchen door.

Any moment she was certain he'd sweep her from her feet, bear her down the corridor and into their chamber. He'd lay her back on the eiderdown pillows and strip away her brother's clothes, revealing the woman he knew she was.

She should let him. To gain the dowry.

Ja, for Gunnar's sake.

A twisted sort of horror gripped her, and she went rigid in Grant's arms. He drew back and looked at her through slitted eyes glazed with desire.

The veracity of her own feelings struck her like a blast of wind off the sea.

Her eagerness to bed him had naught to do with her brother's plight—not by any stretch of her imagination, no matter how much she wished it so. Nay, her willingness had everything to do with her own needs. Needs far past desire.

She wanted him—so very much. His strength fueled her own. His confidence sparked hers to dizzying heights. She needed him, and the truth of it frightened her.

"I…I must go," she said, and pushed him away.

"Rika—"

"Say no more, for I tire of your lies." Oh, but she could listen to them all night. She turned and ran through the kitchen and down the long corridor toward her bedchamber.

Grant's footfalls sounded behind her. Just a few more steps. She skidded into the chamber, slammed the door behind her and threw the bolt.

She exhaled, her heart pounding an erratic rhythm in her chest. Grant's whispered pleas sounded through the heavy timber door.

Rika put her hands to her ears, and ignored them.

George slammed the wall with his fist.

Was he mad? Aye, he was, and 'twas her fault. She tempted him beyond all reason. Stirred his blood to boiling. Befuddled him entirely.

"Idiot," he breathed, and slid down the cool surface of the wall outside her chamber to the rush-strewn floor.

All was quiet, save for the pounding of his heart. He drew a breath and closed his eyes.

"Vixen."

Never had a woman so addled his thinking, or distracted him so easily from his purpose. She was dangerous, and he was a fool. He banged his head backward against the wall, hammering the message into his thick head.

He was a laird, charged with grave responsibilities to clan and king, to his betrothed and her family. How he ever allowed himself to get caught up in this ludicrous scheme was beyond comprehension.

'Twas Rika's fault. Hers alone.

Their heathen marriage was a blasphemy—one the church could ne'er forgive. She'd corrupted his sense of order, his perceptions of right and wrong. She was boorish and brash, and completely unskilled in the feminine arts.

He should loath her, despise her. Feel revulsion at

her artless kisses and cringe at the solid length of her body pressed to his.

"God help me." He felt just the opposite. His desire for her was rich, all consuming.

The madness would end here. He must crush it. Drive it out.

George pushed himself to his feet, nodding his commitment. His eyes burned and his head throbbed. God's truth, he was dead tired. He hadn't slept in days.

MacInnes and his men were likely all abed. 'Twould be easy to slip away. Aye, but was it wise? He had a two-day ride ahead of him, over terrain he did not know. Should he set out in the dead of night he could lose his way.

Nay, there was little point in it now. Tomorrow was soon enough, after a decent night's sleep. He'd wait until they were well away from MacInnes's demesne.

Not one of them—Rika, Ottar, or the other two lads—could ride a horse. They had probably ne'er seen a proper mount until this afternoon in MacInnes's stable. 'Twould be child's play to outrun them on the road.

You gave your word.

Rika's words and Lawmaker's calm visage haunted him. Aye, he'd agreed to their bargain, but under duress. His consent had been snared by trickery and coercion. None that he knew—in his own world—would fault him for breaking his word.

His mind made up, he slipped down the corridor and into the great hall where a dozen men slept on furs and plaids scattered about the floor near the hearth. The peat fire burned low.

George spotted an extra fur and, snaking his way through the snoring pack, collapsed onto it and sighed.

His eyes drifted shut. He willed the tension drain from his exhausted body.

On the morrow he would leave her.

Nothing she could do or say would stop him.

MacInnes's wife roused Rika early from her bed. Had she slept at all? Nay, she'd tossed and turned under the spell of disturbing dreams. Nightmares, really, about her father and Brodir—and him.

Grant.

Her feelings for the Scot contradicted every truth, every conviction she held about men. He was dangerous, clever, and must not be trusted.

Rika snorted. She was the one who could not be trusted. Last night had proved the point. She yielded to his seduction as easily as a smitten maid succumbs to an ardent suitor. Fool. She'd take care to ne'er be caught alone with him again.

Rika dressed quickly, nibbled at the bread and salted fish Mistress MacInnes had left her, and started for the stable. Rounding the corner from the main corridor into the kitchen, she slammed into—

"Thor's blood!" Grant. "Watch where you're going."

"Och, sorry."

She tried to sidestep him, and he her, and again they collided. Heat flushed her face.

"Uh, your pardon," he said, avoiding her eyes.

"No matter." She brushed past him, flustered, and did not stop until she was outside. The wind hit her like a bracing slap. She sucked in a breath and tried to compose herself.

Her mind was made up. Her resolve steel.

"Rika!" Ottar's voice carried from the stable's entrance.

She waved at him as he stood with Erik and Leif just inside the timber doors near five saddled mounts who would bear them to her father's estate.

"They are positively huge," she said, as she approached the steeds, her eyes widening in wonder.

"Fair enormous." Leif slapped one of them, a roan, affectionately on the rump.

"Where's Grant?" Erik said. "The day is clear, but the journey will likely be rough." He eyed their mounts nervously. "We should be off."

"There he is now." Ottar pointed across the courtyard.

Grant and MacInnes walked slowly from the house, deep in conversation. Halfway to the stable MacInnes placed a beefy hand on Grant's shoulder, stopping him. They leaned in close, whispering so that none might hear.

Rika bristled. What on earth were they talking about? Just as her patience ran out, the two clasped hands, then moved quickly to join her and the youths.

Grant helped her to mount the smallest of the steeds—a white mare. Her brother's garments seemed a good choice, after all. She could not imagine riding in a gown. Gunnar's sword hung in the scabbard positioned by her thigh, his hauberk and helm hidden away in a sack tied behind her saddle.

Soon, dear brother, very soon.

Rika settled atop the fidgeting beast and smiled. "'Tis surprisingly comfortable."

Grant handed her the reins. "We'll see how comfortable ye are after a day's hard ride across the moor."

She ignored him, and he turned to assist the youths.

Leif and Erik mounted awkwardly and looked none too sure of themselves as they took up their reins. Ottar surprised them all by vaulting onto his gelding's back and maneuvering the beast out into the courtyard, as if he'd ridden all his life.

"Good man," Grant said, and nodded. He leaped easily onto the back of his own mount, a great chestnut steed whose size and musculature were well matched to the Scot's own powerful build.

Rika followed him out into the courtyard, pleased by the mare's easy response to her direction.

"D'ye know how fortunate we are?" he said to her. "Steeds this fine are rare, and worth more than ye can fathom."

She was just beginning to realize that.

MacInnes slapped Grant's chestnut gelding on the rump.

The horse took off but Grant jerked him to a halt. "Will ye no reconsider, MacInnes?"

Rika frowned. Reconsider what?

"I thank ye, nay," MacInnes said. "Rollo and I dinna get along."

Now this was truly strange. Grant must have asked MacInnes to accompany them. This business with the horses bred more trust than she'd realized. Truth be told, she had thought to ask MacInnes to go with them herself. She would need all the friends around her she could muster in Rollo's cold presence.

"We shall not forget your kindness," she said. MacInnes's wife joined her husband in the courtyard, and for a moment Rika held her gaze.

MacInnes took Rika's hand in his. "There is naught we would no do for the daughter of Lawmaker's heart."

What an odd thing for him to say. A hollow pain welled inside her. She nodded at the two of them, squeezed MacInnes's rough hand, then let go.

Grant led them from the courtyard, snow crunching under the chestnut's hooves.

"Godspeed," MacInnes called after them. His breath frosted his beard. "And dinna worry about the ship. 'Twill be well cared for in your absence. We'll expect ye back in a sennight—a fortnight at most. After that, I canna promise that I willna come a-lookin' for ye."

Rika looked back and waved. A small part of her did not want to leave.

Grant urged the chestnut into a trot. Rika and the youths followed, bouncing along in their saddles. Already her rump grew sore.

Two hours later Grant paused at the crest of a long ridge. It was about time they stopped to re—

"Thor's blood, what's that?" Rika's eyes widened.

"What? Down there, ye mean?" Grant nodded toward the lush sea of greenery below them. "'Tis naught but a small wood. Why?"

She could not take her eyes from it. "It's…nothing like I imagined." A dusting of snow clung to the treetops like icing on a honey cake. "It's…lovely."

He looked at her strangely for a moment, then said, "Ah, right. Ye've no seen trees like this."

"We've not seen trees at all," Ottar said, gaping at the forest.

Grant shivered and waved them forward. "Come on then."

Rika's mount picked her way carefully down the rocky, snow covered hillside. Leif and Erik followed, whining about the cold, their sore behinds and the poor footing. Ottar let out a whoop, then spurred his gelding ahead to keep pace with Grant. The youth had taken to riding as she once had to sailing.

A vision of Lawmaker slipping over the side of the *byrthing* flashed briefly, hideously, in her mind. She pushed the memory away and focused her thoughts on what lay ahead.

Grant had been acting fair strange since they'd left MacInnes's house that morn. He was more than aloof. His manner was stone cold, his eyes hard and calculating. Something was afoot. She read it in his face each time he stopped to study the landscape and gaze at the chart MacInnes had given them.

She felt it each time he looked at her.

Rika bade Erik and Leif draw their mounts up even with hers. "Do you notice how strange he seems today?" she said, and nodded ahead toward Grant.

Erik frowned. "Nay, why? What are you thinking?"

"She's thinking he may bolt," Leif said.

Rika strained her eyes, trying to keep Grant and Ottar in sight as they disappeared into the wood.

"But you have a bargain," Erik said.

"Methinks he intends not to keep it." Rika goaded the mare faster and, a minute later, snaked her way into the cover of the trees. There they were, just ahead. Thank God. She realized her heart had been pounding.

Last night she'd resigned herself to the fact that Grant would likely not honor their agreement—and under the warmth of MacInnes's roof it had been easy not to care. But today, bobbing along on the backs of strange animals in a foreign land, her confidence wavered.

"It's a faeryland!" Ottar grinned and waved her toward them.

Their new surroundings snapped her from her thoughts. It *was* rather like a faeryland. Sun bled through the emerald canopy above them and lit up the snow, drifted high against the marbled trunks of strange trees. Rika exhaled and watched her breath fog the chill air.

"I don't like it," Leif said. "It's too..."

"Closed in," Erik finished.

They were right. The wood was so dense it seemed almost claustrophobic. It would be difficult to maneuver their steeds with any kind of speed, should the need arise. Rika had the unsettling feeling that it would.

She glanced at Grant and caught him staring at her. He quickly looked away.

"Which way?" she said.

"West." Grant urged his mount forward, and they followed, single file, weaving through the trees.

The deeper into the wood they went, the darker it grew. Rika looked up and could no longer see the sky, so knotted were the trees. A couple of times her mare stumbled in the drifting snow. Ottar stopped each time to make certain she was all right.

Grant never looked back.

The light grew flat and white around them, and Rika felt suddenly chilled. She'd worn plenty of clothes—a fur tunic over her brother's woolen one, and her heavy cloak over all. Still, she shivered.

By her reckoning they should be about a third of the way to her father's estate. MacInnes had told them they should expect as much as a day's ride, depending on the weather. Perhaps they should pick up the pace.

She urged the mare ahead, passing Ottar, and drew up even with Grant. "Can we travel no faster?"

Grant eyed her speculatively, as if he was weighing

something in his mind, then shrugged. "If ye like." To Rika's surprise, he spurred the chestnut forward. She shot ahead after him.

"Hey, wait!" Erik's voice sounded behind her.

"Come on," Ottar called. "Keep up, you two."

Grant urged his steed faster, putting more and more distance between them. "Oh, no," Rika breathed, and drove the mare harder.

She heard the comforting snorts and snow-muffled footfalls of Ottar's mount close behind her. A low-hanging branch, heavy with snow, lay in the mare's path. They were moving so fast, Rika had no time to change direction. She ducked—Thor's blood, that was close—and promptly heard a stifled cry behind her.

Ottar.

She glanced back just in time to see him land in the snow on his rump. His gelding immediately bolted.

"Wait!" Ottar called after the beast.

She peered ahead into the dense wood but could no longer see Grant. Damn him, what was he doing? Why did he not wait for them? "Grant!" she called out to him.

No response.

A chilling realization shot through her. He didn't intend to wait. He was giving them the slip. Rika whirled in the saddle as Leif and Erik bounced to a stop beside Ottar. "Help him!" she shouted, then dug her heels into the mare's sides.

"Wait for me!" Ottar cried.

"There's no time!"

The mare shot forward, after Grant, and it was all Rika could do to stay in the saddle. The youths called after her, but she ignored them. After a few minutes, their cries faded to an eerie silence.

The chestnut's footprints were dead easy to follow in the snow. Snaking their way deeper into the wood, they suddenly cut south, to the left, and disappeared up a rise. Bother! Rika fisted the mare's mane in her hands, leaned into the saddle's pommel and drove the mare up the rise.

She realized her heart was pounding. Everything of importance to her was riding on that dowry. She must have it—and to get it, she needed Grant.

At the top of the rise, the mare reared.

"Whoa!" Rika flew backward, arms and legs flailing, and landed hard in a snowbank. "Unh." Before she could scramble to her feet, a rough hand grasped the hood of her cloak and jerked her up.

Grant!

Thank God.

She whirled, ready to tongue-lash him. The words died on her lips. "I-Ingolf," she breathed. Every muscle in her body tensed.

"Good morrow, whore. I knew you'd come this way, which is why I lay in wait. What a boon that your *husband* has left you." Ingolf grinned and raised his fist.

She saw the blow coming, but could not move to save her life. It would end like this then. Murdered in a Scottish wood. Or saved, perhaps, for some crueler fate. Ja, at Brodir's hands.

A war cry pierced the air behind her. Ingolf froze, eyes wide.

"Use that fist and by God I'll cut it off!"

Rika whirled and sucked in a breath. "Grant!"

He stood on the rise below her, his face bloodred. Rasmus dangled from the end of his dirk like a piece of rotten meat.

Chapter Thirteen

He was clearly out of his bloody mind.

George sheathed his dirk and thrust the henchman's limp body aside. A second later, *Gunnlogi* was in his hand.

Why the devil hadn't he insisted MacInnes come with them? He'd have been able to entrust Rika and the lads to the Scot's care and ride on with a clear conscience.

"I shall enjoy this," Ingolf said, and drew his own weapon.

Rika went for her dagger.

"Woman!" George flashed her a stern look. "Stand aside."

She hesitated. He read the bloodlust in her eyes and caught the twitch of her hand hovering a hairsbreadth from her weapon. He was ready, should her emotions overcome her judgment, but they did not. She backed away from them both, her eyes fixed on his.

"Dinna worry," he said. "'Twill be over in a minute."

"Too right, Scotsman." Ingolf lunged.

He deflected the blow, but nearly lost his footing.

Ingolf moved in close and swung a broadsword in a wide arc—Gunnar's sword, George realized.

Here it comes. By God, he was ready. Sparks flew, and the clash of metal against metal split the white stillness as *Gunnlogi* connected with Ingolf's sword.

They pushed off each against the other. "Son of a—" George tripped backward over Rasmus's body. He immediately tried to right himself, but the snow was too bloody deep.

"George!" Rika screamed.

Ingolf's weapon sliced the air.

George rolled left, his heart in his throat. A sharp burn ripped along his shoulder as he raised *Gunnlogi* in a defensive posture. Too late. He smelled his own blood and knew 'twas over. Heat spread from his shoulder.

Ingolf moved in for the kill. George looked into the henchman's murder-glazed eyes as Ingolf smiled and raised his sword.

George.

She'd called him George.

He rallied, redoubled his grip on his sword and waited to deflect the final blow. It did not come. The smile slid from Ingolf's face, and then he was screaming.

George focused his eyes, not believing what he saw. Rika stood behind Ingolf, her face shining with fear, her dagger dripping blood. She shoved the henchman out of her way and fell to her knees beside George.

"Oh, God, George." Her gaze flew to his wound. "Is it bad?"

"'Tis naught—ah!—but a flesh wound." Aye, flesh and muscle. He tried to sit up, grimacing against the pain. "I...I'm fine." But he knew from the sky spin-

ning above him that he was not fine. Thank Christ 'twas
his left shoulder and not the right.

Rika pushed the blood-soaked furs away and gasped.

"It's...no so bad. Let me up." His eyes were fixed
on Ingolf, who was struggling to his feet, though he
bled like a slaughtered pig. George was intent on finishing the job. His head throbbed and his gut heaved.
"Bloody hell, woman, let me up!"

Rika ignored him and pushed him back down into
the snow. Deftly she slit the tunic's shoulder lacing and
tore away his shirtsleeve. "It will take some stitching,
but that I cannot do here."

Too weak to struggle with her, he watched Ingolf
stagger to Rika's waiting mare, dragging Gunnar's
sword behind him.

"I...I must stop him."

Ingolf pulled himself onto the steed's back and shot
away into the wood.

Rika heard the commotion and turned. "Nay!"

George saw her intent and grabbed her wrist. Not for
anything in this world or the next—not even to see his
brother, Sommerled, alive again—would he have let
her go after Ingolf alone. "L-let him go."

"But—"

Ottar's shouts echoed below them. George craned his
neck to see. The three youths were scaling the short
hill, leading their lathered mounts.

Rika glanced back to the place where Ingolf had disappeared into the wood. Blood spattered the snowdrift
where they'd skirmished.

"D'ye want the dowry or nay?" George said.

Her eyes slid to his. "I want it."

"Then let him go. 'Tis more trouble than it's worth
to find him and finish him off."

"But what if he—"

He stilled her with a look. "He'll die by nightfall. No man survives a dagger to the back."

She looked at him for a long moment, then nodded. "Ja, all right, then."

He released her wrist and fell back into the snow.

Ottar topped the hill, gasping and red faced, and stopped dead in his tracks. "Rasmus!" He knelt before the body and searched for a pulse.

"Don't bother," Rika said. "He's dead."

"And Ingolf?" Erik examined the hoofprints in the crimson-tinged snow.

"Gone, on Rika's mount," George said.

"We must find him!" Leif cried.

"Nay, we will not." Rika shot them each a hard look.

George knew her censure was meant to protect the youths. Would he have allowed it, she would have gone off after Ingolf herself. But she'd not risk the lads' lives in pursuit of him.

Ottar knelt beside him, eyeing the wound. "Are you all right?"

"Aye, but it stings like hell." He sucked in air as Rika washed the wound clean with a handful of snow.

"Ottar," she said. "Gather up the horses. Leif, can you and Erik…do something with his body?" She nodded at Rasmus's crumpled form.

"The ground's frozen through," Leif said.

"Ja, but we can bury him deep in the snow to keep the animals off him—though he doesn't deserve it." Erik gestured to Leif. "Come on, let's get it over with."

The youths busied themselves with their tasks.

George settled back and allowed Rika to bandage his wound.

"You were nearly killed," she said to him in low voice so the others wouldn't hear.

"Nearly, but I live still—thanks to ye."

She met his gaze. "What else could I do? Stand by and watch him murder you as he did Lawmaker?"

"Most women would have." Why had he not noticed before how beautiful her eyes were?

She tightened the bandage until he winced. "I'm not like most women."

"Aye, that's the God's truth."

She looked away, and he fixed his gaze on her mouth, her lips cherry-red from the cold. The urge to pull her down on top of him and kiss her was near overwhelming.

"Why did you come back?" she said softly.

A stab of remorse twisted inside him. "What d'ye mean?"

"You know very well what I mean. You meant to leave us." She looked at him, not accusingly, but with resignation. "Didn't you?"

He had, in fact, but had found that he could not. Only after he'd turned around to find them again did he spy the strange tracks in the snow. It didn't take him long to put two and two together. Had Ingolf hurt her, he would never have forgiven himself.

Ottar knelt beside them in the snow and broke the spell. Rika's face tightened.

"What have ye got?" George asked him, eyeing the rolled parchment.

The youth unfurled the chart MacInnes had lent them. "How much farther to Rollo's estate, do you reckon?"

"No far." George allowed his eyes to linger on Rika's tense features as she finished bandaging his wound. "If we hurry, we should reach it by sundown."

Rika sat back on her heels and met his gaze. "You intend to keep to our bargain then?"

He ground his teeth, avoiding giving her an answer.

"Must I dog your every step to make certain of it?" She flashed her eyes impatiently at him. "Say now, Grant—ja or nay. Will you or will you not keep your word?"

"So, it's back to Grant, is it?"

Her cheeks flushed a pretty shade of pink.

Leif and Erik stopped their work, awaiting his answer. Ottar went stock-still.

George didn't have to think about it for very long. *"Ja,"* he said, mimicking her speech.

Her brows arched in surprise and what he thought was a touch of amusement.

"I will keep to our bargain."

The youths grinned.

He told himself he'd do it because he'd promised. Because she was a woman alone and needed his protection. Though given what had just transpired, he wasn't doing a very good job of it. She'd saved his life, which was no small thing. He owed her something for that, at least.

Rika rose and offered him her hand. He took it. For a split second the memory of her body writhing beneath his, the taste of her kisses, the slick heat of her, flashed across his mind.

And hers.

He read it in her eyes, saw it in the blush of her cheek, felt it as her fingers softly closed over his.

She pulled him to his feet and abruptly turned away.

The youths mounted their steeds and George did the same, taking care not to pull at his wound.

"What about Rika?" Ottar said. "She has no mount."

"Gunnar's sword!" Rika whirled toward the place where Ingolf had disappeared with her mount. A frown creased her soft brow. "His helm and hauberk, too. All were tied to the mare's saddle!"

"It canna be helped," George said, and reined his steed beside her. The look of abject misery on her face nearly undid him. "Come, ye shall ride behind me, lass." He offered his right hand to her.

She hesitated, then took it, and he pulled her up behind him.

"Hold tight," he said. "The ground is rocky. I wouldna see ye unseated twice in one day."

She gripped him about the waist, and he felt the comforting weight of her breasts against his back. They turned into the setting sun and rode in silence.

His breath frosted the air, which was so cold now it burned his lungs. Shafts of red-gold light set to sparkling the crusted snow amidst the trees. Rika edged closer.

Mayhap he was fooling himself.

Honor, duty, obligation—aye, they were each a formidable motive to stay with her and see their bargain to the end.

But were any the true reason he tarried?

Rika jolted awake as Grant reined the chestnut to an abrupt halt at the edge of the wood. How could she have let herself drift—

"Thor's blood!"

Grant shot her a backward glance. "My sentiments exactly."

She unlaced her hands from his waist and wiped the sleep from her eyes to make certain she was not dreaming. Nay, she was not. The stone and timber structure rose up from the moor like a dark bird of prey unfolding its wings against the bloodred sunset.

"It's a castle!" Ottar said.

Grant snorted. "'Tis a bloody fortress."

Erik and Leif pulled their mounts up short and exchanged wide-eyed looks. "This is it?" they said in unison.

Grant shrugged. "Dunno."

Rika slid from the chestnut's back into the crusted snow. Her breath fogged the icy air. "Ja, this is it—my father's home."

"How d'ye know?" Grant said.

A chill shot up her spine, and she pulled her cloak tighter about her. She could not take her eyes from the foreboding structure. "I just do."

She was vaguely aware of Grant dismounting. He pulled her aside, out of earshot of the others. "We dinna have to do this, ye know?"

"Wh-what?" She shrugged off her unease and snapped to attention. "Ja, we do. I must have my coin."

"Why? It's of little import now."

She frowned, not understanding him.

"Ye heard MacInnes as well as I. There is naught he would no do to protect ye and yours."

"What do you mean?"

Grant looked at her for what seemed an eternity before answering. "Brodir," he said finally. "That's what I mean."

"Oh."

"His henchmen are dead, and the man himself un-accounted for. Why return to Fair Isle at all? By your own admission, all those whom ye loved are either dead or gone from there."

Grant was right, but there was more to it than that.

"MacInnes would take ye in a heartbeat," he continued. "He is well connected from what I can tell—and boasts five score men of his own. Under his protection, ye'd have no need of the coin."

Or of me, his eyes seemed to say.

Ja, MacInnes would take her, as if she were a cow to be shielded from reivers. Hmph. It was clear Grant was anxious to be on his way. A bride waited for him in Wick.

Rika had considered more than once that day enlisting Grant's help in freeing Gunnar. The hardness of his eyes in the failing light wiped the thought from her mind for good.

"You don't understand," she said coolly.

He glanced at the darkening sky, gone crimson at the edges, then arched a brow at her. "Enlighten me."

She was not about to tell him the truth of things. Not now. What business was it of his? They had a bargain, plain and simple, and he swore to uphold his end. Must they have this conversation at every turn of events?

"The coin buys my freedom from Brodir, ja, but also ensures my independence—" she tipped her chin at him "—from any man. So you see, Grant—"

"Aye, I see." His lips thinned into a hard line.

They were so close. Nothing would turn her from her purpose now. She must cinch his commitment one last time. "You're afraid," she said, and nodded at the dark fortress.

"What?"

"That's why you try to dissuade me."

His eyes blazed, and she knew she'd won. Men were so predictable.

Grant whirled toward the youths who had tethered their steeds just inside the wood. "Mount up," he barked. "The light's nearly gone."

Stars blinked at them from a field of velvet cobalt as their horses clomped along the cobbled walk leading to the castle's bailey.

Rika tensed as Grant conferred with the sentries. Two of them brought torches from a nearby fire to get what she supposed was a better look at her. God knows what Grant had told them.

Their eyes widened as they surveyed her garb, for she had staunchly refused to don even the simplest of the gowns Mistress MacInnes had lent her for the journey. Ridiculous. Did these folk really expect women to ride beasts the size of MacInnes's mounts while garbed in normal attire?

From the amused looks she received from her father's men, she supposed they did.

Rika had ne'er been inside a castle. She'd seen a few on her trips to the southern Shetlands with Lawmaker. But nothing in her experience prepared her for the size and opulence of Rollo's hall.

Grant seemed not at all surprised by the rich interior of the room. She noticed he was on his guard, however, watching every doorway and taking particular note of the collection of fine weapons—both Norse and Scot— displayed on the walls.

It occurred to her this dower money was of little

consequence to a man of Rollo's wealth. Where had he made this fortune?

"Who did ye say ye were?"

The stern, high-pitched voice startled her. Rika whirled, her hand moving instinctively to the hilt of her dagger.

"What, would ye slay me in my own hall?"

Rika opened her mouth to speak but found no words. The woman standing before them was like no other she'd e'er seen. She was middle-aged—older, mayhap—with skin as white as the chalk cliffs of Fair Isle. Her hair glistened black as a raven's wing and was done up in some fantastical arrangement. It did naught, however, to improve the sourness of her expression. Her gown was what most surprised Rika. 'Twas fashioned of a fine, shimmering fabric that bore not the slightest resemblance to the homespun to which Rika was accustomed.

Grant cleared his throat ceremoniously. "Lady, may I present Ulrika, daughter of…" He shot Rika a quick glance, and she nodded. "Daughter of Rollo."

The woman blanched. "That canna be."

Rika stood tall and tipped her chin high, though the woman was so short it hardly made a difference. "I am who he says. Who, may I ask, are you?"

The woman narrowed black eyes at her. "I am Catherine Leonard, mistress of all ye see here."

"Then you are…" Ottar's words died on his lips as Catherine raked her gaze over him.

"Rollo's wife," she snapped. "Who else would I be?" She trained her eyes on Rika's mannish garments and her expression grew even more sour. "What d'ye mean dressing like this?"

"I was…" Thor's blood, would she allow this crone

to treat her so ill? Rika tipped her chin so high she had to look down her nose at the woman. "It's for riding."

Catherine snorted. "Ridiculous."

Grant inched closer to Rika and, to her surprise, slipped his arm around her shoulder. "Aye, 'twas a difficult journey and—"

"Who might ye be?" Catherine said. "'Tis clear ye're no one of them." She flashed her eyes at Rika and the youths.

"Nay, I'm a Scot. I'm also her…husband."

"Ye dinna say." Catherine sized him up.

"My name is Grant—George Grant. Laird of a clan to the southeast, near Inverness."

Catherine's brows shot up. "Really? My husband will be pleased to make *your* acquaintance at the least, then."

Rika would stand no more of this base treatment. "Now see here, we've come all this—" Grant pinched her arm. "Ow! Why did you do—"

"Aye, it is with your husband that I have business," Grant said. He shot Rika a warning look.

Fine. She'd let him handle the crone if that's what he wished. But she'd take no more of this abuse. She'd suffered enough of it as a child under Rollo's care and would suffer no more.

"Well then," Catherine said. "I will have someone show ye to a suitable chamber." She glanced at Ottar, then at Leif and Erik, who had not dared utter a peep since their arrival. "As for the lads, they can sleep in the hall."

Rika supposed this was as good as any arrangement she might expect, and did not protest. Besides, Grant still had a death grip on her arm.

"Our thanks," Grant said. "Ye are most gracious."

Catherine shrugged. "I dinna have much choice, do I?" Her gaze slid to Rika again, and this time she glared back. "Ulrika, is it? Rollo will be surprised, indeed."

They waited nearly an hour in the hall, during which time a score of Catherine's kinsmen—or servants, she knew not which—flurried about them setting up benches and tables in preparation for the evening meal.

Rika sat alone on a stool by the enormous hearth, drumming her fingers on her leather-clad thighs. There had been no sign of her father, or of anyone who had shown them even the simplest hospitality. Her patience was nearly at an end.

Grant sat at a nearby table in whispered conversation with Erik and Ottar and Leif. From what she could overhear, he seemed to be instructing them in how to behave in this strange and unwelcome place, and in what to do should all not go as planned.

His face was swathed in the warm glow of the fire, his slate eyes sharp. A tremendous calm radiated from his confident demeanor. The youths looked up to him, respected his judgment. Ottar especially. She marveled at this change in him.

In all of them.

They were in Grant's world now, and must rely on him to do as he promised and see them safe away with her dowry intact. What choice did she have but to trust him?

Muffled laughter echoed off the high stone walls of the hall. Rika turned toward the arched entrance. Two women, younger and more delicate versions of Catherine, swept into the room. Her daughters, no doubt. Sisters. Each was robed in more of the same fine fabric that had made up Catherine's gown, but in colors so vivid Rika sucked in a breath.

Their beauty and elegance was not lost on Rika's companions. Grant rose so abruptly he nearly upended the bench on which he sat.

"Good evening," he said, and smiled warmly at them. Ne'er had she seen such a smile grace his lips before.

Rika was suddenly aware of her own torn and soiled clothes—men's clothes—and how her dirty hair hung in dull, lifeless hanks about her shoulders. Absently she twisted the bronze bracelets circling her wrists.

Ottar and Erik and Leif scrambled to Grant's side, hastily adjusting their damp garments and raking hands through their disheveled hair.

What, did they think these women princesses?

They were pretty, she'd grant them that. Nay, they were more than that—they were beautiful. And the magnitude of that beauty shone in Grant's eyes.

Heat flushed her face. Without thinking, Rika shot to her feet. All eyes turned to her. The young women gasped, their bright eyes round as saucers.

Rika felt the familiar sting of embarrassment under their scrutiny. She was a freak, she did not fit. Especially here, in this haven of beauty and finery. What of it? No more would she shrink under another's scorn. That time was over. She strode to Grant's side, elbowing Erik out of the way.

"This is my...wife," Grant said. "Your...sister."

Rika fisted her hands at her sides and scowled at the two of them. She was no sister to these peacocks. The women—maidens surely—eyed her, openmouthed, up and down. Up mostly, as Rika towered over them by nearly a foot.

"Ye...ye are Ulrika," one of them said—the elder of the two, Rika guessed.

She would have thought her identity obvious. The servants had been yammering and casting her strange looks since her arrival. "Ja, I am she. Ulrika, daughter of Fritha—and Rollo."

Their eyes grew wider, if that were even possible.

"And we are—"

Rika silenced Ottar with a raised hand. "We have rested here with neither food nor drink for nearly an hour," she said to the maidens. "Your mother mentioned that a chamber would be prepared."

Grant shot her a look of censure, but Rika ignored it.

The other sister, the younger, finally found her tongue. "Oh, our pardon! Aye, your chamber is ready." She gestured for Rika and Grant to follow. "Come, I will show ye the way."

The elder sister stayed behind. As Rika quit the room, she noticed that Leif and Erik and Ottar surrounded her like whelps to a fresh teat. Grant dogged their escort's heels up a flight of stairs with equal interest.

Rika's face grew so hot she thought surely her blood would boil. She must contain herself. Now was not the time to fall prey to feminine emotion. That was for the weak and the foolish.

And she was no one's fool.

"Here it is," the maiden said. She batted her lashes demurely at Grant as she gestured to an open door off the main corridor.

Rika peeked into the finely appointed room. A smallish bed draped in plaids and furs was tucked into a corner near the hearth. She snorted and shot Grant a disgusted glance. But he was not looking at her. His eyes were for the maiden, and hers for him.

Rika pushed between them into the chamber, teeth clenched, and fists balled at her side. Why this anger? What were these feelings welling inside her so wholly unbidden?

Grant seemed not to notice her distress, and she was glad of it. "I'll be with ye shortly," he said, not looking at her. "If this kind lady will show me to the kitchen, I shall bring us back something to slake our thirst."

The maiden blushed prettily and, had she and Grant not departed a second later, Rika might have slapped the color right out of the woman's delicate face.

She slammed the heavy door behind them. "Little harlot." What, did the vixen think to seduce him? Grant had plainly introduced Rika as his wife.

And what about him? Husband, indeed. He was like all men. *Something to slake our thirst.* More like something to slake his lust.

Rika whirled away from the closed door and her breath caught. "Thor's blood!" Staring back at her from across the room was her own image. What on earth…

Of course!

It was a looking glass.

She'd seen one once in the Shetlands, but never one so big. It was nearly as tall as she. She approached it cautiously with slitted eyes, on her guard as if the vision looking back at her would suddenly jump out. Moving closer, she frowned.

Was it any wonder Grant preferred the blushing maid?

She ran a hand along her sun-bronzed cheek, across

wind-chapped lips that, to her, seemed over-full. Crouching, she took in the rest of her image. She forgot sometimes, particularly in Grant's company, how tall she truly was. And her hair. It looked far worse than she had imagined in the hall. A rat's nest came to mind.

A small stool was positioned before the silvered glass. Rika collapsed onto it and absently pulled her dagger from its sheath. Before she even knew what she was about to do, her fist closed over a hank of hair.

She gripped the dagger.

What did it matter that she was not beautiful? When had she begun to care if Grant did or did not find her pleasing? Had he ever looked on her with the same longing she read in his eyes a moment ago?

Once, perhaps, on their wedding night.

A thin film of tears glassed her eyes, shimmering back at her from the looking glass. She tilted her face into the amber firelight and, out of the corner of her eye, caught the white reflection of Brodir's handiwork.

It was a formidable scar, indeed.

"It doesn't matter," she breathed.

No man, least of all Grant, would ever want her. In truth, she'd be far better off were her countenance even more repugnant than the silvered glass proved it to be.

Lawmaker always said she had courage.

Did she?

Her hand shook as she slid the flat of the icy metal blade along her cheek. Holding her hair away from her face, she rolled the dagger's hilt ever so slightly.

And sucked in a breath.

Blood welled at her temple.

"Sweet Jesus, Rika, what are ye doing?"

Grant!

She nearly jumped from the stool. A flagon of mead

and two cups shattered on the floor at his feet, scattering into a thousand pieces. The dagger slipped from her hand and landed point first in the soft timbers.

In a flash he was kneeling by her side. "What have ye done? Here, let me see that cut."

"Leave me alone." She jerked away from him.

"Are ye daft?"

"Ja—to have wed you in the first place. Thank God it's nearly over."

She caught his look of incredulity in the silvered glass before them. He tried to dab at her cut with a bit of cloth torn from his shirt.

"Don't touch me!"

"Why the devil not? Ye did as much for me when I was injured."

She glanced at his bandaged shoulder. "Ha! Methinks you would have preferred one of Catherine's pretty peacocks to act as surgeon."

"What?"

She jerked out of his grasp and flew to the narrow window. This was not a conversation she had intended to have with him.

"Is that what this is about?"

"I'm sure I don't know what you mean."

He grabbed her arm and wrenched her toward him. The whoreson was actually smiling.

"You're jealous," he said.

"I am not! What nonsense."

To think that seconds earlier she would have marked herself. For what? To prove she had the grit to abandon even the smallest chance Grant would favor her. She needed not that impetus. If he were the last man standing, she'd not want his favor.

He grinned at her. "Aye, ye are. Just look at your face. 'Tis red as an autumn apple."

He tried to grab hold of her chin, and she slapped his hand away. "Stop it! Don't touch me." She glared at him and his grin widened. "Wh-what's an apple?"

"Ye *are* jealous." He tried to brush her hair from her face. "Here, let me see to that cut."

"Nay!" She batted him away.

"'Twill likely leave a scar."

"Ja, and why should I care? What's another scar?"

He grabbed her around the waist, and she struggled against him.

"I told you to stop it! Leave me—"

A roar echoed from the open door, and both of them froze. Rika's heart beat a tattoo in her chest as her gaze raked over the vision in the doorway.

Rollo. Her father.

He was a formidable presence, yet smaller than she remembered him. But then the last time she'd seen him she'd been but two and ten.

Catherine lurked behind him in the corridor, her face a mask of pure hate. The shattered flagon, Rika's dagger, the blood welling along her cut—nothing escaped Rollo's attention.

"What did I tell ye," Catherine said smugly. "Is it her or nay?"

Rollo eyed Rika up and down, ignoring Grant completely. Grant's hands slipped from her waist, and the two of them faced their host. Rika felt her knees quiver beneath her breeks.

"Ja," Rollo said. "It's her all right." He took in her disheveled and dirty appearance, then stepped toward her. His hand flew up, and Rika instinctively cringed.

Grant's arm went around her waist, as if to remind

her that he was there and she was under his protection. She had to admit that, without him, her tenacity might have faltered.

She pursed her lips, tipped her chin higher and met her father's shrewd gaze.

Slowly Rollo traced the line of her scar from ear to chin. He grazed the skin where she'd cut herself, and blood came away on his hand. "You've all but lost the look of your mother," he said quietly.

For the briefest moment, she thought she read something else in his eyes—something besides the scorn she was prepared for. Ja, there it was.

Regret.

"Methinks she favors *ye* in her countenance," Grant said.

Rollo snapped out of his trance and narrowed his blue eyes at the Scot. "Who the hell are you?"

Rika held her breath. Grant's arm tightened about her, buoying her confidence. "He is my husband," she said simply.

"What?" Rollo turned on Grant. "What trickery is this?"

"'Tis the truth." Grant stepped between them, pushing Rika behind him. Both men were matched evenly in height and build. "The lady is my wife. We were wed on Fair Isle nearly a fortnight ago."

Rollo narrowed his eyes, placing Grant under the same haughty scrutiny Rika had suffered each day of her life in his care. "Grant—of Inverness, so my wife tells me."

Catherine's eyes flashed a murderous sort of satisfaction.

"East of Inverness, aye." Grant held Rollo's gaze and did not stand down. Rika was impressed.

Her father was impressed, too. She could tell by the way he nodded almost imperceptibly as he looked Grant over. Nay, she did not think he was even aware he did it. "Why have you come?" Rollo said finally.

"I've come for what's mine." Grant flashed her a quick look. "Her dowry."

Rika froze, each muscle taut as a fiddle string.

Her father roared a string of curses, and still Grant held his ground. "You are not the man I chose for her. Where is Brodir?" He trained his eyes on her again.

Her heart pounded so fiercely, surely it would burst from her chest. "He's… I mean, I don't exactly—"

"It matters not," Grant said. "I am her husband, and by rights her dowry is mine."

Rollo narrowed his eyes at him. "You'll ne'er get it. Not while I live."

Oh, God. What now? She feared it would come to this were Lawmaker not with them. They'd come so far, paid so dearly. It must not end like this. Gunnar's freedom, mayhap his very life, hung in the balance. She must do something, and quickly.

"Fine," Grant said.

"What?" Rika's eyes nearly bulged out of their sockets.

Grant crossed his arms and shrugged at her. "That's fine with me."

Rika stared at him, openmouthed. Catherine, on the other hand, puffed up like an exotic bird and gloated in the doorway.

"It is?" Her father's thick blond brows knit in confusion.

"Aye," Grant said. "No dowry, no marriage. Ye can have her back." He grabbed her roughly by the shoulders and thrust her into Rollo's arms.

''This is outrageous!'' She pushed back from her father's brawny wall of a chest and whirled on Grant. ''What do you mean by it?''

''Just what I said.'' He crossed his arms over his chest and cocked a tawny brow at Rollo. ''No dowry, no marriage. Take her—she's yours.''

Chapter Fourteen

Ne'er had he heard words so foul uttered from so pretty a mouth. Once her wrath was spent, Rika didn't speak to him for nearly two days. George smiled to himself, recalling the magnitude of her fury.

"Something amuses you?"

He glanced at Rollo from across the *tafl* table. "Nay. I was just thinking of my wife."

Rollo snorted. "I find naught about her amusing." He shot a quick look at Rika, who sat by the enormous hearth absorbed in some needlework she'd borrowed from one of Catherine's daughters.

George caught himself staring at her many times that evening. To secure the dowry, she'd transformed herself into everything a proper Christian wife should be. The result was shocking.

Catherine had provided her an ill-fitting gown of plain, pale wool. Too short and too tight, it bared her slender ankles and hugged the lithe curves of her body. Her hair was clean and plaited into one thick braid.

'Twas odd to see her wearing no weapons. After witnessing the incident before the looking glass, George had confiscated her dagger. That had angered her, but he would not relent.

The change in her public demeanor was nothing short of revolutionary. She made a show of deferring to him in all matters. What little she did say was swathed in honeyed words and usually of no consequence.

Though her submission was feigned—an act designed to secure Rollo's favor long enough to gain her coin—George should have enjoyed it all the same.

He did not.

He knew at what cost to her pride she played this uncharacteristic role. The dowry meant much to her. Far more than he'd first suspected. What plan did she have for the silver? Mayhap none.

Her mere possession of the coin ensured her independence. That, all along, was what she'd said she wanted. In the beginning, he hadn't understood the import of her freedom. But he himself had lived in a kind of bondage these past weeks, and had found it near intolerable.

Aye, he understood her motives well.

Rollo moved a game piece and grunted satisfaction. "You are certain you would not prefer equal shares of cattle and land?"

George met the Norseman's gaze. "In lieu of the silver? Nay, I have need of the coin."

Rollo grunted again, then called for another flagon of mead.

It had been like that between them these past two days and nights. George's gamble had paid off. Naught but the threat of leaving Rika in his care would have coerced the intractable Norseman to hand over her dowry.

George glanced again at Rika. They were two of a kind, father and daughter. Stubborn. Headstrong. Used to getting their own way. God's truth but she did favor him in appearance. He hadn't been lying that first night.

Rollo was a powerful-looking man. Tall and fair-haired, and in tremendous physical shape for one so far past his prime. Rika had his eyes—sharp and so icy a blue their gaze chilled a man right down to his bones.

There was more they shared in common, and if either took the time to look, they'd see it, plain as day. Both carried inside them a bitterness born of hate and pride, and no small amount of fear, though neither would have admitted it.

For Rika, the wounds ran deep. She had been wronged, by the two most important men in a young woman's life—her father and her betrothed. Would that George had known these things sooner.

He thought often of the tale MacInnes had told him, about the chaste love shared between the young Law-maker and Fritha, and how it twisted Rollo's heart into something dark and cold.

Rika looked up from her needlework and caught George staring. Her cool smile sent a shiver through him. Though she was again speaking to him, in private she was distant, icy as the day he first met her.

He hadn't told her yet that Rollo would likely give over the coin. He was saving it for when her mood improved. Mayhap he'd catch her alone this eve before she retired. George rubbed the small of his back. This sleeping on the hard floor had to end.

"Your move, Grant," Rollo said, jolting him from his thoughts.

"Ah, right. Sorry." He eyed the stretched sealskin board, then moved one of his attackers.

Lawmaker's *tafl* lessons had proved valuable after all. In fact, all that George had learned from the islanders served him well in Rollo's company. Leif and Erik had been right. The man was shrewd and well schooled.

Over the past two days he'd engaged George in all manner of sport and gaming for the purpose of sizing him up, George knew. *Tafl,* swordplay—at which he was not his best given his shoulder injury, which was nearly healed—a bit of hunting in the forest, even a sweat together in Rollo's sauna.

The Norseman had constructed a bathhouse in the castle that resembled much the one on Fair Isle. A vision of Rika naked and perspiring flashed across his mind. He shook off the thought and turned his attention back to their game.

He was surprised to find Rollo staring at his broadsword. "How came you by that?" Rollo nodded at the weapon.

George wondered that he hadn't asked about it before. 'Twas plain Rollo knew the weapon. "*Gunnlogi?* It was given me," he said simply.

"And the giver? Where might he be?" Rollo pretended to study the board, but George knew the question was far from casual.

"Lawmaker is dead."

Rollo looked up and their gazes locked. "When?"

"On the journey here. There was a storm." He thought it best not to elaborate on the circumstances of the elder's death. None had mentioned Brodir or his henchmen since the night of their arrival.

"Were you not given a family sword at your wedding to my daughter?"

"I was. Your son's, in fact." George held the Norseman's gaze in hopes of seeing some flicker of emotion in those unreadable eyes. He did not.

"Where is it, then?"

"Stolen. Along with one of our mounts."

Rollo ran a beefy hand over his bearded chin. "The weapon was once mine—and my father's before me. 'Tis of no import now."

George picked his words carefully. "The weapon meant a great deal to your daughter. She mourned its loss most grievously."

Rollo remained silent, but George watched his gaze drift to the hearth where Rika sat sewing. After a while, he said, "How came she by that scar?"

"Och, 'twas an accident. She cut herself the evening we—"

"Nay, not that one. The evil looking scar that runs from ear to chin." Rollo traced a similar line along his own throat. "Was it you who marked her?"

George leveled his gaze at him. "Nay."

"Who then?"

"Methinks 'twas the man to whom ye betrothed her."

For the barest moment, he read a flicker of anger in Rollo's eyes. Then the Norseman let out a bellowing laugh. "Aye, well, he's not the first man who's been tempted to slit her throat."

Nor the last, George thought.

Rollo's expression sobered as he continued to look at Rika. "You really think she favors me?"

He was treading on dangerous ground, but could not help himself. "Who else?"

The light in Rollo's eyes went out. "He's dead you say. Lawmaker."

George nodded.

"Aye, well they are together at last then." Rollo rose stiffly from the *tafl* table, leaving their game unfinished.

They meant Fritha and Lawmaker. Rika seemed not to hear them, or if she did, she took not her father's meaning.

"About the bride-price," George said, remembering what Lawmaker had told him.

Rollo dismissed the topic with a wave of his hand. "I care only for your allegiance, should I e'er have need of it."

George thought this generous, though it hardly mattered, as his marriage to Rika was likely to end within the week. The distance between Rollo's castle and his own near Inverness was great, and likely he'd ne'er meet the Norseman again.

"The hour is late," Rollo said. "I would find my bed."

Rika looked up as her father lumbered from the hall. He spared her not a glance.

"Thor's blood, what now?" Rika peeked out the open door of the castle. Snow from an afternoon storm flurried across the bailey, sending a chill clear through her.

"Archery, by the look of it." Leif nodded at the straw butts erected near the stable.

Rollo handed Grant a bow and a quiver, then slapped him on the back.

"It's deadly cold out. What's my father thinking? And Grant's injury—he'll open the wound."

Erik shrugged. "He is relentless in his quest to discover a sport at which Grant does not excel."

"We could be here for weeks if that be the case."

Rika turned her back on them and made for the warmth of the hall.

"Why don't you just tell him?" Erik said, dogging her steps.

Rika snorted. "I will not." She'd been over this with Lawmaker and the youths a dozen times before they set sail from Fair Isle. "I do not need my father's help." She'd go to her grave before she'd ask anything more of him beyond what the law decreed he owed her.

Leif pulled up a bench for her to sit on, and all three of them settled before the blazing hearth fire. "Gunnar is Rollo's only son," he said. "Surely if he knew of his imprisonment…"

Both of them looked at her with huge liquid eyes. She was unmoved.

"Rollo cares naught for his son—or for me. If he did, he would have ne'er abandoned us in the first place."

Leif took her hand in his. "Perhaps if I just mentioned that Gunnar—"

"One word and I'll cut out your tongue." She jerked her hand away.

She didn't want Rollo's help. She didn't need it. The silver was enough. And were there a penny left over after Gunnar's release, she'd send it back to him were there not a chance he'd use it against her in some way.

"At the least will you not confide in Grant?"

"Grant?" Not once had she considered it. "The Scot cannot be trusted."

Erik's face brightened. "He's had a score of opportunities to abandon our cause, should he wish to—but he has not."

"Besides," Leif said, "he's your husband." She

shot the youth her iciest look, but it did naught to deter him. "He's behaved as one."

Erik nodded vigorously. "Were it not for Grant's intervention, we might all be dead."

The ambush in the wood three days ago burned fresh in her mind.

"You cannot fault him, Rika," Leif said.

Nay, she could not, as much as she would like to.

"And while I do not pretend to know all there is between you, with my own eyes I have seen how highly he regards you."

"Ha!" The *regard* Grant held for her was capricious at best, and expressed only on those occasions when he thought to get her between the furs.

"We are but three now," Erik said. "And none of us knows the way of things here, or the lay of the land."

"With Ottar we are four." Rika glanced at the *tafl* table in the corner where Ottar sat tittering with Catherine's youngest daughter.

"Ottar knows naught of our true purpose." Erik's gaze strayed to the smitten youth. "As was your wish."

Rika nodded. "Lawmaker and I thought it best to keep it from him, but soon we must tell him our plans for the silver."

She had, in fact, thought to tell Ottar days ago, when first they landed on the mainland. But the closer he grew to Grant, the more she feared he'd betray her confidence. And she was more determined than ever that Grant not know.

The Scot would tell Rollo in a heartbeat.

She watched the youth and the maid together. The dark-eyed girl sat rapt as Ottar spun some preposterous tale. Rika had to admit the sisters were sweet and well-meaning. They'd been naught but kind to her these three days. She thought it nothing short of amazing, given the shrewish behavior of their mother—and her own coolness toward them.

Rika's ears pricked as the castle door crashed open. She heard her father's bellowing laughter followed by some unintelligible comment from Grant. The two of them blew into the hall laughing, their cheeks ruddy from the cold.

Grant shook his head like a dog, spraying snowflakes across the *tafl* table where Ottar sat with the maid. She giggled and chastised him. A knot caught in Rika's throat as Grant smiled at her.

God's truth, the girl was lovely. Fresh, unspoiled beauty coupled with a gentle grace. What more could a man want? Apparently nothing, as the maid had the admiring eye of every male in the room.

Rika's face grew hot. She felt suddenly conspicuous, as if she didn't belong there. Why, she did not know, for neither Grant nor her father seemed to notice her presence.

Mayhap she'd lie down before the evening meal. She started to rise, and Erik caught her hand. "Tell Grant of our plan," he said. "Ask his help."

Not this again.

"The man is a skilled diplomat," Erik said. "We will have need of such talent."

Leif turned his attention back to her. "Do it, Rika. For Gunnar's sake."

Gunnar.

She squeezed Erik's hand, then let go. "I will think on it," she said, and turned to leave.

As she crossed the room, Grant's gaze slipped to hers

for the briefest of moments. Was that a smile breaking at the edges of his mouth?

Her father put his arm around him and whispered something in his ear. Grant turned to him and grinned. How alike they seemed to her. Not in appearance, but behavior. It was almost as if Grant had transformed himself into a younger version of her father these past three days.

Mayhap it was the Scot's way of winning Rollo's favor. Whatever it was, she didn't like it.

"Where are ye off to, wife?" Grant called out as she passed them.

Rika shot him an icy glance and did not answer.

He turned to Rollo and shrugged. Her father snorted, and they both laughed together.

Her hands balled into fists as she quit the room.

If Grant were the last man on earth, she'd cut her tongue out before she asked his help. They had a bargain, nothing more. Once Grant delivered his end of it, she'd be done with him. And her father.

That evening, Rika felt no closer to her goal than she had when first they arrived. Her patience was at an end.

"You've eaten almost nothing," Grant said to her.

She toyed with a bit of bread, then tossed it to one of the dogs lying by the hearth. "I'm not hungry."

Catherine eyed her from across the supper table, then turned her gaze on Grant. "Methinks a missed meal or two willna harm a woman of your wife's…shall we say…stature."

Thor's blood, how much longer must she sit here and suffer the crone's insults? Rika snatched up her cup and drained it.

Grant immediately refilled it from the flagon on the

table. "Just smile and ignore her," he whispered into her ear.

Rika clenched her teeth behind upturned lips. Behind the pleasant mask her blood boiled.

"So, Grant—" her father paused to devour a slab of meat dangling from the end of his dirk "—what think you of my daughters?"

Rika froze.

All eyes turned to Grant. To her surprise, he slipped an arm around her shoulder. It was the first time he'd touched her in days. The warmth of his hand caused her pulse to quicken. "My wife is a unique wo—"

"Nay, not her. My stepdaughters, Celeste and Karen." Rollo grinned at the blushing sisters who sat between Erik and Leif.

Catherine shot Rika a triumphant smile.

Had Grant not tightened his hold on her, Rika might have lunged across the table and stuffed an entire roasted hare down the woman's throat.

"Easy," Grant whispered between smiling lips. He squeezed her once, then his hand slipped from her shoulder.

"D'ye no find them lovely?" Catherine said.

Grant raised his glass to her. "No as lovely as their mother, but aye, they are most fair."

Catherine tittered, and Rollo roared with pleasure.

Rika wanted to wretch.

Could she fathom a way to free Gunnar without the dowry, she would have quit the hall that instant, mounted the first nag she saw, and put a dozen leagues between her and her father—and Catherine, and Grant—that very night.

The crone beamed at her daughters. "They will make fine wives, will they no?"

Erik and Leif and Ottar gazed moonfaced at the maids, and answered in unison, "Ja."

Rika's cheeks blazed against her will as Grant looked with unfeigned delight on the sisters. Damn these ridiculous feelings! Why did she care that he—or any man—admired them? They were as he said—most fair. Nay, beautiful.

Exactly what she was not.

There it was. The truth. Rika toyed with the hammered bracelets circling her wrists. Humiliation burned a slow path to her face.

"'Tis a pity your wife does not favor her mother," Catherine said to Grant.

Rika's gaze shot to hers.

Catherine's eyes burned into her like live coals. "I have heard Rollo speak many times of Fritha's delicate beauty."

Rollo put down his dirk.

"Aye, but 'twas a blessing for ye and your brother that Fritha died young," Catherine continued.

Rika rose stiffly from the table, her hands fisted so tight her nails dug into her palms. Somewhere at the edge of her awareness she felt Grant's hand close over her wrist.

"After all," Catherine said, "what child should suffer a whore for a mother?"

Rollo shot to his feet.

Rika caught the barest hint of anger in his eyes. A deadly calm washed over her. "What did you say?"

Catherine shrugged. "Why I simply meant that—"

"Enough!" Rollo slammed a fist on the table.

Celeste and Karen gasped. The youths froze, eyes wide and darting from Rollo to Grant, as if the Scot would intervene.

He did not.

After a moment, he let go her hand.

Her father looked at her then, and a lifetime of unspoken emotion passed between them.

Whore.

'Twas not the first time her mother had been labeled so, though it had been years since Rika had heard the accusation. The last time, uttered from her father's own lips, had been mere days before Fritha's untimely death.

"Why?" she whispered, as she looked at him.

Rollo said nothing and, after a moment, the small measure of warmth that had glassed his eyes, was abruptly gone.

Rika drew a calming breath and strode from the hall, forcing herself to slow, measured steps. She'd had enough. More than enough.

There must be another way.

Mayhap she'd take MacInnes at his word. Ride back to Gellis Bay on the morrow and seek his help in freeing her brother. She must think. Clear her head. Temper her roiling emotions.

A chill shot through her as she made her way down the drafty corridor past the kitchen. Her feet stopped of their own accord before the bathhouse door.

A sauna.

Ja, that was exactly what she needed.

She'd cleanse her body and her mind of the events of the past few days.

A comforting warmth drew her in as she opened the heavy door and stepped across the threshold. Rollo had constructed the bathhouse as an addition to the castle. 'Twas similar in style to the one on Fair Isle, but larger, boasting three separate chambers.

The fires were lit each day. Wood fires. A luxury Rollo could well afford, given the castle's proximity to the forest and so much timber.

With relish, she dispensed with the uncomfortably tight gown and shift Catherine had loaned her, dropping them purposefully onto the packed dirt floor.

She stepped into the smallest of the chambers and a cloud of fragrant steam engulfed her. Before settling onto the wide, padded bench, she slid the privacy bolt into place across the door. Not that she expected company.

A vision of Grant, naked and sweating, flashed across her mind.

"You must forget him."

She tossed the ladle aside and poured the entire bucket of herb-laced water over the bed of white-hot stones. The water hissed and spit and sputtered, throwing up a shield of aromatic steam. "Ah." She breathed deep and sank languidly onto the bench.

She must accept the fact that Grant's usefulness to her was at an end. True, he'd gotten them this far, but he'd ne'er secure the dowry. Not now. Her father was toying with him—enjoying turning Grant away from her.

It didn't matter. She didn't care. She couldn't. She'd seen how Grant had looked at Catherine's daughters.

"Would that I were half as fair," she whispered.

"Would that ye were half as patient."

She nearly jumped from the bench. The sauna door banged shut. "Who's there? What do you mean by—" She sucked in a breath as Grant stepped naked out of the steam and knelt before her. In a flash she drew her knees to her chest and wrapped her arms around them, shielding herself from his roving eyes. "What are you doing here?"

"I fancied a sweat. Ye might have waited for me."

"How did you get in here? I bolted the door."

He smiled. "It slides from both sides. Did ye no notice?"

She hadn't, and it annoyed her. He had surprised her twice now bathing, and that was two times too many. "Go away. I wish to be alone."

"Ye lie."

His hand edged across the bench to her foot. Her pulse quickened as his fingers slid over her ankle.

"What do you want from me? Isn't it enough that you and my father and that shrewish bitch humiliate me in front of my own kinsmen?"

His smile faded. "I was no party to that woman's ill behavior."

"Ha!" She jerked her foot from his gentle grasp and fought to maintain her composure. "You delighted in it."

"Nay." His gaze slid over her body.

"Don't look at me!"

She willed herself rise from the bench and leave. Why, oh why, did her body not respond to her mind's command? The moist heat, the intensity of Grant's gaze, her nakedness—all fueled her discomfort.

"Ye are more beautiful than any woman I have ever seen."

Her heart stopped.

Unwillingly she met his gaze. "Do not mock me."

"I would never do that, Rika." The sincerity in his voice disarmed her.

Hot tears stung her eyes. Why did he torment her?

She bit her lip and fought desperately to control the tempest of emotions whirling inside her.

Oh, what she would give to be able to trust him. Just this once. To believe his words. Rely on his strength to bolster her own.

Never in her life had she sought help or comfort from a man. Never had she felt the need that ached inside her, shaking the very tenets of her existence.

She gazed into his eyes and instantly realized her mistake. Should Grant reach for her now, she'd abandon her convictions and fling herself into his arms.

Nay, she must not. She could not.

The dowry. She must focus on the dowry.

"My coin," she said abruptly. "I must have it. When will you ask my father to—"

"Your dowry matters not a whit."

Of course it mattered. It meant everything. If she could not get her hands on it—

He moved closer—so close the damp hair on his chest grazed her knees. Beads of perspiration dripped from his face onto her bare thighs. "Ye think to protect yourself by claiming it. That with the silver gone, no man would want ye."

Her breathing grew labored. Steam swirled up around them, curling her hair and heating her skin to near burning. Why did he look at her with such hunger?

"No man would," she heard herself say.

His eyes held hers in their steely grip as he peeled her hands from her knees. Slowly, with purpose, he removed the hammered bracelets from her wrists and cast them to the floor.

Why did she not stop him?

Sparks shot through her as his lips brushed across the scarred pulse points at each wrist.

"You're wrong," he whispered, and drew her into his arms.

Chapter Fifteen

The passion in her eyes was his undoing.

George eased Rika back onto the bench and kissed her. He told himself 'twas purely physical, this burning, the hunger, the overpowering need to possess her.

"Nay, we should not." Her arms twined around him defeating her feeble protest.

"Why not?" He kissed her again before she could answer. Oh, she felt good in his arms.

"S-someone might come in."

"Let them. We're marrit, are we no?"

She looked at him, her face a radiant fusion of desire and fear, and in that moment he knew at long last he'd melted the ice maiden's stringent resolve.

Perspiration sheened her burning skin. His hands glided over ribs and rounded hip. Slowly he ran his tongue across her throat, tracing her scar from ear to chin.

She closed her eyes and drew breath.

"So salty," he breathed, "so hot." He moved atop her, their bodies melding in wet, silken heat.

She wrapped her legs around him and pulled him close. Her response fueled his desire.

"Slow," he whispered between kisses, fighting for control. He was so hard he thought he would burst. His manhood pulsed against her thigh in excruciating anticipation.

"Love me," she whispered.

His heart stopped.

Her lashes fluttered open and what he read in her eyes mirrored his own confused emotions. Nay, he told himself, it could not be. It must not be. 'Twas lust he felt, nothing more.

Steam infused with a heady tinge of juniper blazed into his lungs. He lost himself in her eyes, the feel of her hands roving his body, and gave himself up to the moment.

"I would pleasure ye beyond your wildest imaginings." His mouth sought hers in a violent kiss, designed to drive this unbidden tenderness from his heart.

He was an animal, a predator, and she his prey. The fierceness of her response thrilled him, but made him wonder who was stalking whom.

She writhed under him, her breasts thrusting upward toward his mouth. He indulged her need and his hunger. She moaned softly as he suckled each nipple hard.

"Oh, George," she breathed, and the sound of his Christian name on her lips spurred him on.

He tasted his way across each rib, over the soft flat plane of her belly. When his tongue blazed a salty path to her sex, she gasped.

"Spread your legs," he said.

She looked at him, her eyes glassed with desire, her face suffused with heat. After a moment, she obeyed, and he plundered the slick, salty heat of her like an animal gone mad.

"George!" she cried out, and bucked beneath him.

His hands closed over her hips to still her. He continued even as she begged him to stop. In a frenzy, he swept her with him to the brink of madness. When her protestations turned to cries of pleasure, he drove her over the edge.

A second later he buried himself inside her, his loins burning for release. They came together in a blaze of passion and heat. Their tongues mated in wild abandon, mimicking their fierce coupling.

There was no going back.

He closed his eyes and, somewhere at the edge of his awareness, heard himself cry her name.

"Look at me," she commanded.

He willed his eyes open. His name spilled from her lips. That, and the raw emotion he read in her face drove him to his own ecstasy.

Later—how much later he did not know—he pulled Rika up with him and sat her across his lap. "There's something I meant to tell ye, but I got…distracted."

"What?" She lay languidly in his arms, looking at him through a veil of white-gold lashes.

How could he have ever thought her anything less than beautiful? "Your dowry—the silver."

"What?" Her whole body went rigid. She gripped his neck so tight he thought she might crush the life from him.

He eased her arms away and smiled. "I have it. Your father's promised it to me on the morrow."

She screeched with sheer joy and wrapped herself around him like one of the serpents that had graced their bridal cup. Her reaction was like a dull blow to his gut.

The coin meant much to her. More than he'd hoped. Why did this surprise him? From the beginning she had said 'twas all she wanted from him. They had a bargain. He had met his part of it, and she hers.

Why then, did he feel this emptiness?

She peppered his face with tiny kisses. He pushed his confused emotions aside and succumbed to her affection. The feel of her naked body twisting atop his rekindled the fire in his loins.

Lust.

That was all there was between them. All there ever could be.

He kissed her hard and pulled her down on top of him, hell-bent on proving it to himself.

Rika woke with a start, her heart pounding. "Where am I? What is this place?" She sat up in the dark, blinking at the glow of a wood fire, confused by her surroundings.

Ah, of course. She remembered now.

Late that night, after their lovemaking and when all were finally abed, Grant had carried her from the sauna to their shared bedchamber. Only this night, he refused to sleep on the floor.

"You're dreaming," he murmured sleepily, then drew her down beside him, fitting her tight against his nude body.

The man ran hot as a smith's brazier.

Though she was already overwarm, he pulled another fur coverlet over them both and brushed a kiss across her earlobe. "Go back to sleep."

His hand closed gently over hers, their fingers intertwined. She lay there in the comfortable harbor of his body until his breathing slowed.

He was asleep.

She, on the other hand, was wide-awake.

Firelight bathed the chamber in a cozy glow and flickered red-gold off the hammered metal of their wedding bands. She drew Grant's hand to her breast and held it there.

He was not at all what she had expected. Lawmaker had read Grant's character true from the first, from the moment they found him washed up on the beach. The old man was gifted that way. God, how she missed him.

Would that he had been her father and not Rollo.

Grant had surprised her every step of their journey together. Few men in her life had his integrity. Lawmaker was one. Her brother, Gunnar, another.

And no man, save Grant, had made her feel so cherished, so wanted—even if it was only for a night.

The first time he made love to her in their bridal bed on Fair Isle, she'd thought it all chance. That his passion for her, his tenderness, was a result of too much mead.

But tonight in the sauna he'd had all his wits about him. She had not known it could be this way between a man and a woman—that she could feel the things she felt this night.

An aching need for intimacy. The joy of pleasuring and being pleasured. Passion. Mutual surrender.

Love.

For she did love him.

And the fruit of that realization was fear.

She turned in his arms so she might look at him in the firelight. He barely stirred. Ne'er had she seen him so at peace. His tousled hair spilled gold across the pillow. She reached out and brushed the thin braid at his temple away from his face.

How could she have let down her guard?

Love was the most dangerous of emotions. Not because it muddled a woman's thinking, as she'd once believed—but because it proved exactly the opposite.

It lent a clarity of purpose she was wholly unprepared for.

She listened to his breathing, watched the slow rise and fall of his chest, drew his scent into her lungs, and knew she would do anything he asked of her.

"Dangerous," she whispered, and traced a finger along his lower lip. He twitched.

And if he asked nothing?

What then?

Of what consequence was her love?

Here in his own world—her father's world—Grant seemed too much like Rollo, and that saddened her. He was far too casual, detached, unmoved.

Oh, she had moved him this night, and he her. But all men responded to such pleasures of the flesh. Grant didn't truly care for her. How could he?

She'd forced him to marriage as a way to buy his freedom. A bargain between two strangers, nothing more. Why, the man had been bound for his own wedding when Rika snared him for her own purpose. Even now, his bride waited for him in Wick.

Rika's throat constricted.

A bride—a virgin—bred for a Scottish laird, and to Grant's specific tastes. Biddable, demure. Small and delicate, like Catherine's young daughters.

Rika's gaze lit on her scarred wrists.

She asked herself again, of what consequence was her love for George Grant? It served only to distract her from that which mattered most.

Gunnar's freedom.

She'd set out to bring her brother home, and do this she would. Beyond that, she could not think. There was nothing left for her on Fair Isle. Not now. Gunnar would take his place as jarl, and all would be as it once was.

Only she was changed.

Grant had changed her.

He opened his eyes, and a lazy smile curled at the edge of his mouth. Her chest tightened. "What are ye doing?" he whispered.

"Looking at you."

He drew her into his arms, and she gave herself up to his gentle lovemaking. This one night she would pretend that he loved her. That he was her husband and she his wife, and that there was no tomorrow.

George rolled onto his stomach and buried his face in the pillow. Rika's pillow. "Mmm." It smelled of her.

Light streamed in from beneath the window cover and splashed across the timber floor of their bedchamber. He'd overslept. No matter. It had been the first night in weeks he'd truly slept.

Since the last time he'd lain with her.

"Rika," he said, but knew she wasn't there. He edged a toe to the other side of the bed and felt only the cool linen sheet. She always did rise early.

He threw off the fur coverlet. The chill morning air shocked him fully awake. God, he felt good.

And then he remembered.

Who he was, and why he was here—and why he must leave.

He slid the pillow over his face, blocking out the light, and again breathed her fragrance and the lingering scent of their lovemaking.

'Twas useless to try to make sense of his feelings.

Honestly, he didn't know what he felt. He caught himself wondering what things were possible should his clan, his king, and the Sinclairs all come to think him dead.

That he should have such a thought made his gut twist in shame. What had she done to him that he would think, even for a second, to shirk his obligations?

He launched the pillow across the room and rolled onto his side. And then he saw it, lying there on the chest by the bed.

Her wedding band.

Ten minutes later he was dressed and standing before her in her father's stable. She was dressed in her traveling clothes—her brother's clothes, he had come to understand.

"Your ring," he said, and offered it to her. "Ye…left it."

The stiffness of her demeanor puzzled him. Just hours ago, in his arms, she'd been so affectionate—nay, more than that. She'd exuded a tenderness, a guileless passion, and something more. Something that had stunned him.

Love.

Aye, he was certain of it.

But this morning, he was not so sure. How could he be? No woman had ever loved him before. Women obeyed him, feared him even. Aye, as they should.

Shouldn't they?

He didn't know anymore. One thing he was sure of—no woman in the whole of his life had ever looked at him the way Rika had last night.

Watching her now, he read nothing in those cool blue eyes. They were dead. Lifeless. What had happened to so change her? Suddenly he felt ridiculous. A rush of heat flushed his face.

She glanced at the ring in his open palm and shrugged. "I meant to leave it. It's usefulness to me is finished."

Her words stung more sharply than any wound he'd e'er suffered. His eyes widened before he could hide his reaction. "Oh." His fist closed over the ring, and he stuffed it awkwardly into the pocket of his breeks.

Ottar passed him, lugging a saddle. George looked past Rika into the dimly lit stalls and saw Erik and Leif readying their horses. "Where are they off to?"

"They?" Rika said. "You mean *we*. We're leaving. All of us. Within the hour."

"So soon?" He would have thought they'd tarry at least another day.

"I will not spend another night under my father's roof." Her lips thinned to a hard line.

"But, your father. What must he thi—"

"I told him you had urgent business."

"Business? What bu—"

"In Wick."

He stopped breathing. Her gaze was so cold, her expression so hard, he could scarce believe she was the same woman who had cried his name in ecstasy just hours before.

"That is where you wish to go, is it not?" She arched a white-gold brow at him.

"Aye, but—"

"And I have affairs of my own to deal with." She knelt beside the pile of saddlebags at her feet and pulled a small chest from under them.

"The silver," he said, recognizing the chest Rollo

had shown him last night just after Rika had fled the hall.

"Precisely. It was waiting for us this morn in the hall. She lifted the lid and ran her hand over the coins. Only then did her eyes show signs of life. She smiled, and George felt suddenly sick.

"So," he said, "our bargain is concluded."

"Ja."

Just like that. So simple. She looked at him, waiting, and for a moment he could have sworn she wanted him to protest. His head spun. The words left his lips before he could bite them back. "And...last night?"

She held his gaze, and he knew —twas by sheer will alone. He could see her grinding her teeth behind lips swollen from his kisses.

"Last night was..." Color tinged her cheeks. "I thought I owed it you, is all. You secured my dowry, and I was...grateful." She closed the lid of the silver chest and rose, hefting it with her.

"You're saying ye did it for the coin?"

"Ja."

His gut roiled. When she turned toward their mounts, he grabbed her arm. "But ye didna know about it before, when we—" he whispered so that the youths would not hear "—made love."

For a second their eyes met, then she pulled away. "How much longer?" she called to Ottar.

The youth peeked over one of the geldings. "Nearly ready. Your father's provided us another mount." He nodded at a black mare. "To replace the one Ingolf stole."

"Good," Rika said.

George stood there, stunned. The bloody woman acted as if there was nothing between them. As if he was a stranger she had hired to transact some dirty business for her.

Aye, that's exactly what he was.

She lifted the silver chest onto the mare's well-padded back. Ottar secured it tight. "There," she said, and turned to address him. "Are you ready, Grant?"

He nodded, not knowing what else to say.

"Well then, you'll wish to bid my father goodbye, no doubt. At least make a show of it. Go ahead. We'll wait for you here."

"Ye dinna wish to say goodbye to him?"

Rika snorted. "Good riddance, you mean?" She patted the silver chest. "I have what I want. There is nothing more to say."

Aye, that was more than clear.

He left her there in the stable and returned to their chamber to gather his few possessions. He felt dirty. Used. Like a tavern wench who'd not yet grown used to her trade.

A short time later, the five of them sat mounted in the courtyard, awaiting their host's farewell.

Rollo stood on the castle steps with the dour Catherine. George knew their departure pleased her. Her daughters huddled behind her, shivering. Christ, 'twas cold. George raised a hand in farewell.

The Norseman nodded. His gaze strayed to Rika—his daughter, whether he believed it or nay. Her face showed the strain of the past few days. She would not look at him.

Mayhap if George had told her about Fritha and Lawmaker, she'd understand, even forgive, her father's monstrous behavior. Without a word, she drew herself up in the saddle, head high, and kicked her mount to action.

Nay, she would never forgive, nor did she want to understand.

Rollo watched her until she rode out of sight. His arm slipped from Catherine's shoulder and, at the last, George read the pain in his eyes.

"Farewell," George called to him.

"And to you, Grant."

George reined his mount into line behind Ottar and the others, and met the Norseman's gaze once more.

"Take care of her, won't you?" Rollo said.

George smiled bitterly. "Aye, I will—if she'll let me."

With but an hour of daylight to spare, Rika reined her mount to a halt just beyond the great wood. George pulled up beside her. The weather had been mercifully mild. Cold and clear with but a light wind blowing off the sea.

George cupped his hands and blew hot breath into them. "Why have ye stopped?" he asked her.

"We're here," Rika said.

Ottar shot her a puzzled glance. "Where?"

"The crossroads." She nodded to the path leading north back to Tom MacInnes's house. George strained his eyes and thought he could almost see the white-washed structure hugging the cliffs.

So this was it then.

Rika pointed east to a faint path meandering up and over the moors. "There lies Wick, or so the chart says."

"You would leave us, truly?" Ottar said. "After all…" The youth's face clouded. "After everything?"

Leif and Erik looked hard at Rika, as if she would intervene. George knew she would not.

"Our bargain is concluded," she said. Her voice had that familiar hard edge to it. Good God, the woman was cold as ice.

"But—" One stony look from Rika and Ottar's mouth snapped shut.

"Grant's bride awaits him in Wick." She tipped her chin at George. "Does she not?"

Their eyes locked, his searching, hers icy.

"Aye, she does." He pulled the rolled chart from his saddlebag and unfurled it. "Two days' ride, methinks. No more."

Leif and Erik nudged their mounts in close, straining to see the map.

Erik snaked his hand between them and ran it over the parchment. A stubby finger lingered on the jagged coastline near Dunnet Head.

"A day at most," Leif murmured.

George frowned. "A day to where? MacInnes's house is but an hour—"

Erik snatched his hand back, and Rika shot him a look that would freeze water. The youths exchanged loaded glances. What the devil was going on here?

"I will see ye all safe to MacInnes's house," George said, "before I take my leave."

"You shall do nothing of the kind." Rika turned her mount away from him. "It's just down the hill. Besides, it will be far easier to explain your absence to MacInnes now, without you, than for you to take your leave of us in his presence."

"Rika's right," Erik said.

Ottar nudged his gelding closer. "But why do you have to go at all? Why not come back to Fair Isle with us?"

"Ottar, that's enough," Rika said. "Grant has a life

of his own. A clan. A bride. Is that not true?'' She arched a brow at him.

'Twas the second time she'd asked him that. She knew the answer, so why did she ask? George met her frigid gaze, searching for a sign. Did she wish him to stay? Was that it? She pursed her lips and tipped her chin at him.

Nay, she wanted him gone.

And he was daft not to want to go.

''But you're married,'' Ottar said. ''And with Law-maker dead, there is no elder to speak the words to undo the bond.''

Rika snorted. ''It matters not. I shall never wed again, so I need not the divorce. As for Grant—'' she looked him up and down as she had that first day in the courtyard ''—it was never a proper Christian mar-riage, and therefore does not exist.''

''Just like that,'' George said.

''Ja, just like that.''

Her arrogance and easy dismissal of him proved too much. ''Fine. I'll be gone then.'' He rolled the chart and thrust it at her. ''Give this to MacInnes. I've no need of it. I know where I'm going.''

She handed the parchment to Ottar who stuffed it into a half-full saddlebag. ''Good. Well then, Grant. I bid you farewell—and Godspeed. I am certain your…bride…will be pleased to see you.''

''Aye, that she will.'' He reined his mount east, then pulled him up short, remembering something. He fished it out of the small leather bag tied at his waist and weighed it in his hand before tossing it to her.

She caught it, and when she realized what it was, her face turned to stone.

''The brooch,'' George said. ''Your *morgen gifu.*''

"I told you, I do not—"

"Take it. In payment for last night."

Her eyes burned into him like white-hot daggers. By God, she was cold-blooded. A man could break himself against the rock that was her heart.

She kicked the black mare into a gallop and rode north across the moor, her white-gold hair flaming out behind her catching the last rays of the setting sun.

Ottar raised a hand in farewell, his boyish face twisted in sorrow. Erik and Leif bid him goodbye and Godspeed.

George turned away from them, away from her, and spurred his mount east toward Wick.

Chapter Sixteen

This was going to be harder than she had thought.

Rika crouched behind a tumble of broken rocks as the quarry below them materialized in the gray light of dawn. Heavily armed guards rousted a pack of laborers from a barracks and herded them toward the foul-smelling slag heaps on the perimeter of the camp.

She blew a hot breath into icy hands and strained her eyes against the mist shrouding the whole of Dunnet Head. Where was Gunnar? What if she'd been wrong about his whereabouts? What if the conversation she'd overheard among Brodir's men had been staged on purpose to mislead her?

Nay, her brother was here, somewhere.

She could feel it.

What remained of a stone and timber castle sat on the edge of the cliff overlooking the sea and served as the quarry's headquarters. That much she and the youths had been able to discern from their precarious perch on the moors above.

She jammed a hand into the pocket of her cloak and gripped the silver brooch Grant had delivered as a parting token yesterday morn.

In payment for last night.

The sting of his words seemed no less sharp today. She ground her teeth, recalling the coolness of his expression. What more had she deserved? It was she who had turned a cold shoulder to him.

Perhaps if she'd trusted him, shared the truth about Gunnar, told him of her love...nay, how could she have? Such trust flew in the face of all her instincts. Besides, he would have laughed at her. Surely.

She pulled the silver brooch from her pocket and marveled at the workmanship. Her gaze strayed to the dirt caked under her broken fingernails and the callused wind-burned texture of her hands.

''Hmph.''

Surely he would have laughed.

She watched as the guards directed their prisoners, prodding them with short spears and sharpened sticks. The crack of a lash kissing bare flesh made her jump. She didn't know whether to hope Gunnar was among them or not.

One thing was certain. Her confidence in freeing him, were he here, would have been tenfold greater were Grant crouched here beside her among the rocks. Strange that she should feel that way. With Brodir, with her father, with all men to some extent—save Lawmaker—she felt weakened, less than what she was.

But with Grant by her side, she had felt near invincible. Almost as if it were the two of them, together, against all the evils of the world. Only now did she realize it.

She remembered that feeling, its power, and pondered the mystery of how such a thing was possible between her and any man. Perhaps she'd been wrong about love—and loving. All her life she'd known naught but despair and weakness to come of it.

Until now.

Yesterday, in her father's courtyard, as she stole one last glance at the man who'd sired her, she thought she caught a glimpse of something else in Rollo's eyes. Something besides his obvious relief at her departure.

What was it she saw?

Rollo was a man who she knew did nothing he did not wish to do. He relinquished the silver—a small fortune, really—and in her heart Rika knew there was more to it than Grant winning him over with games and verse and idle banter.

Did Rollo care for her after all?

Perhaps a little. Even Norsemen grew soft in their old age. And were it true, did that wipe away the years of neglect and open contempt he had wreaked on her and Gunnar and their mother? Could she ever forgive him for that?

Lawmaker used to tell her that one day, when she understood Rollo better, she would forgive him. Would that the old man were here to help her make sense of her feelings.

"Look, he comes!"

Ottar's whispered warning jolted her from her thoughts.

"Where?" She scanned the paths leading from the quarry for Leif's slight form.

"There," Erik said, and pointed.

"Ja, I see him. Let us hope he bears good news."

Ottar and Erik edged closer to her as the three of them peeked between the rocks at their fast-approaching kinsman.

"I still can't believe you kept it from me all this

time.'' Ottar shot her a brooding look. ''I could have helped in the planning, maybe even persuaded Grant to—''

''Stop it,'' she said. Her instincts had been right. Ottar would have told Grant straightaway. ''I told you. The fewer who knew our true plan, the better. Brodir's men see all on Fair Isle.''

''Ja, they found out anyway, didn't they?''

She frowned at him, not wishing to remember what had happened in the storm. ''It's over now. They are dead.''

''But Grant might have helped—''

''It's better this way. He has his own life, and we ours. Besides, we have no need of him.'' If only she could make herself believe that.

The three of them slid back out of sight as Leif jogged up the path leading to their hiding place behind the rocks. As soon as he topped the small ridge, Rika pulled him down beside her.

''Gunnar—is he there?'' She held her breath and searched the youth's bright eyes.

Leif grinned. ''Ja, I saw him.''

A cry of joy escaped her throat before she could control it. She crushed the startled Leif to her chest in a bear hug. ''Thank God! Oh, thank God!''

''Methinks the Scot's Christian ways have rubbed off on her, eh?'' Ottar said. Erik grinned.

''Oh, stop—the both of you.'' She pushed Leif away and thumped Ottar affectionately on the forehead. ''You know very well I keep both the old ways and the new.''

''You never let Grant know that.'' Ottar arched an accusing brow at her.

She ignored him and turned to Leif. ''How fares my

brother? Tell me everything.'' Her hands were shaking. She'd clutched the silver brooch so tightly it cut into her palm. She quickly pocketed it and bade Leif tell them what had transpired between him and the quarry master.

"Gunnar is thin, but moves with purpose," Leif said. "He is in reasonable health from what I could tell."

"It's a miracle." She shook her head, afraid to believe. "Did he recognize you? Does he know we're here?"

"Nay. I caught just a glimpse of him, and I don't think he saw me."

"Where is he?" Rika scrambled to her feet and fixed her gaze on the prisoners working the quarry. "Show me."

Leif pulled her back down. "Don't show yourself. It's dangerous."

He was right, but she didn't care anymore. Her brother was alive!

"Besides," Leif said, "he's not among the other workers, but inside—in the castle."

"The jailer," Erik said. "Will he deal?"

Leif grinned. "He will. It's not often the quarry master's offered a fortune in silver for the release of one man—and a Norseman at that."

Rika could scarce believe their luck. "When? When shall we make the trade?"

"Now," Leif said. "The quarry master waits for us below."

She shot to her feet and started for the horses tethered behind them in a copse where the open moor met a small wood.

Ottar caught her up. "Let me go, Rika. You stay here. It's too dangerous."

"Nay." She waved him off, and cast warning looks to Erik and Leif, who followed. "I shall go. The three of you stay here."

"But—"

"Should I not return in an hour's time..." She paused because she didn't know what to tell them. Her pride, her innate distrust of men had kept her from enlisting even MacInnes's help. She'd been wrong, perhaps, not to share her secret with him.

It was too late for that now. Gunnar was alive, and that's all that mattered.

Ottar started to argue, but she ignored him. Gorse and dead thistles tore at her garments as she snaked her way into the copse. Where were the horses? Hadn't they left them right he—

"Looking for something?"

Rika froze in her tracks. Ottar and the others smacked into her from behind.

She knew that voice, and the deep timbre of it made her blood run cold.

"For this, perhaps?" A huge, battle-clad Norseman stepped from the thicket, her silver chest tucked neatly beneath his arm.

"Brodir," she breathed, and fought the overwhelming urge to flee. The youths crowded speechless behind her.

Somewhere close she heard the high-pitched whinnies of restless horses and Ingolf's unmistakable laughter.

Brodir smiled.

Rika knew that smile and what it meant. The hair on her nape prickled.

After a day's hard ride, George waited anxiously in a small but lavishly furnished chamber for August

Sinclair to return home from his hunt and bid him welcome.

In the winter garden below his window, a dark-haired maiden swathed in ermine and brocade tittered with her sisters over a bouquet of dried roses.

Anne Sinclair.

His bride.

He gripped the edge of the window casing and watched her. Truly she was beautiful. Milky skin, soft delicate features, a virginal blush about her cheeks mirroring the pale pink of the roses she crushed to her breast.

She was as promised—all any man could want in a bride.

Yet he was wholly unmoved.

His gaze shifted to his silver wedding band and its smaller twin—Rika's ring—circling his little finger. He'd not had the heart to cast them away.

"Good God, you're alive!"

He spun toward the voice. August Sinclair stood in the open doorway of the chamber, openmouthed, his face twisted in astonishment.

"Aye," George said, "it seems that I am."

"But…" Sinclair eyed him warily, as if he did not believe George was real.

"We were shipwrecked."

"S-so we heard."

"Ye know then, about my men, and my—"

"Aye, 'twas a terrible tragedy."

Sommerled's gentle face flashed in George's mind. His gut knotted in pain and remorse. "I…I washed ashore on Fa—on an island, and had a devil of a time catching a vessel home." 'Twas best, he thought, not to reveal too much. "I…I came as soon as I could."

Sinclair stepped closer. His expression of disbelief faded to one of concern. Nowhere was the relief, or the anger, George expected to see.

"I apologize for the inconvenience I must have caused ye and your family. The wedding was planned for more than a fortnight ago, and ye must have gone to great trouble to change—"

"Nay, dinna fash about it." Sinclair waved a hand in dismissal, but continued to frown. He paced the floor of the chamber, stroking his short beard, as if he were considering something of great import.

"Your daughter," George began.

"Aye, she's in the garden—" Sinclair stopped short "—but dinna go to her just yet."

George relaxed, grateful for this small reprieve. He was nowhere near ready to meet the lass. His head was still spinning from the events of the past weeks. In the back of his mind he wondered whether he could get out of it all together—the marriage, the alliance, everything.

God's blood, what was he thinking?

'Twas his duty, his destiny. All the plans were made. One short month ago—it seemed like a lifetime—he couldn't wait to meet his bride and seal the bargain.

Why, then, did every instinct tell him to quit this place and go?

He caught himself toying with Rika's wedding band, and stuffed his hands into the pockets of his breeks to stop from fidgeting. Too well, he knew where he wished to be, and 'twas not in the arms of a dark-haired maiden in a castle in Wick.

Sinclair resumed pacing, apparently lost in thought, and George used the time to consider his own situation.

He stepped again to the window, drawn by Anne's pretty laughter.

How could he not want her?

Mayhap she was not so fair as first he'd thought. He narrowed his eyes and studied her more closely. Aye, she was…too small, her skin too white, her features too fragile. He couldn't imagine her strong enough to weather a long walk, let alone a day's ride. Surely not a sea voyage. And she'd probably never handled a weapon in her life.

Nor did she look very bright. In fact, the king had mentioned her lack of education, as if it were a boon. Likely, she knew nothing of the weather or the sea or the stars. For certain she would have no head for chess or other strategic pursuits.

Why then, he wondered, did William the Lion speak so favorably of her? She was not at all remarkable.

Remarkable.

Hadn't he and Lawmaker discussed that very topic? He couldn't rightly remember their conversation, but he had the nagging feeling that the old man had been trying to tell him something.

Anne's silly chittering pulled him out of his thoughts. He sucked in a breath of chill air and knew what he must do. Hang the consequences. He turned to the chieftain. "Sinclair, we must speak plain."

Sinclair stopped pacing and joined him at the window. "Aye, there is something ye must know. When we thought ye dead, we made other arr—"

"Before this goes further, I would have ye know my feelings about this marriage."

"Grant, what I have to say ye may no like, but—"

"Not that I wish to compromise our alliance in any way. It's just that I've changed my—"

Sinclair raised a hand to silence him. "We thought ye dead. We made other arrangements."

His brows arched of their own accord. "What?" Saint Columba be praised if it were true!

"Besides, she's in love with someone else."

Both of them turned at the sound of the feminine voice. Mistress Sinclair, whom George had met on his arrival, whooshed into the room and joined them at the window.

"That has naught to do with it," Sinclair said. "'Twas a business arrangement and—"

"For pity's sake, August, that has everything to do with it." Mistress Sinclair nodded to her daughter in the garden. "Just look at her. She's smitten."

The three of them gazed down at Anne, who now sat alone in the garden on a stone bench, caressing the dried petals of her bouquet.

George blinked, speechless. Never would he have expected this to go so easy. Still, once William the Lion got word that he lived, he might find himself right back in the thick of this arrangement.

"Now May, I told ye no to meddle in the affairs o' the cl—"

"Who is the man?" George said. Mayhap he could somehow turn the situation to his advantage.

"That's the strangest part of all," Sinclair said. "It happened so quickly, after all of us thought ye dead. In truth, methinks 'tis a better match all around and serves our political purpose as well."

He shook his head, now totally befuddled.

"Why, there he is now," Mistress Sinclair said.

George's gaze slid again to the garden, and his heart stopped.

A fair-haired youth dashed breathless across the snow-dusted flagstones into the open arms of Anne Sinclair. The bouquet of pink roses spilled from her lap.

"Sommerled," George breathed.

Rika stood on the crumbling battlement of the ruined keep and shivered against the waxing wind. The setting sun lent a pinkish cast to the snow-covered moors and the scarred earth of the quarry.

She turned toward her jailer. "I should have finished you when I had the chance."

Ingolf grinned at her. "You may yet have another. When Brodir's done with you he's promised me a go." Rika gritted her teeth as Ingolf traced a dirty finger across her throat. "Take you my meaning, whore?" She slapped his hand away, and he laughed.

"Enough!" Brodir stepped onto the battlement from the stair leading down, and nodded at his henchman. "Find the quarry master and see that he's done what I've asked."

Ingolf scurried past him like a rat. When his footsteps faded on the stair, Brodir turned his attention to her.

"Think you to keep me prisoner here?" she said, determined not to let him intimidate her.

Brodir lumbered toward her. She'd forgotten how big he was. She was tall, yet he towered over her by a head and outweighed her by seven or eight stone.

"For a while." He smiled—that terrible smile. "Until I tire of the scenery—or of you."

"You have my silver, what more could you want from me?" She regretted the question the moment it slid from her lips. He loomed over her, and by sheer will alone she held her ground.

"Have you forgotten so soon?" One beefy hand closed over her braceleted wrist and squeezed.

She gritted her teeth and looked him in the eye.

"I'm hurt," he said in a mocking tone. "After all, we were...betrothed."

"No longer. I am already wed."

The smile slid from his face, and he released her. "So Ingolf has told me. He's a Scot, ja?"

Her pride got the better of her fear. She tipped her chin at him. "He is. A chieftain."

"A chieftain? Well." He circled her slowly. "So, where is he, this husband of yours?"

Heat burned her face despite the frigid wind whipping at her hair and garments. "He's...away. On business."

"What, he leaves his wife alone to exchange her fortune for some worthless chattel. Think you, woman, I'm a complete fool?"

"My brother's life is far from worthless."

Brodir laughed. "His life is over—at sunset tomorrow."

Her blood froze in her veins.

"And the lives of those sniveling whelps you dragged with you from Frideray."

Rika stepped in front of him, and a look of surprise washed over his dark features. "Touch them and I'll kill you," she said.

"Ha! What's this?" His gaze raked over her. "Men's garments do not a warrior make. Think you to slay me? With what, your bare hands?"

She reached instinctively for weapons that were not there. Brodir shrugged, grinning, and for the first time she noticed the sword hilt protruding from his shoulder baldric.

"That's Gunnar's weapon. Give it to me!" She lunged and he caught her arm in a death grip.

"So it is. A present from Ingolf. By rights your husband should have it. I repeat my question...where is he?"

He released her, and she fell back against the crenellated wall of the battlement.

"I told you, he..."

"He left you, didn't he?"

She scrambled to her feet, burning at the comment.

"Ingolf told me. He was betrothed to another. A Scot. One of his own. And as soon as he might, he left you—for her."

Heat flushed her face. Rage and shame twisted inside her like a vortex.

"Smart man."

She went for the dagger belted at his waist, but he was ready for her. In a matter of seconds he had her immobilized, lifting her off her feet and turning her in his arms so that she faced out overlooking the quarry. Fruitlessly she struggled against him.

"Look!" he commanded. "Look your last on your brother." With his free hand he wrenched her jaw toward the barracks below them.

Slave laborers marched two abreast from the slag heaps toward their ramshackle barracks. In the dying light her eyes searched for familiar faces. There! Ottar and Erik and Leif. And with them—ja!

"Gunnar!" she cried, just as Brodir clamped a hand over her mouth. A disturbance broke out among the laborers. She fought to see, kicking and scratching, biting at Brodir's filthy hand. The stench of him was near overpowering.

"Enough!" he raged, and dropped her on her feet. "There! See him! Take your last look."

She leaned out over the battlement, trembling, scanning the ranks of laborers, calling her brother's name. A host of guards broke up the skirmish near the barracks entrance, and as the slaves were herded inside, one paused and raised a hand to her in recognition.

"Gunnar," she breathed. Her hand shot up. Joy and despair wrenched her heart. Gunnar was pushed inside the barracks, along with the others.

"You see?" Brodir said. "There is naught to be done. I made the same mistake with your brother as you did with Ingolf. I should have killed him when I had the chance."

She turned on him, seething. "You mean when first you kidnapped him."

"Exactly. But I thought a good long stint in this hellhole might do him some good. He always was a weakling."

"He was your jarl."

Brodir snorted. "He was soft. Not a fit leader for our folk. I did what had to be done and have no regrets. Except one. Would that I had seen Lawmaker die."

She stood there looking at him, incredulous, wondering when her fear of him had changed to hate and, finally, pity. The power he once held over her had vanished, yet he was no different. The same selfish, ignorant man.

She was the one who had changed. Loving Grant had changed her. That she could no longer deny.

Brodir sensed her transformation, and the edgy fu-

sion of wariness and disbelief she read in his dark eyes
fueled her courage.

"You cannot harm me now, no matter what you do
to me."

The last of the pale light faded to gray, and in that
eerie twilight he smiled the smile reserved solely for
her.

"Oh no?" he whispered, and closed the distance between them.

Her last thoughts before he herded her below stairs
and toward his makeshift bedchamber were of Grant.

George.

Thank God he was safe in Wick.

A dozen regrets raced through her mind, but sending
him away was not one of them. Were he here with her
now, he'd be dead—or worse.

She mustered her strength and followed Brodir to the
bed.

George pushed the food around on the trencher he
shared with his brother. He was not in the least hungry.
Rare beeswax tapers burned low in the great hall, and
his hosts, the Sinclairs, seemed anxious to find their
beds.

"More ale?" Sinclair said to him halfheartedly from
his place at the head of the table.

"Nay," he said absently. "I prefer mead."

"Mead?" Sommerled stared at him, wide-eyed, his
dirk loaded with meat and poised before his mouth.
"Ye've always hated mead."

"I...I know." He shrugged, not wishing to discuss
it.

Anne sat rigid and silent between Sommerled and
her parents. 'Twas obvious to George that his miracu-

lous return from the dead gave her no cause to rejoice.
August Sinclair had swiftly agreed with him that afternoon, given the circumstances, to postpone all discus-
sion of their impending marriage until the morrow.

Needing some diversion from the whole affair, he
turned to Sommerled and bade him tell the tale of his
rescue one more time.

"I told ye," the youth said matter-of-factly between
bites of bread and roasted mutton, "I was plucked from
the sea by a passing frigate bound south from Shetland
to Wick. 'Twas sheer bloody luck."

George shook his head. Still, he could not believe it.
He rumpled Sommerled's blond hair, unleashing a tiny
fraction of the joy he felt.

"No more," his brother said, laughing.

"'Tis a wonder the lad didna freeze to death," Sinclair said.

"I nearly did." Sommerled grinned. "I was stiff as
an icicle when they hauled me aboard."

Emotion clouded George's thinking, and a film of
tears glassed his eyes. He swiped at them with the back
of his hand. "I need some air." When he rose from the
bench, Sommerled rose with him.

"Aye, me as well. Besides," the youth said, stuffing
his dirk into its scabbard and leaning close to whisper,
"there are things I would speak this night for your ears
alone."

"Until tomorrow, then." Sinclair nodded at them
both, and his wife smiled tightly.

As George turned to leave, he caught the look of
despair Anne flashed his brother. Sommerled's face
clouded, and the lass quickly lowered her eyes. The
exchange was not lost on her parents.

"Come." George placed a hand on Sommerled's shoulder. "There are things I, too, wish ye to hear."

A few minutes later they found themselves in the winter garden where first George spied his bride and her groom of choice, his younger brother.

Before he could speak, Sommerled grabbed his arm. "Truly, George, had I known... At first, I didna consciously woo her. I was out of my head, delirious, after the wreck."

"Aye, lad, I know ye were." He pushed the distraught youth down onto the stone bench.

"The Sinclairs took me in. Anne herself hovered over my bed each day until I was fit. When they told me none had survived, I—"

"Easy. Easy lad. It's over now. We are alive and well, the both of us."

"Aye, but—"

Sommerled's voice broke and George could stand it no longer. He knelt in the snow and gathered his brother into his arms. They wept like children.

"Forgive me," Sommerled said, his breath hot on George's ear.

"Nay, stop it." He broke their embrace and settled next to him on the cold bench. "'Tis ye who must forgive me."

Sommerled frowned in the moonlight. "For what?"

"For...for no saving ye myself." There, he'd said it. The sin had been gnawing at him for weeks. Over and over he relived it. Mayhap now he could atone and lay it to rest.

They looked at each other for a long moment.

"I saw ye caught in the rigging. There was naught to be done. Besides—" Sommerled grinned "—I didna think ye could swim."

His eyes widened. "At the time I didna think so either." Never would he forget pulling Rika from the sea. "But, aye, I can and I do."

Sommerled started to laugh, and the sound of it caused George's heart to swell with joy. He could not help but laugh with him.

"A fine pair o' sailors we are, eh?"

"So ye forgive me then, brother?" George held his breath, but knew already he was absolved.

"Of course I do, ye silly twit. We're here, aren't we?"

"Aye, we are, but the next time we go a-traveling 'twill be by steed."

"As for the clan," Sommerled said, "I told ye, I sent word home of the wreck weeks ago. As for this marriage idea, the elders proposed that I should take your place—and Sinclair agreed, o' course—but the king's no been approached, and now that ye're back, well, 'tis only fitting that—what I mean to say is that of course I'll step down."

"Whoa, laddie. Catch your breath." He wrapped an arm around Sommerled's shoulder. "So the elders thought it a fine idea for ye to marry Anne?"

"Aye, they did."

"And Sinclair agreed?"

Sommerled nodded.

He held his brother's nervous, wide-eyed gaze until he could feel the lad fidget under his scrutiny. Then he smiled. "And from what I've seen today in this very garden, methinks the lady was well pleased with the idea."

He watched as Sommerled fought the smile curling at the edges of his mouth. Were there more light,

George knew he'd see his brother's cheeks flushed ripe as cherries.

"Well, aye…if ye must know…she took to the idea after a week or so."

"A week? Christ, lad, ye're slipping. I would have thought ye'd have had her wrapped around your finger from the very first day."

"Aye, we did get on well from the start."

George nodded, satisfied. "Then, 'tis all settled. I shall step down, and ye shall have your bonny dark-haired bride."

"But, the king. What shall we d—"

"Leave William to me. I have a way with him, but he'll have to be dealt with in person. A missive willna suffice."

Sommerled exhaled in relief. "Oh, George, ye dinna know what I've been through these last hours."

"Aye, I know." He idly twisted Rika's wedding band on his little finger.

Sommerled's gaze was drawn to the hammered silver band, and his fair brows knit in confusion. George quickly stuffed his hand into his pocket.

Too late.

"Those rings. They're twins. What are they?" Sommerled poked at his pocketed hand.

"They're nothing. Just something I picked up."

Sommerled's frown deepened, then all at once he jumped from the bench, his young face alight with recognition.

George's stomach did a slow roll.

"Ye're marrit!" Sommerled cried. "That's it, isn't it?"

He looked at his brother sheepishly and shrugged.

"Good God, what the hell happened out there?"

George shot to his feet and started down the flag-stone path, Sommerled dogging his steps. "I dinna know anymore. Damn the bloody woman! If only she—"

"Who is she?" Sommerled jumped in front of him and blocked the path. "Tell me. Where did ye meet her? Is she a Scot?"

"Nay, nay." He shook his head and waved his brother off. "The truth is, she's a Viking. A Norse-woman. There, I've told ye. Are ye happy now?"

His brother let out a whoop that George was certain would wake the entire household. "A Viking! Is she fair? Can she fight? I've heard their women are cou-rageous and wicked tall."

"Aye, she's tall, and courageous. And fair, but in a different sort of way. Ye wouldna understand."

He didn't understand it himself. He told himself he would put her out of his mind for tonight. But now his head spun with naught but thoughts of her.

"Ye're in love!" Sommerled cried.

"Shut it!" He clamped a hand over his brother's mouth, but Sommerled pushed it away.

"Ye are, aren't ye? Ye love her, this Viking woman, this…"

"Rika," he snapped. "Her name is Rika." He met his brother's gaze. "She's my wife and, aye, I love her."

The words seemed to hang there on the breeze, ring-ing in his ears. He could hardly believe it, himself, and was compelled to speak it again. "I love her."

There. He'd said it.

'Twas true.

It had always been so, from the first time he saw her

looming over him on the beach. From the very first words she spoke.

He is perfect.

Nay, she had it all wrong. She was the perfect one. And he'd left her. Like a fool he'd left her, alone in a foreign land with naught but boys to protect her.

"What have I done?" he breathed.

Sommerled didn't hear him. He was going on and on about some other Viking tale. Something he'd heard on the hunt that day. "…and this silly woman offered a fortune in silver for the prisoner, but—"

"What?" He grabbed his brother by the collar of his fur wrap. "What did ye say? What woman? What fortune?"

Sommerled wrested out of his grip. "Calm down. If ye'd listen, I'd tell ye. 'Twas today on the hunt we met him—one of Sinclair's kinsmen newly come from the quarry at Dunnet Head."

Dunnet Head.

He grabbed Sommerled by the arm, dragged him back to the bench and pushed him onto it. "Tell me. What woman? What was her name?"

"What in bloody—"

"Tell me!"

Sommerled looked at him as if he were a madman. "Dunno. Only that she came to the quarry with a chest full o' silver to buy the release of one indentured slave. Her brother."

Brother.

"Gunnar, son of Rollo. Was that his name?"

Sommerled nodded. "Aye, that was it all right. But how did ye know?"

An overpowering anxiety coiled tight inside him. "And the woman—what happened to her? Did she make the trade? Did she free him?'' A hundred small mysteries that had nagged at him for weeks suddenly made sense.

''Nay, she didna. The silver was snatched from her very hands by some big Viking bloke. 'Twas her dowry, they say, and he her betrothed.''

George's heart stopped for the second time that day.

''Can ye imagine?''

He could, and a sick horror washed over him.

''He took her and the lads she had with her for slaves.''

''What? She works the quarry?''

''Nay, no her. Just the lads. She's...what did Sinclair's kinsman call it? Aye, I remember now. 'Tis a Viking custom.''

''What?'' He grabbed his brother and shook him near senseless. ''What's the whoreson done with her?''

Sommerled's face tightened, as if he just that moment realized who the woman was. ''They...they say she's his...bed slave.''

Chapter Seventeen

He would never forgive himself for leaving her.

George slapped the lathered stallion's rump and it shot forward into MacInnes's stable. The man himself stood in the courtyard, his mouth agape.

"Ho, lad, what have ye got, a bee in yer bonnet? What the—"

"There's no time!" George half dragged him into the stable. Sommerled dismounted and followed them inside.

A minute's worth of explanation on George's part and MacInnes had the whole of his household in an uproar. In seconds they'd selected fresh mounts. He'd known the Scot would help them.

"Ye rode all night?" MacInnes said.

"Aye." George shaded his eyes against the dawn.

"'Twill be cold and clear today. We should make good time." MacInnes pulled himself into the saddle of a tall gelding and raised a hand in farewell to his wife, who stood in the courtyard wringing her hands.

"Godspeed," she called out as the three of them, along with twenty of MacInnes's men, guided their mounts out the gate and spurred them west toward Dunnet Head.

Please God, keep her safe until I can get there.

For the first hour they made good time as the path was gentle and nearly free of snow, but were forced to slow their pace when they entered the wood.

"Damn it to bloody hell!" George shot MacInnes a nasty look. "Can we no go around?"

"The wood? Aye, we can, but 'tis farther out of our way. If we stick to the path we'll make the quarry late tonight."

George swore under his breath.

"Besides, now is an excellent time for ye to tell me the whole of it." MacInnes arched a peppered brow at him.

Sommerled lowered his eyes and dropped back with the others, and George was grateful for it. He would not have his brother suffer again the tale of his stupidity. MacInnes flanked him, and as they cantered through the wood George recounted the whole of his adventure with Rika and her folk.

MacInnes listened without comment, but George could tell by the occasional snort that not all of the tale was new to him.

Finally he said, "Ye knew more than ye let on, that day we quit your house for Rollo's."

MacInnes shrugged. "'Twas all conjecture on my part, but aye, I knew something was amiss from the start. A newly wedded man doesna sleep on the floor of his wife's chamber with her in the bed."

They exchanged a look.

"Besides, I had ye followed to Rollo's castle, and again when ye left there. On the way, my kinsmen lost yer tracks, and didna come upon the place where blood was spilled until ye'd gone.''

"What? But how, without our seeing—''

"Remember, lad, this is my birthplace, and ye are but a visitor. I know all that goes on for twenty leagues.''

He cursed himself silently for the hundredth time that day. Was he a complete idiot?

"When ye split up three days ago on the road above my house, and ye rode south and she west, I knew for certain ye'd lied to me.''

"I never—''

MacInnes raised his hand. "Well, no lied exactly, but kept the truth o' things from me.''

"I didna know the half of it myself.'' He drew a breath and ground his teeth. "Bloody woman.''

MacInnes laughed. "Aye, I'd tan her hide were she my wife.''

He swore again.

"Dinna fash, lad. I know this Brodir. 'Tis no the killing he fancies, but the power that comes of domination.''

That came as no surprise to George. A dozen tiny moments with Rika flashed across his mind. Her irrational fear on their wedding night, her shame when she realized he'd discovered Brodir had bound and abused her.

Above all, her driving need for control, that damnable pride, and her relentless focus on winning—all of it made sense to him now. Aye, she sought power as a way to thwart those who would oppress her.

He smiled bitterly. In truth, her quest for independence drove her to take on the worst traits of those who had used her ill. Would that she could see it. He, himself, was not immune to such sensibilities.

Did he not once wish for a wife whose love would be measured by the magnitude of her submission, and her loyalty ensured by blind obedience?

Mayhap he was not so unlike Brodir after all.

"What about this Anne Sinclair?" MacInnes said, wrenching him from his thoughts. "Ye are pledged to her. What d'ye plan to do about it?"

In recounting the tale to MacInnes, he'd skipped the part about discovering that Anne and Sommerled were in love. 'Twas best not mentioned until he squared things with their king. He glanced back at his brother and frowned. "I know not. I have other matters to put right first."

"Aye, that's the truth. But have a care, lad. William the Lion is no a man to be trifled with. A chieftain's marriage is made on the bargaining table, no in the heart. And a pagan wedding will mean naught to your king."

"Is he no your king, too?"

MacInnes grinned. "There are benefits to dwelling in a land so remote it escapes the interests of kings, both Norse and Scots."

What he wouldn't give to be so overlooked. The edge of the wood came upon them without warning, and George spurred his mount faster. MacInnes dropped back with Sommerled and the rest of the men, and George urged his steed to a gallop.

Why in God's name had he left her?

How could he have been so blind to the truth?

Rika's character alone should have made him realize there was more at stake in this dowry business than merely buying her own freedom. She had flaws, God knows, as did he, but reckless selfishness was not one of hers.

He'd thought from the first that a sea voyage in the dead of winter was madness, that they risked far too much—their very lives. A vision of Lawmaker dragging Ingolf over the side into the sea replayed itself in his mind's eye in hideous clarity.

And for what? A chest of silver so that Rika, daughter of Fritha, could be rid of her appointed husband? Nay, she would ne'er have risked her kinsmen's lives on her own account.

He could kick himself for believing such a lame tale. Why did she not tell him about her brother?

"She doesna trust you, ye fool," he muttered to himself, and kicked his mount faster.

And without trust, there could be no love between them.

Not that there was much chance of that. He was no great prize, after all. Hadn't she made that clear to him on a dozen occasions? Her cold dismissal of him at the crossroads that last day haunted him still.

The steed stretched out onto the open moor, and George breathed deep of the chill air. Hoofbeats pounded in his head, and his heart kept time.

The wind was mercifully mild and the sun warm, but the day was half-gone and he feared what he would find at the end of their frantic journey.

Bed slave.

"Rika," he breathed, and his gut twisted in anguish.

"George." She whispered his name to herself as if, by doing so, he would miraculously appear.

Not that she wished him here in this awful place, but

were she to see his face once more it would give her the strength she needed to do what must be done.

The door to the crude bedchamber creaked open on rusted hinges. Rika froze, prepared for another round with Brodir. She'd not seen him since early that morn and had had plenty of time to think on her vengeance.

But the pair of dark eyes peeking tentatively into the chamber were not Brodir's.

"Ottar!" she cried. "What are you doing here? He'll kill you if he finds you with me."

The youth burst across the threshold, eyes wide with shock as he surveyed the damage to the room—the result of Brodir's rage—and her state of undress.

"Don't just stand there, cut me loose." She nodded at a dagger above her, stuck deep into the timber wall over the bed.

Ottar's face bloomed red with rage. Tears filled his eyes as he severed the bonds that pinned her to the foul and stinking bed. Rika's heart went out to him.

"I—I'll kill him," Ottar said in a voice shaking with a man's anger and a youth's fear.

She sat up carefully, feeling the circulation return to her hands, then massaged her raw wrists. She had truly thought Brodir would kill her. But, nay, that was not his way, was it?

"H-here," Ottar said, handing her the crumpled garments Brodir had stripped from her body the night before. He turned away while she quickly dressed, and she heard him choke back a sob. He was only six and ten, she reminded herself.

"It's all right." She rose and squeezed his shoulder. "It wasn't so bad this time."

He turned on her. "How can you say that? The monster. He…he…"

She willed him look her in the eye. "He *didn't*."

"He…didn't?"

She smiled and shook her head. "Nay, he…couldn't. I don't know why." She recalled similar instances on Fair Isle. It was not the first time Brodir's incapacity had spared her his abuse. "When he found himself unable, he flew into a rage."

Ottar's face brightened. He swiped at the tears streaking his cheeks.

Footfalls sounded in the corridor outside, and they both snapped to attention. Ottar brandished the dagger and stepped in front of her. She held her breath as the sounds got louder, then died away.

"That was close," she said. "We must get out of here before someone else comes." Suddenly it dawned on her. "How did you get in here? There are guards everywhere."

He smiled at her. "When I found out you intended to trade the whole of the dowry away for Gunnar's release, I pocketed a handful of the silver and—"

"What? How could you do such a—"

He grabbed her arm to still her railing. "Not for myself, for God's sake. For us. I thought we might have need of some coin on the journey back to MacInnes's. Lucky for me, I was overlooked when we arrived. The guards searched only Leif and Erik. Anyway, I bribed my way in here to find you."

God, how she loved this reckless, courageous boy. "You might have been killed, you idiot."

"We'll all be dead by nightfall if we don't get out of here. I heard the quarry master tell that very thing to one of his guards."

"Ja, Brodir said as much to me last night." She

looked Ottar in the eye. "Tell me, how fares my brother?"

"He is well, truly. I was with him myself this afternoon. He is beside himself with worry about you. I fear if we get out of this, you will suffer both his joy and his anger."

Rika nodded. "I knew he'd not be pleased to see me here, but I could not, while I lived, leave him here, alone, to wither and die."

Ottar smiled. "He knows that. You two are much alike. Come now, we must flee this place and go for help."

"Help? Where?"

"To Tom MacInnes's. We can steal back our horses and—"

"Nay, it's much too far. We could never ride there and back in time to save the others."

"To your father then. Rollo's castle is but a few hours' ride."

She shook her head, but knew Ottar was right. They needed help. Nothing she could do or say now would change Brodir's mind. Why he hadn't already slain Gunnar was hard to fathom.

Perhaps he enjoyed the drama of dragging it all out, prolonging her agony a few hours more, making certain she knew her brother would die and all that they had suffered to free him was in vain.

"Whoreson," she breathed. "I will kill him myself."

Rika wound her braid atop her head and secured it with a thick sliver of wood from one of the crude benches Brodir had smashed to bits in his rage the night before.

Together they peeked around the edge of the cracked door. The corridor was empty.

"Wait." Ottar retrieved something from the floor by the bed. "Here, you forgot these."

Her bracelets.

His face flushed scarlet. She stared at the hammered bronze circlets for a long moment, rubbing her scarred wrists. "All right, give them to me."

Ten minutes later they were in the quarry, hiding among the heaps of fetid slag. The sun was not yet set, and a host of laborers slaved at the other end of the open pit.

"You should have listened to me, Rika."

A guard patrolled too close for her liking, and she shoved Ottar's head down. "What do you mean?"

"You should have trusted him. You know who I'm talking about."

She did. Grant.

"The man's your husband."

She snorted, but her heart wasn't in it. Ottar was right. She should have trusted Grant with the truth. He would have aided her in her cause. Not because he loved her—for how could he? But because that was his way.

He was a good man.

The best of all men.

"MacInnes, too—and your father. They love you, though you cannot see it or you refuse to believe it, I do not know which. All of them would have rallied to our cause had you but told them the truth of things."

She slumped beside him, unable to protest. It was her own fault they had come to this. Her pride and fear were twisted so tight inside her, they'd blinded her to things even a youth of ten and six could plainly see.

Oh, but there was more, more than Ottar could fathom. Her fierce independence, this visceral need to conquer, to win, to prove her worth in a world where all save a few had considered her worthless. That's what had landed them all in this mess.

Her cheeks blazed hot with shame.

"If only I'd told him," she whispered.

Ottar shook her. "It's not too late. Send word to Wick when we reach your father's."

"Nay, Grant has his own life—and a new bride." Would that she could turn her heart to ice to stop the pain.

"*You* are his bride, the wife of his heart, no matter what bargains he need keep for king and clan. I've watched the two of you together for weeks now. I know him, and I know you."

She looked at him and a film of tears stung her eyes. "Lawmaker would have been proud of you, were he here this day."

"You love him," Ottar said. "Admit it."

"Ja." She nodded. "I do."

"Well then—"

A whoosh cut the air above them, and her heart jumped to her throat. They both looked up to see the butt end of a Viking spear protruding from the slag pile where they hid.

"I knew you'd not go far," a chillingly familiar voice said behind her.

Rika scrambled to her feet, wrenching the dagger from Ottar's belt before he could stop her. She knew it would come to this, and she was ready.

More than ready.

"Brodir," she said, turning on him. "How good of you to join us."

* * *

"Where's the bloody fog when we need it?"

George crouched low beside MacInnes and peered over a tumble of rocks and down into the quarry. A score of guards hovered around a bonfire outside the slave barracks. More patrolled the southern perimeter.

"Aye," MacInnes said, and spared a look at the clear dark sky. "We'll have no cover tonight."

"Christ, it stinks to high heaven." He wrinkled his nose at the stench wafting from the slag heaps below them. The fresh salt scent of the sea did naught to disguise the fetor.

"Sulfur—and copper and lead, as well."

Behind them on the moor a horse whinnied. "Keep those damn nags quiet," he hissed at MacInnes's men.

"I had no idea there would be this many." MacInnes nodded to the guards below. "It's been years since I've been to this wretched place. Methinks some o' them must be Brodir's men."

"Aye, and from what Sinclair's kinsman told us, this Brodir holds the quarry master in his back pocket."

"Are ye certain she's down there?"

"Aye. Dead certain." The description Sinclair's kinsman had given of the Norsewoman left no doubt in his mind.

"There's nothing for it then. There are too many o' them and too few of us. We must wait until your brother returns with Rollo and his men. 'Twas a good idea to send for him. Let's hope to God he's of a mind to come after his daughter—and his son."

"He'll come, but I willna wait on him."

MacInnes arched a brow in the soft moonlight. "Ye canna think to—"

"I can and I will. My wife's down there—in the

hands of a beast." He locked gazes with the Scot. "Are ye with me?"

MacInnes grinned in the dark. "Aye, but we'll have to be bloody ghosts to slip past the guards unnoticed. We canna take them openly. The fewer go in, the better."

George checked *Gunnlogi* for the dozenth time. "All right then, let's do it."

MacInnes picked two of his men to go with them. To the others he said, "Wait here. If we're no back with her by the time Rollo arrives—"

"We'll be back." In his mind's eye George pictured the layout MacInnes had described. "Come on. We'll take the path leading off the slag heaps. From there we'll snake to the castle."

MacInnes nodded.

George took off at a run, skirting the perimeter of the quarry, taking care to avoid the guards, making his way toward the pale glow of torchlight that marked the ruined castle where he was certain Rika was held.

Pray God, she was still alive.

MacInnes and the others dogged his steps. In minutes they reached the crumbled seaward side of what once had been a fine stone and timber structure. They'd been damn lucky thus far.

Now, how to get inside without being seen?

It didn't look as difficult as George imagined 'twould be. After all, the quarry and castle headquarters were designed to keep people in, not out. At the end of the workday the slaves were rounded up and secured in their barracks.

Few prowled about outside the castle. The only guard who proved too sharp to elude in the dark, now slumped to the snow-covered ground, his throat slit.

George sheathed his bloodied dirk and dragged the body behind a pile of rubble.

A moment later his ears pricked. Footfalls and the laughter of approaching men. George dropped to the ground. MacInnes and his men ducked into the slag heaps flanking the path. Had they been spotted? Nay, he didn't think so.

There were six of them—Brodir's men, he guessed, given their speech and attire. Another few yards and George would be discovered. MacInnes and his men were on the opposite side of the path, cut off from him. Damn!

He had but one chance, and he took it.

Lightning fast, George slipped around the corner of the ruined castle, dirk in hand. No one was about. Seconds later he came upon a side entrance that was unguarded and clearly not part of the original construction. MacInnes had been dead right about that. He could kiss the man.

George slipped inside, his heart in his throat, and crept silently along a corridor toward a splash of torchlight and the murmur of voices. Turning the corner into a dark alcove, he stopped dead.

Rika stood rigid in the chamber directly across from him, hands fisted at her sides.

Thank Christ! He wanted to shout it from the rooftops, but bit his tongue instead. He willed himself not to move, for fear she'd see him and give away what little advantage his stealth afforded him.

Behind her stood—Ingolf! What was the blackguard, immortal? This time he'd make certain the murderer got his due. With him stood another of Brodir's henchman.

Beside them, lashed to the timbered posts supporting

the mud and stone wall, were four youths, three whom he knew. Ottar, Erik and Leif, who looked surprisingly healthy given their situation.

The fourth lad had not fared so well. Dried blood matted his white-gold hair. He hung there, unconscious or dead—George couldn't tell which, beaten bloody at any rate. His resemblance to Rika was startling. Tall and fair, if a bit thin. No surprise, given the hellish conditions he'd no doubt survived these long months in bondage.

Gunnar, son of Rollo. Rika's brother.

She cast a glance in the youth's direction and her eyes saddened. In that moment George understood everything. Were it his own brother who'd been held here, he would have done anything to have freed him.

Lied. Killed. Anything.

Aye, he understood her well, and his heart swelled with an aching visceral love.

Slowly he unsheathed *Gunnlogi*. Torchlight bounced off the fine metalwork of the blade, bathing the carved runes in fire. Would that Lawmaker had bestowed him with the knowledge to invoke the magic the weapon was rumored to hold. George would have sold his very soul for it.

"Will you deal?" Rika said to a shadowed figure at the edge of George's field of view.

"Why should I?" The figure stepped into the light and George sucked in a breath.

Brodir.

Sweet Jesus, he was huge. Garbed in Viking battle gear, and all muscle by the look of him. The Norseman raked his dark eyes over Rika's form and laughed.

George felt the blood rage hot through his veins.

"I have you—and him." Brodir nodded at Gunnar's slumped body. "Why should I deal?"

Rika stepped toward her captor, and George held his breath. "Because if you let them go—" she gestured to the youths "—all of them, I will give willingly all that you would have from me by force."

Ottar began to protest.

George closed his eyes and gritted his teeth to still the sickness rolling up from his gut. Steady, he told himself. Bide your time, man. Choose the right moment. He drew a breath and opened his eyes.

Erik and Leif joined the youth's protest until Ingolf landed a fist in Ottar's belly.

Brodir snickered and stepped toward her. Rika held her ground. "But that would take all the pleasure out of it." He slid a thick finger across her scarred throat. George redoubled his grip on his broadsword.

In a move that startled them all, Rika sprang backward. Out of the corner of his eye George caught a flash of light.

"She has a weapon!" Ingolf started forward; Brodir called him off.

George moved into the corridor, his heart pounding.

"And I know well how to use it." Her eyes blazed murder as she circled Brodir like a predator.

Wait, George commanded himself. Wait for the right moment.

"Come on then." Brodir waved her toward him.

"Rika, no!" Ottar cried.

She ignored him and moved forward, graceful as a cat. One more step and George would put a stop to it.

Brodir cocked his head and frowned. Rika stopped in her tracks, apparently confused by his expression. George waited. One second more.

To his surprise, Brodir pointed at the silver brooch pinned to Rika's rumpled shirt. 'Twas the first time George noticed it. His throat constricted and his heart swelled.

"I remember that," Brodir said. "It was your whore of a mother's."

Rika's eyes widened ever so slightly. Aye, she remembered, too. George watched as the confusion in her face dissolved, hardening to recognition, then clarity. She tipped her chin at the Norseman. "My husband gave it me."

Brodir laughed.

"As my *morgen gifu.*" A proud smile bloomed on her face, and George's chest tightened with love for his beautiful and courageous wife.

The grin slid from Brodir's face. He raised a beefy hand as if to slap her. Rika, true to form, God love her, stepped toward him and tipped her chin higher, blue eyes blazing.

'Twas time. George sprang into the light wielding *Gunnlogi.* "Lay a hand on her and you're a dead man."

Chapter Eighteen

She was dreaming.

Ja, that explained everything.

"Grant!" Ottar cried, snapping her out of her stupor.

Rika blinked, believing him a vision, and drank in the glorious sight of the Scot. Nay, he was no dream, but flesh. "Thor's blood, what are you doing here?"

Grant's eyes flicked to hers for the barest instant. "I would ask ye the same—wife." He nodded to the corridor. "Move behind me, now."

Wife.

His voice was so commanding and her brain so addled by his unexpected appearance, her feet began to move before she realized his intention. "How did you know?"

"Had I any sense, I would have—"

Ingolf and his henchman shot forward, weapons drawn. Rika froze.

"Hold!" Brodir called, then grinned wickedly at Grant. "So, this is the husband, ja?"

"*Ja.*" Grant glared at him and raised *Gunnlogi* higher.

"Do not!" Rika stepped out from behind him, brandishing her ridiculously short dagger. "This is my fight, not yours."

Grant's eyes widened. He stared at her in disbelief, as Ingolf and his man slid closer, snickering. "Ye canna mean that. Ye expect me to stand by and let ye—"

"I do." She drew herself up and leveled her gaze at him. "There is a score to settle here—my score."

Brodir's grin widened.

"But…" Grant shook his head, incredulous. "Ye're my wife, and your battles mine. And if ye think I'll stand down while this blackguard yet lives—" he nodded at Brodir "—ye dinna know me."

Ingolf lunged.

Rika was ready.

She spun as he grabbed her, and his dark eyes popped wide. His breath was foul. She recoiled as he slid to the floor, the hilt of her dagger protruding from his chest.

Grant had not stood idle. Ingolf's henchman, a Norseman she did not know, lay slumped at his feet. *Gunnlogi* dripped blood.

Ottar and Leif and Erik struggled against their bonds, shouting encouragement. Rika spared a quick glance at her brother, but he did not stir. "Hang on," she whispered to him.

All at once, Brodir advanced on them, his face twisted in rage.

"Dinna touch her!" Grant said, and raised his sword.

Brodir stopped short.

"Your business is with me, for I stole her from ye."

Rika moved toward her husband. "Nay, I told you, I would slay him myself."

A terrible smile curled the edges of Brodir's mouth.

Oh, how she longed to wipe it from his face with her blade.

"Aye," Grant said, "and conquer the whole bloody world on your own while ye're at it?" His anger startled her. "That night on the ship, Lawmaker went over the side of his own accord." He kicked at Ingolf's dead body. "And no just to thwart this whoreson. Ye know that, don't ye?"

Their eyes locked, and a chill snaked up her spine. She did know.

"He did it so that I would have no choice but to...trust you."

Grant nodded, and pain colored his expression.

"Foolish old man," she breathed.

"No so foolish, Rika."

"Enough!" Brodir slid a double-headed ax from the belt at his waist, and backed Grant toward the wall where the struggling youths were tethered.

Rika swept her dagger from Ingolf's chest and moved with them. "George, you do not know him as I do. He'll kill you. Please, let me—"

He ripped the dagger from her grasp and tossed it to Ottar who had managed to free one hand. In seconds, all three youths were freed, but the dagger the only weapon between them.

Brodir called out toward the empty corridor.

"Coward," Grant said. "Can ye no disarm me on your own? Must ye call for help like a woman?"

Brodir let out a war cry and lunged at him. Rika froze, her breath caught in her throat. Grant deflected the heavy ax stroke, but just barely.

"Get her out of here!" he cried, and nodded at the youths. "And her brother. MacInnes waits for ye outside."

Brodir lunged again, and Grant turned his attention full on him.

"Nay!" Rika rushed forward. Ottar caught her and dragged her back. "Let me go! I must help him!"

"Get her out!" Grant's face contorted into a hot meld of rage and courage.

Ottar dragged her, kicking, toward the corridor. Leif and Erik followed, bearing Gunnar's limp body between them.

"You fool, he'll kill you!"

Nay, he would not.

George lunged and Brodir backed off, affording him the chance to glance at Rika as Ottar dragged her from the room.

"George!"

George.

How he'd longed to hear her call him by his Christian name. His heart nearly burst for love of her. "There are things of which we must speak—but later."

"I love you," she breathed. Her words seared his soul.

Ottar jerked her down the corridor, and she was gone.

Dawn crept over the snow-dusted moor surrounding Rollo's castle. Rika steadied herself against the stone window ledge and gazed west into the mist toward Dunnet Head.

Did her husband live or die?

The anxiety of not knowing would surely drive her mad.

"Get some sleep," Ottar said. "You've been standing at that window since we arrived yesterday morn.

She fought the crushing exhaustion bearing down on her. "Nay, I'm fine," she said absently.

But she was not fine.

She fisted her hands and opened them again to stir her blood and stave off the chills. Each time a horseman materialized out of the fog on the moor below, her stomach tightened in anticipation. And each time, as she realized it was not him, a sick feeling washed over her.

"He lives," Ottar said. "You must believe in him."

She did believe in him, at long last. Too late, perhaps. The clash of Brodir's ax against George's sword still rang in her ears, and gnawed at the tenuous hope she clung to for her husband's safe return.

"The nerve of my father." She strode to the heavy timber door and beat it fruitlessly with her fists for the hundredth time. "To lock me in like this."

A weak laugh drifted from the bed.

"Gunnar," she breathed, and rushed to her brother's side. His color had returned, and he looked much improved from yesterday when, after constant tending, he finally roused from unconsciousness. She touched her finger to his battered head, and he winced.

"It's for your own good, sister. I would have locked you in myself had Rollo not beat me to it."

"Thor's blood, I hate him!"

Gunnar smiled in that gently admonishing way she used to love. "Nay, you merely make a show of it. As does he."

Still, she could not believe her father had come for her. George had sent his brother to fetch Rollo, and he'd come. Just like that. George, too. And MacInnes. She shook her head, afraid to believe what their aid implied.

"Our mother's brooch." Gunnar clutched at her tattered shirt.

Twice Catherine had bade her don something more suitable, a gown, but she'd refused. She must be ready to ride, should an opportunity arise for her to escape this ridiculous incarceration.

She shook off her dark thoughts and smiled at her brother. "Ja, it was hers. I remember now. I didn't... before."

"You mean, when Grant gave it you?"

She shot him a surprised look. "You know?"

"I told him," Ottar said, and helped Gunnar to sit up in the bed. "You did drift off a little last night."

"What else did you tell him"

"Everything." Gunnar arched a fair brow at her. "All that he knew."

She flashed angry eyes at Ottar. He merely shrugged.

"Lawmaker gave it to her, you know." Gunnar nodded at the silver brooch. "Long before Rollo wed her."

"What?" Her hand shot to the brooch, and she clutched it protectively. "Lawmaker? But—"

"They were in love," Gunnar said.

She felt her eyes pop wide as saucers. "Fritha and Lawmaker?" A thousand tiny snippets of memory screamed through her mind.

"Ja. Before she and Rollo were joined." Gunnar frowned. "What a tragedy—for all of them."

Her mouth dropped open. She shook her head, but knew in her heart it was true. It dawned on her that perhaps Grant had known, as well.

"But...when did you learn this?"

"Lawmaker told me the day I became jarl."

"And you kept it from me?" Anger sparked inside her. "Why didn't Lawmaker tell me?"

"Would you have wanted to hear it?" Gunnar took her hand in his and moved it to his heart. "Could you have understood it, Rika?"

She looked at him, and knew the answer. "Nay, you are right. I was not ready to know." In her mind's eye she held George's strong, tender face. Her heart swelled. "But now I understand."

Gunnar's hand tightened over hers. "Ja, methinks that you do." He loosened his grip and turned to Ottar. "I owe you much, friend. My life—and my sister's."

"Nay." Ottar rose and strode to the window. "It is Rika who deserves your thanks—and the Scot."

"Grant."

"George," she breathed.

"You love him." Gunnar smiled at her, his eyes brimming with the affection she'd so long missed.

She nodded weakly.

"Look!" Ottar cried from the window.

Rika leaped to her feet. "Is it he? Does he come at last?" She raced to the window and pushed Ottar aside. "Where? Where is he?"

Ottar pointed into the mist, and a second later she saw him. "There!" she cried.

But the man who rode into the heavily guarded bailey was not her husband. Her heart plummeted for the dozenth time. Rollo lifted a gauntleted hand to her in greeting. Two score men followed on lathered mounts and filed toward the stable.

"It is our father," she said, and turned to Gunnar. "He is alone."

Rika sat stiffly on a stool near the blazing hearth fire and waited for Rollo to appear. Her hands were like ice, and would not be warmed. A feeling of dread so powerful it made her nauseated descended on her like the reaper himself. The door to the chamber creaked open, but she did not look up.

Footfalls sounded on the plank floor. The heady aromas of mead and tobacco confirmed her father's arrival. She would not meet his eyes.

"Daughter," he said. "I have brought you something."

Still, she would not look up. Her hands fisted in her lap. Her eyes fixed on the fire. Rollo fidgeted beside her, as if he were retrieving something from his pocket. She held her breath, and he dropped it in her lap.

The sunstone.

George had worn it around his neck e'er since the storm at sea.

The world spun. She closed her eyes, certain that for the first time in her life she would faint. "He...he is dead then." Her fingers closed over the crystal and squeezed.

"Dead?" Rollo's voice boomed above her. "A bit torn up, but far from dead. What kind of a wife has so little faith in her husband's—"

"He lives?" Her eyes flew open. She shot to her feet and grabbed her father by the front of his fur wrap. "Oh God! Where is he? Is he hurt? Thor's blood—"

"Easy, girl." Rollo peeled her hands from his chest and shook her until she got a hold of herself.

Her breath came in short gasps, and she worked to control it. "Tell me. Tell me everything."

"Ja, I'll tell you. But sit, and calm yourself."

He pushed her down onto the stool and Ottar shoved a cup of mead into her hand. She drank, and breathed, and felt her blood slow to a mere race.

"And for you, son," Rollo said, and turned to Gunnar. "I have this." To Rika's surprise, her father unsheathed a familiar weapon.

"Your sword," Gunnar said, and accepted the weapon from him.

"Nay, yours." Rollo grinned. "I took it off a dead kinsman—a snake unfit to call himself a Norseman. 'Tis said my daughter slew him." He turned to Rika and his smile widened. "Well done, girl."

It was the first time in her life her father had ever praised her. She held his gaze and offered him the beginnings of a smile in return. There was much about him she now longed to understand—and perhaps forgive. But first she would know how her husband fared.

Holding the cup, her hand began to tremble. "What of Grant?"

"Ah, Grant. He's gone."

"What?" Ottar cried.

The cup slipped from her hand and shattered on the flagstones.

"Ja," Rollo said. "He and his brother."

Sommerled. Rika had heard from MacInnes of the youth's miraculous return. But gone? She shook her head. "Where?"

"Back to Wick."

Her blood screamed to a halt in her veins. "Wick?" she breathed. "But then…"

"I know not why." Rollo shrugged. "It seems there is some duty there to which he was bound. But he asked you to wait for him here, until he can return and explain."

A deadness enveloped her from the inside out. "Those were his words?"

Rollo nodded.

There are things of which we must speak—but later.

She moved awkwardly toward the table near Gunnar's bed. On it rested a silver chalice, now empty of the wine she'd used to tend her brother's wounds. Lifting it to her face, she gazed at her own reflection. All she saw was that hideous scar staring back at her.

She'd been right about Grant, after all. He was a good and honorable man who would not abandon her to her enemies.

But he did not love her.

"But surely—"

Her hand flew up to quiet Ottar. "Leave me now. All of you. Please. I would have some time to myself." Gunnar started to rise from the bed. "Nay, not you, brother. There is much we have to discuss."

Gunnar looked at her, and she saw pity in his eyes.

"I would sail for Frideray as soon as you are able," she said to him quietly.

"Not until the spring, surely," Rollo said.

Ottar eased his way past him. "And not before Grant returns?"

Rika shrugged. "Our folk have need of a jarl, and have long hoped for Gunnar's return. You know that, all of you."

Rollo grunted. "Come, boy," he said to Ottar, and clapped a hand on the youth's shoulder. "Let us leave these two to catch up. And I could use a meal and a boatload of mead."

Ottar cast her a forlorn look, and followed Rollo from the chamber.

"Will you not wait for him?" Gunnar said, after they'd gone.

Her heart iced over, and the familiar feel of it fueled her resolve. Once, the deadness would have also buoyed the strength of her convictions, but not so to-day.

"Nay," she said, halfheartedly. "I think not."

A sennight later, Rika stood at the *byrthing's* stern and breathed deep of the cool salt air. A light breeze toyed with her thick braids. The day was warm, the sun brilliant against a field of clear blue sky.

It was a good day to sail.

"Are you sure, sister?" Gunnar willed her look at him, but she would not. "We can wait. Another week. Two even. Spring is nearly on us."

She fingered the sunstone hanging from her neck and scanned the southern horizon one last time. "Nay. The weather is fair, and the tide is turned. Let us take our leave of this place."

Gunnar nodded and turned to join the others—Ottar, Erik, Leif, and a half-dozen of her father's men—who stood ready to cast off. Ottar had not spoken to her all that day, and now refused even to look at her.

Stupid boy. What did he expect her to do? Wait like some desperate, love-struck fool for a husband whose only purpose in returning was to tell her he had taken another to wife? Nay, she would forgo that humiliation.

She was not the kind of woman he wanted, but knew now that she did not wish to be otherwise. She was Ulrika, daughter of Fritha and Rollo. Would that Grant could have loved her for who and what she was, as she loved him.

Sunlight glinted off the hammered bronze bracelets circling her wrists. Without another thought, she removed them and cast them into the sea.

When she turned around she caught Ottar's bitter

smile. He nodded, and she smiled back, her heart full to aching.

The anchor raised, Gunnar called for them to push off. Leif shouted out the strokes, and her father's men put their backs into the oaring. Ottar and Erik stood ready to hoist the sail. A hundred feet into the bay, she turned for one last look.

"MacInnes," she breathed. The old Scot stood on the dock, beside his wheezing horse. "Hmm, that is strange."

"We took our leave of him this morn," Gunnar said, joining her at the stern. "I wonder what—"

"Ja, but he waves us back. Look." She raised a hand, acknowledging they'd seen him.

"He calls to you. What is he saying."

She shook her head. "He says my name, but I can't make the rest of it out."

Another rider topped the ridge above the bay. Rika squinted against the sun and tried to make him out.

"Who is it?" Gunnar said.

"I know not."

But she did know, and her spine prickled.

"Whoever he is, he's got the devil in him. At that speed he'll break his neck."

The rider's black steed thundered down the ridge and across the moor, heading straight for the dock.

"Grant!" Ottar cried.

Rika stopped breathing.

It *was* him. She saw him clearly now. He wore a belted plaid, the same as the first time she'd seen him washed up on the beach at Frideray.

"Turn around!" Gunnar cried, and the men instantly stopped rowing.

"Nay, do not." Rika clutched her brother's arm. "Do not, I beg you."

"But—"

Gunnar shot Ottar a warning look, and the youth clapped his mouth shut.

"Rika, are you sure?" Gunnar said.

A dozen rational reasons why they should just sail on raced through her mind, clashing with the knot of emotions welling inside her.

"Ja," she said, then shook her head. "Nay. I don't know." She realized she was trembling, and clutched the *byrthing's* top rail to steady herself.

Her breath caught in her throat as Grant flew past MacInnes and drove the black steed clear onto the dock. Grant pulled him up short just before the poor beast plummeted into the water. He slipped from the saddle and stepped to the edge.

"Rika!" she heard him call. He frantically waved her back.

"Well?" Gunnar said.

She shook her head, gripping the top rail so tightly her hands began to cramp. "I...I don't know."

Ottar and Erik and Leif stood behind her, silent, but she could feel their anxiety. Her father's men waited for Gunnar's command, oars in the air.

A minute passed, or was it an hour? Each second twisted her stomach tighter. And then Grant did something that shocked them all. He threw off his weapons and—

"Thor's blood!"

"He jumped!" Ottar cried.

Rika gasped.

"Look, he swims toward us." Leif pointed at the flailing Scotsman. "Well, if you call that swimming."

The crazy fool! What was he thinking? He can barely swim a stroke.

"It seems your husband does not take kindly to your leaving." Gunnar cocked a sun-bleached brow at her.

She leaned out over the top rail, straining to hear what it was that George shouted. Terns and gulls cawed overhead, drowning out his words. Rika's heart swelled to bursting as he thrashed across the water toward her like a salmon desperate to make his way upstream.

And then she heard it.

His voice clear, his words unmistakable.

"I love ye!"

Her breath shot from her lungs in a tortured sort of gasp.

"Told you," Ottar said behind her. "Nay, but you wouldn't listen, would yo—"

"Ottar, shut up," Gunnar said.

A second later she was balanced precariously on the top rail, her eyes fixed on the man swimming toward her.

"That water's wicked cold, sister, but methinks you do not care."

She jumped.

And gasped as the icy water shocked her to her senses.

"Rika!" George cried, and then nearly went under.

"George!" She cut through the water toward him, the whoops of her kinsmen spurring her faster.

They collided, shivering, and then his arms were around her. "R-Rika, I…l-love…ye," he said, teeth chattering from the cold, and breathless from the long swim.

Over and over he said the words as he peppered her face with kisses, his lips warming her icy skin.

"But...your wife. What will she—"

"Ye are my wife." He cupped her face in his hands, and she wrapped her legs around him in the frigid water. "My brave, bonny wife. A remarkable woman, and I will have no other."

"But...Anne Sinclair...your king—"

He stilled her with a kiss. "The Sinclairs and the Grants are joined, and William the Lion is well pleased."

She tried to make sense of his words but could not.

He smiled, and she remembered something her father had mentioned in passing.

"Your brother!"

"Aye, 'tis a good match, and why I had to leave Dunnet Head straightaway—to square things with king and clan before I found my head on the block." He brushed her lips with a kiss. "Did ye no get my message to wait?"

Her cheeks warmed under his scolding gaze, but now was not the time to explain the fears that had driven her to leave.

"I, too, had things to put to rights," she said.

"Your father."

She nodded. "There is much I have yet to reconcile in my own mind, but we parted with peace between us that will lead, in time, to forgiveness." He started to sink, and she pulled him up. "Come," she said, "we are closer to shore than the boat."

She looked back at her brother and the others. All of them were smiling. Gunnar waved—a gesture of farewell.

"Bring her for a visit in the summer," he called.

George raised a hand in acknowledgment.

Together, they swam for the beach. MacInnes stood

grinning on the dock, hands fisted on hips. They washed ashore, shivering and drenched to the bones.

George pulled her close, and she clung to him. His heart beat fierce against her breast.

"Say it," he breathed. "What ye said at the quarry."

She looked into his eyes and felt the warmth of his love melt all of her doubts. "I love you."

And then he kissed her.

"Lawmaker was right about everything, wasn't he?" she said, when finally their lips parted to draw breath.

"Aye, he was a wise man."

She would remember him always, with love, as a daughter remembers a father. Sun glinted off the silver brooch pinned at her shoulder, and she smiled.

Together they watched as the *byrthing* sailed out of the small bay, north toward Fair Isle. But she found herself thinking of other shores, and wrapped her arms tight about her husband's neck.

"Scotland is beautiful in the spring," he said, as if he read her thoughts.

"I have oft wondered about that."

He gazed at the brilliant blue sky. "Aye, and the thaw is coming. I feel it."

"So do I."

And truly, she did.

* * * * *

*Be sure to watch for
Debra's next Harlequin Historical,*
THE MacINTOSH BRIDE,
on sale summer 2001

Travel back in time to America's past with wonderful Westerns from Harlequin Historicals

ON SALE MARCH 2001

LONGSHADOW'S WOMAN
by **Bronwyn Williams**
(The Carolinas, 1879)

LILY GETS HER MAN
by **Charlene Sands**
(Texas, 1880s)

ON SALE APRIL 2001

THE SEDUCTION OF SHAY DEVEREAUX
by **Carolyn Davidson**
(Louisiana, 1870)

NIGHT HAWK'S BRIDE
by **Jillian Hart**
(Wisconsin, 1840)

AWARD-WINNING AUTHOR

GAYLE WILSON

presents her latest
Harlequin Historical novel

ANNE'S PERFECT HUSBAND

Book II in her brand-new series

The Sinclair Brides

When a dashing naval officer searches for the
perfect husband for his beautiful young ward,
he soon discovers he needn't search any
further than his own heart!

Look for it in bookstores in March 2001!

Available at your favorite retail outlet.

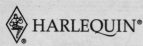

HARLEQUIN®

makes any time special—online...

eHARLEQUIN.com

your romantic life

•—Romance 101——————
♥ **Guides to romance, dating and flirting.**

•—Dr. Romance ——————
♥ **Get romance advice and tips from our expert, Dr. Romance.**

•—Recipes for Romance ———
♥ **How to plan romantic meals for you and your sweetie.**

•—Daily Love Dose——————
♥ **Tips on how to keep the romance alive every day.**

•—Tales from the Heart———
♥ **Discuss romantic dilemmas with other members in our Tales from the Heart message board.**

Finding Home

New York Times bestselling authors

Linda Howard
Elizabeth Lowell
Kasey Michaels

invite you on
the journey of a lifetime.

Three women are searching—
each wants a place to belong,
a man to care for her,
a child to love.

Will her wishes be fulfilled?

*Coming in April 2001
only from Silhouette Books!*

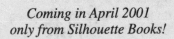

Where love comes alive™

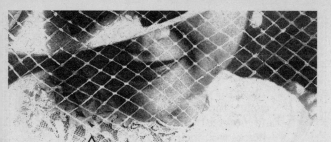

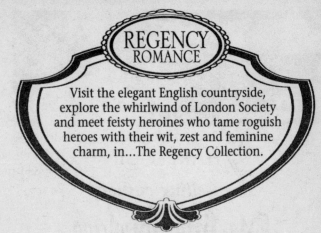